BLUEBERRY MANOR

-HOPELESS MAZE-

BOOK 01

ISBN:978-0-692-07365-0
Library of Congress Control Number 2018935683

Cover designed by HPP Designs
678-938-3869

BLUEBERRY MANOR
-HOPELESS MAZE-
BOOK 01

BY

AMINA CAPRICE ANDOLINI

DEDICATION

Dedicated to Momma Caprice (1935-2008)
Dragonfly (1943-1971)
Family and Unconditional Friends on this
Side and the Other

ACKNOWLEDGEMENTS

I would like to acknowledge all misunderstood, underestimated, and undervalued artists. I thank those who believed in me more than I believed in me. Thank yous and side-eyes to my daughter Tiara, sister Shirley, and brother-in-law Emmett Superstar for dragging me to Larry Dodson's book signing where I met my editor, Shelia E. Bell. I thank my son, Christian, for keeping me grounded. I thank my father, I thank the shoulders, backs, ears, kind words, financial support, and vibes of innumerable family members and a few friends. I thank Light Beings, Lightworkers, Empaths, and am so very grateful to Mario Puzo (1920-1999), Marlon Brando (1924-2004), Francis Ford Coppola, Robert DeNiro and Oreste Baldini for their parts in Vito (Andolini) Corleone's existence.

Special thanks go out to each of the characters of Blueberry Manor (especially the Charlemagne family) for forcing me to deal with their madness for over thirty years, for not allowing me to sleep regular hours at times, for bogarting my energy and occupying most every thought. NO THANKS to my wacky thyroid, though she has a hand in my super weird imagination, so I guess I thank her too.

Hopeless Maze

Shelia Marie Odell

I'm crying to the future
'cuz the present looks so bleak,
in spite of this,
I'm so meek at my peak,
I unease...
I don't know why I'm weak,
I don't know what I seek.

I have an idea,
don't like it here,
dreams sear with every tear,
people take them away,
people stay in a daze,
blocking the sunrays.
Why do we get to stay
another jacked up day
in a hopeless maze?

hitting brick walls,
trying to find a way out,
don't know what life is really about
until we're gone...
Where did we go wrong?
Not much to say,
another jacked up day
in a hopeless maze.

Wednesday, May 31, 2006
Reims, France

Long business trips, Suntilian Devils, and the nostalgia of coiling around crowded houses of sparkling wine and vineyards was his realm of sanity. He imagined that's where he was three days ago, in the realm of sanity, not staring at the human manifestation of nostalgia. He imagined the taste of his mother's soft cake and coffee served in the dining room, his father's digestive bitter served outside by the mirrored lake.

Fifty-three-year-old Joseph Charlemagne did not remember leaving the meeting at his equestrian estate three days ago. He came into consciousness while staring at a group of purple orbs. The orbs took him to the walkway of the château, through demon-inhabited deciduous trees to the left of the outer wall, through the cool breeze that blew in the mirrored lake's essence. Paranormal spheres took him in the manor house through the great hall, music room, up to the library and drawing room where he stood in front of a window waiting for sunrise.

He looked over the naked estate, formerly one of the biggest tourist attractions in France. The large stone fence riddled with graffiti, the wrought iron gateway opened to a white square-shaped barbican. It contained a dead bank and several large ticket booths that once housed hundreds of travel consultants. He followed the walled road that led to the gatehouse where the humming noiselessness of spas, relaxation rooms, and a malt shop reminded him of his uncle's Roman bathhouse. City walls connected the gatehouse to three towers and a keep. There was a landscaped maze, sometimes mistaken for a crop

1

circle, in the bailey, where BJ Valenteen, one of the senior managers of the estate, witnessed an altercation between Joseph's wife and one of his best friends almost six months ago.

Visions of the past three days washed through Joseph's psyche like truth serum. Joseph and his associates had been flying around on the corporate oonta-oont jet for a little over one day from Whangarei, New Zealand to the United States—New Orleans, Louisiana, and from New Orleans to Le Bourget, France. After the business end of the trip, they spent the rest of their time in the nightclub area, which took up more than half of the jet's second floor.

Sunday, May 28, 2006
The Corporate Jet

Half-asleep and half-awake in the master suite's lounge area, Joseph blurted, "Who's there?" He saw the hint of a tall black man with an English style three-piece suit and matching overcoat draped over his shoulders. His eyesight focused quickly, like an unexpected optical zoom. "Big Theon!" Joseph jumped off the bed, hurried a handshake, and wrapped his arm around Big Theon's neck.

Big Theon slapped Joseph on the back then punched him in the small of it. He said, "You still got it," while tightening his lips over quivering gold teeth.

Joseph kept his composure. "You can do better than that, Theon. I haven't seen you in months." They threw light punches.

Big Theon spoke in Joseph's ear. "Mr. Charlemagne, there was a video call."

"What do you mean *was*? And you're supposed to be stuck in somebody's office, Mr. Chief Information Security Officer."

"Like you, I got a vibe. It drew me out the office." He put two fingers next to his right temple, an old signal Joseph remembered. "I saw your son on one of the monitors in the boardroom."

"Kenneth on video call?" Joseph laughed. "He wants to do some video conferencing, huh? Why not my cell?" He patted his pockets, but all he could find was a torch lighter.

"Sir, they took your business and personal phones."

Joseph mouthed a few obscenities while hitting his right fist

2

against his left palm.

"Don't stress. I took care of 'em." Big Theon held Joseph's personal phone. "I have Kenneth on the line right now."

Joseph could hear Kenneth screaming through the phone, "Christel has crossed the goddamn line again!"

Joseph said, "Thank you, Theon. I can vividly see Kenneth's spit flying; blood vessels popping all over the place. Taking this call makes me a little nervous." He took his phone from Big Theon's hand.

Big Theon smiled. "I know, Joseph, but this is Kenneth's fifth attempt at calling you." Before he could close the door all the way, Joseph imagined Big Theon's eyes, cold and questionless, dressing down the bodyguards, exotic dancers, and the entire human resources department.

After ending the call with Kenneth, Joseph screamed at a pitch only glassware could understand. He heard bottles shatter, bodies drop, and slide across the floor—more like scrapes and scrubs—as the personal security detail drew guns. Exotic dancers scrambled, stilettos broke, tassels bounced off light fixtures. He heard piercing screams as he smashed heavy furniture against the master suite's door, ripping it off its hinges. Bodyguards grabbed fire extinguishers, assembled weapons, ugly exotic dancers strode through splinters.

Joseph stumbled out of his room, teeth bared. "Why the hell am I just now finding out about this? My son called five goddamn times and nobody thought it best to give me the phone?"

There was silence throughout the jet. One of Joseph's personal assistants continued to shuffle papers while a close protection officer straightened his tie.

Cahlus-Azari, a young bodyguard who had just awakened from several hours of oblivion rambled to another. "So what if Kenneth called five times." He protected his eyes from the lights with his hand. "I feel Mr. Charlemagne shouldn't have received the call. It was unnecessary stress too soon."

"Unnecessary stress," said a security officer, "Cahlus-Azari! You're the moron who took Mr. Charlemagne's phones and put everything on mute, huh? Good thing Big Theon caught on and slapped you shitless. You should always put his family through."

A bodyguard, overly muscular with a box fade haircut said,

3

"Did he say 'too soon'? We're only twenty-five minutes away from the aircraft hangar home." He tapped another bodyguard on the shoulder. "I heard the chefs were already there....Yessir. I can taste those seasoned chicken legs."

As other bodyguards talked amongst themselves, Joseph shouted, "Shut the hell up! I can hear all of you."

A member of the security staff hissed at a male exotic dancer, "Nightshade, you know what to do, Sweet Cakes." Nightshade slid his knuckles down the security guard's cheek before rolling a cart containing a fried oyster po-boy, dressed, a seafood platter, wine, and a Cajun martini to Joseph.

Joseph smiled a little. "What the hell is this?"

Nightshade explained how they ordered several boxes of food during a stop in New Orleans.

"I don't remember going to New Orleans."

Nightshade smacked his lips. "You had insomnia, Mr. Charlemagne, sir. When you finally fell asleep, we didn't wanna wake you." He doubled over with forced laughter. "You know how you get when you party too hard, Mr. Charlemagne, sir." He looked around, "You know how we all get, right!" He tried to make everyone clap their hands in agreement.

Everybody's imagined laughter and applause made Joseph's head throb. He held his beating temples. "Who the fuck asked you to humor me?" He snapped and shook Nightshade's shoulders repeatedly. "Why the hell are you laughing at me?" One of Joseph's personal assistants calmed him and apologized to Nightshade.

"Oh, Mr. Charlemagne, I'm not laughing *at* you. Nobody's laughing at you. Aren't we still in celebration mode?" Nightshade asked, voice trembling, tears pooling in his dimples. After he wiggled away from Joseph's grip, he smoothed his bare chest. A member of the security staff handed him a multicolored handkerchief.

The sight of the handkerchief broke Joseph's mania. "I apologize. I didn't mean, I mean... my anger isn't directed at you. How long was I out?"

Nightshade sniffed. "A few hours."

Joseph massaged his forehead. "It doesn't matter." When staring at the po-boy, he thought about Peacemaker Rag, a jazz song written

BLUEBERRY MANOR

and performed by his Grandma Ginger, sung to him by his grandfather.
"When jazz funerals were brass band funerals (or funerals with music) and po-boy sandwiches were peacemakers..."

Peacemaker Rag (by Ginger Cook-Bianchi)
say goodbye, three hours' time
second line, 'longside the pine
every time, they brag on yo' bag
I go mad... Peacemaker Rag

bordello? what crime is that?
second cat, keep fallin' flat
sweeney time, all blood in the bath
It's so bad... Peacemaker Rag

let George be jake
I'm out'ta this place
up to date, on time's and space
let 'em brag!
on grands, and vamps, and bags
I'm not mad... Peacemaker Rag
Flamin drag... Peacemaker Rag

Joseph turned on his portable air conditioning unit, slithered down in a split, an unusual V-shape, that looking back was impossible to do while not underneath the horrors of his past. He thought about that night in 1925, pulled at his collar, and whimpered. He was standing right there when his Grandma Ginger saw her baby, Prudenzia, Joseph's mother, for the first time—a baby that set off a chain of breakdowns all because she looked more white than black.

He cupped his hands over his ears and bawled around in a fetal position, feeling every seize, the barbiturates, every broken bone, and hearing the Serpent's commencement.

All the bodyguards could do was to make sure he couldn't hurt himself during the flashback, which looked more like an awful seizure—one that could shake the whole crew out of their shocking, drunken oblivions.

AMINA CAPRICE ANDOLINI

Ginger blurted out twelve "fuck-yous" in five different languages. Two of which were unknown.

"She didn't do well during delivery, and to have an accident that severe shortly afterwards should have killed her instantly. We'll have to take Mrs. Bianchi to surgery right now." Doctor Rossi clapped his hands at three zoned out nurses. "Fretta!"

As they wheeled Ginger to surgery, she looked at baby Prudenzia and hissed, "SSS-SSS-Serpent Race!"

Sunday, May 28, 2006
The Corporate Jet

Joseph screamed at the bloody visions until he could see pure purple Energies beam out of his third eye. His Spirit popped above him. He could see his physical body crouched between the corner and the air conditioning unit. The crew looked at him, some cried, others removed all dangerous objects. Big Theon made sure the aircraft hangar home housed a mobile clinic as well as two party busses and three stretch limousines.

Joseph drifted to his mother's childhood in Spirit; felt shock when a group of children found Grandma Ginger's burnt corpse in the neighborhood park. He felt as if he was one of those children. He could see his grandmother partially hidden under a rose bush. Somebody's baseball was brave enough to roll on the crunchy black grass. The broken vine was an obvious (failed) attempt at hanging herself.

He could feel his mother's pain. He felt it when children and ill-spirited adults teased her about Grandma Ginger's death. They teased her for twelve years. He understood why Grandfather Joe and his mother moved to a different part of Italy. They made the drive from Castrovillari to Reggio in order to catch a train to Ventimiglia, forty minutes or so from Nice, France. He understood why his mother passed for a white woman. He watched as she fled to Nice, traveling further north over a period of four years with the hope of settling in Paris.

BLUEBERRY MANOR

Joseph's Spirit returned to his body. He moaned, "Christel could never understand my loyalty. If she did, she would not have chased everyone away from the estate. The tenants, some of the cooks, some of the servants and keepers of the grounds." He struggled to get "I'm co-cold" out of chattering teeth. Samantha, one of Joseph's personal assistants, wrapped a green army blanket around his shoulders. He grabbed Samantha's collar and screamed, "It's a hopeless maze. Don't you see? While on this business trip, Christel destroyed my vision!" He put his head on Samantha's lap. She massaged Joseph's temples. In spirit, he trekked down the narrow path leading to the House of Dijon alongside his mother. Joseph saw his mother pull a small card that another escort, one that already had far too many drinks, and too many parties to attend, had given her as a gift. He read the address, "1111 Myrtille Village," and watched his parents meet for the first time in the summer of 1946, in Dijon, France.

Summer of 1946
Dijon, France

P rudenzia sunk in a mud hole, grabbing a weak branch on the way down. "Hot diggity damn dog!" She felt weird, as if a sheet of wind chimes jangled throughout her psyche. It felt slightly less original than déjà vu, or it could have been a mild form of epilepsy. Perhaps she had also hit her head on a tree. Otherworldly knowledge of her Byronic hero's arrival moved her style in a not-so-innocent manner. "Aren't you a pistol? You come with your own theme song?"

Jean-Pierre pushed his fingers against his lips as if he was a blushing teenage girl. "Perhaps."

Prudenzia looked up, amazed that there was a real person standing over her. "Are you Augustine-Baptiste?" She looked at the card the other escort had given her.

Jean-Pierre rolled his eyes. "No, I'm his brother. His little brother." He held out his hand. "I'm Jean-Pierre. I'm sorry if I seem aloof, but I've developed a headache due to all the perfumes in the House of Dijon."

"Where's that?"

Jean-Pierre pointed at the mansion behind him. "It's like several wicked concoctions."

Prudenzia grabbed his hand, dusted her puffed dress and red and white pinafore with her hands. Her white stockings, black shoes, and white gloves were covered in mud. "Augustine-Baptiste's fantasy is ruined. He told me to deck out in this god-awful mess of a dress. I look like a little girl."

Jean-Pierre frowned. "That's exactly what my brother, the pervert, was going for."

Prudenzia cocked her head. "No fooling!"

"What's your name, Cookie?"

8

"Prudenzia Bianchi is my name. Why do you care? I've been summoned by your brother."

"Such an odd name for a beautiful girl."

"I'm named after several parentela."

John-Pierre tested the weak branch Prudenzia broke.

"That's kinfolk," she blurted, then complimented all of her family members. "They are some of the most beautiful people you'll ever meet."

He avowed, "I think I've already met her." Jean-Pierre took a seat on the wrought iron bench and signaled Prudenzia to sit beside him. "My family forced me to come to my brother's gathering. They want me to find a wife but I don't see how. I can't see through the charm."

"You chicken? You have beef with perfume?"

"No. I'm alluding to certain women, call girls, and their style." He took a drag from a fancy cigarette. A huge puff of smoke accompanied his wheezy "Ha."

Prudenzia teased, "What's wrong with call girls? You got something against them and perfume?"

"I have nothing against nothing. From what I know, it's bad business."

"Maybe you haven't met the right one."

Jean-Pierre wore a big toothy grin. "I guess not."

"I've been drifting around for so long I've forgotten what it's like to be around normal people."

"Normal people," Jean-Pierre jerked his head back, "What do you mean by that?"

Prudenzia enjoyed the smell of his cigarette too much. Her eyelids went droopy. A cheesy grin, slow and overconfident, wrinkled her perfect brow. "It's such a relief to be with normal intentions, normal expectations, and people with real goals."

"Where are you from, Denzi?" Jean-Pierre lit another cigarette. "Can I call you Denzi?"

Prudenzia coughed. "Sure. My father calls me Denzi." She looked at her arm, pale skin shining brighter than Jean-Pierre's, eyes a shade or two lighter. Her hair, a lighter shade of brown.

A picture of Prudenzia's father floated from the edge of her pocket to the ground. Jean-Pierre picked it up. "Who's this?"

She pulled at her collar. "He's the..." She went blank. Every attempt at word building felt vicious, as though words caught themselves in the mangles of her throat or squeaked off her head's plastic nothingness.

Jean-Pierre looked at her, then at the picture again. "You look just like him, but—"

"But what?" She could hear her heart beat in her ears.

"He looks like he could be a black man. One of those black men mixed with white. Some in my family act as if they don't know, but I have a pretty good way of judging."

"You judge people?"

"No. I can tell is all."

She looked at her skin, pumped her fist in the air, almost punching Jean-Pierre's chin. "He's the son of the help and he's my best friend, so don't go speaking ill."

"No, no, I'm not speaking ill. Those things don't bother me. As a child, I used to get in trouble for conversing with the help," Jean-Pierre smiled, "especially the black girls."

"You like black girls?"

"I have nothing against black girls; however, they're different from us. The culture, the struggles, everything. I'd rather not imagine their differences while dealing with xenophobes. I'd rather go with what I know."

"It's true, black people have different struggles, but they aren't as different as you're making it out to be," said Prudenzia, "and what xenophobes are you talking about? Your folks racist?"

"No. They're just used to a certain life. One in which foreigners are destructive and offensive. They think black people are foreigners and should go back to..."

Prudenzia held her chest. "Back to where?"

Jean-Pierre shifted his eyes to the ground. "Back to Africa."

"Then they ARE racist!"

"No. They were raised to distrust whatever's different, to guard against threats to their lineage. It's something they do without giving it real thought. It's deep-rooted."

"I guess Jean-Pierre's making excuses for his racist family is all," she whispered. Prudenzia didn't like the feeling of reassurance in Jean-Pierre's explanation. That warm, gentle tenderness gave birth to an irksome question. *Should I tell Jean-Pierre about my past? Hell no! I can't. I'll surely send him away.*

"What's wrong, Denzi?" He grabbed her hand. "You look clammy and paler than before."

She jerked away. "I know your parents are proud of your brother, Augustine-Baptiste, cavorting with black escorts at the House of Dijon and all."

"Our parents don't know about this place. They wouldn't believe Augustine-Baptiste or I would stay here anyway. Look at the round front porch, windows in the attic, the cellar. My mother would seize. It's unbelievably tiny compared to the castle in Paris."

"The castle!" Prudenzia looked at the house. "The House of Dijon is huge. You mean the castle in Paris is bigger than that?"

"Sure. The House of Dijon is for bachelors and parties in the boondocks. Right now I live with my parents. I'll get my own castle when I marry."

"Right now, I stay in a big house with needy women." She looked Jean-Pierre up and down. From his reckless desert-sand hair, longer and rowdier than anyone she'd ever met of his class, to his fair skin with olive undertones. His hazel eyes complemented his lean, muscular frame. His odd cigarette complemented his mesmeric mouth. "They'll tear you apart. You look like a cake boy."

"What's a cake boy? My brother calls me cake boy bitch all the time."

"Never mind what it is."

"What about you? Would you tear me apart, Denzi?" He cupped her dimpled chin.

She turned pink. Nobody had ever asked her opinion of anything. She looked to the sky, feeling as if she'd been a good girl because the Universe had sent her a friend.

"Denzi, let's get lost. Why don't we run off and get hitched?"

"Cool down! Aren't you a gas? You have to court me with sweet treats." She was surprised at how easily those words slid out of her mouth. She began daydreaming about her feelings, their life's journey, his god-awful jazz cigarettes. She also thought about her past. Again, she wondered if she should tell Jean-Pierre about her struggles, her anything, or, if she should wipe the slate clean.

He clapped his hands. "You in there, Denzi?"

"I'm sorry Jean-Pierre. I apologize for drifting off."

"Nobody's using the House of Dijon."

"So?"

"So I'm moving you in. Nobody will ever know you're there." Jean-Pierre pinched Prudenzia's cheeks. "Look at you blushing."

11

AMINA CAPRICE ANDOLINI

Prudenzia pretended to fight him. "Where will you live?"
"Depending on how we mesh, I'll move in with you." He clutched Prudenzia's hand as they walked toward the House of Dijon. "Denzi, I've already set a date for three months and some change down the road. You know, depending on how we mesh."
"Look at you, planning in advance." Prudenzia laughed.

Sunday, May 28, 2006
The Corporate Jet (Le Bourget, France)

Joseph's Spirit fell in his body through the crown chakra—feet first. It took him a while to focus on the now, that he was still in his corporate jet, on the way to Le Bourget. His son's words bounced around his weightless head. *Christel has crossed the goddamn line again!*

In his mind, he slammed his fist through a table. *Christel must understand my loyalty!* Joseph squawked internally. His eyes worked the cream colored ceiling and back down to the caramel brown carpeting with flecks of gold throughout. He wondered where all the furniture went. *Some will never understand how hard my parents worked to restore the barren estate they were given for punishment.* "My grandparents *were* racists," he mumbled, "they hated Mother Denzi after they discovered the secrets of her past." He massaged his forehead as he thought about the murder of his father's second wife, and how it helped his parents regain their fortune.

He spoke aloud. "Why'd she do it? Why'd Christel ruin my sanctuary? Why does she make me grieve Blueberry Manor's barrenness time after time?"

When they arrived in Le Bourget, Joseph caught a glimpse of his aircraft hangar home before his doctors and security team whisked him off to the mobile clinic. After the isolated glaze in his eyes had left, he found himself in the stretch limousine, the one with the nightclub and bar inside. His grandmother's song, Peacemaker Rag boomed throughout his psyche. He could hear it as clearly as he could feel the flatness of nightclubs, neon lights, and strange looking women. He poured himself a drink. All he wanted to do was stop reliving horrific events of his past and get to the bottom of how Blueberry Manor grew to be a hopeless maze in only six months, during his flights to and from New Zealand, the United States, and France.

Sunday, May 28, 2006
The Equestrian Estate (Le Bourget, France)

hen Kenneth arrived at the equestrian estate in a solid silver sports car and diamond encrusted suit, he saw two of his sisters, twenty-nine-year-old Michelle and twenty-four-year-old Bree, smiling at him. "What are you fucking handbags smiling at? Did Christel's ignorant ass send you here?"

Michelle's face went dull. "If you attended a goddamn meeting, you'd know Bree's been COO of this place and board member for five years and I've been on the board for eleven years."

"Dad's lost his damn mind doubling up on my CEO training. I haven't had time to attend a bitchass meeting. You'd think the old man's about to retire, or die."

Michelle poked Bree in the rib. "No time for bitchass meetings but you have had time to squeeze in a few modeling sessions. Get'cho shiny car and shiny suit wearing—" She took out her camera phone. "Gotta get a picture of this shit."

"Consider yourself lucky," said Bree, "have you spoken with Dad since he left the oil refinery? I called yesterday, just to check, but I couldn't get through."

"I finally got him." Kenneth laughed. "He was red fucking hot at Christel and some dumbass new guys that didn't wanna give him the video call. Either Dad or Big Theon will kick some asses at the meeting. I'm thinking that bitchass, bobble-headed, drunkard Cahlus-Azari has his nose in the situation."

"Again?" Michelle said.

"Yep. And I can't wait." Kenneth did a camel chest move. "Dad's about twenty minutes away from the hangar home. Him and the 'love to love you' crew." He finished with a version of the Egyptian Figure Eight, and

13

laughed. "You blind harpies can't see my professional male belly dancing moves."

Michelle said, "I'm glad I'm blind."

Bree looked at the sky, hand cupped above her eyes. "The *oonta-oont* jet? No wonder. Surprised you were able to get at the 'mighty realest' or speak to Dad at all. You know how they get when Sylvester's blasting."

"All those old dopeheads know how to do is drink, do the fatman dance, and fall the fuck out," said Michelle, "and they deaf as fuck. Surprised they heard the call at all."

"That's the point. They didn't hear the call," said Kenneth. "I had to deal with their incompetence."

"Wow," Michelle and Bree said in unison.

"Wow, Kenneth. You've finally run into people who don't know you or don't give a shit," Michelle said.

"I've run into a lot of somebodies who don't know me, and obviously, they don't know Dad either. What I don't understand is where were the personal assistants?"

"They'd just left the oil refinery," said Michelle, "they're probably swamped."

"They need to be. Keeping the new fuckers in line is one of their jobs now. Big Theon has oomp-fucking-teen new jobs. In fact, Big Theon's whole family is the best at knowing what to do and when to do it. That's why I'm trying to get two of his sons and three of their cousins to work for me."

"That's stupid, Kenneth. What the hell do you need with all those people on the payroll?" said Michelle.

"I'm gonna be CEO, dumbass."

"And what does all that have to do with Dad's drinking?"

"Drinking is a part of the job. See, he shouldn't have to worry about none of this shitness right here. If I had Dad's power right now, I'd hire a crew just to beat Christel's fucking ass."

"Could that be why they didn't want to give Dad the video call," said Bree, "because they didn't want him to worry?"

"They didn't give him the video call because they're a bunch of fucking assholes. You know Dad's rule... ALWAYS put us through, no matter what." He whispered, "Dumbasses."

Michelle laughed. "Coming from you. You're a drunk-out-the-ass drunk your damn self. You take classes on drunkenness and hair of the

14

dog, too?" She slapped her knee in jest.

"Look who's talking, chimney head ass. You needa leave that Kryptonite alone. Killer weed lookin' ass."

"That's enough, Kenneth," Bree said.

"No! Dad drinks to relieve stress," said Kenneth, "do you know how many fucking jobs he has? He's a workaholic, and then has to put up with Christel's ass."

"So," said Michelle.

"So, we're multi-billionaires," said Kenneth. "He doesn't have to be a workaholic." He glared at Michelle. "Do you know how many jobs he has?"

"What, you think I'm a fucking Mary Jane plant? I know how many goddamn jobs he has." Michelle raised her voice, "I'm on the goddamn board. And Dad should be here but he's somewhere drunk on a plane."

"Right now we're here because of Mom's nonsense, not Dad's drinking," said Bree.

Michelle said, "He's an alcoholic is what he is."

Kenneth waved his hand around. "I'm not studying you, Michelle, and I'm not studying Christel's ass either. Dad should have strangled the bitch a long time ago."

Michelle and Bree gasped in unison. "Kenneth!"

Kenneth hunched his shoulders. "I can't stand the bitch. And I wanna see what Dad does when he finds out what she's been doing for the last six months. While he's been in New Zealand, she's been driving the tenants crazy with her lousy ass-out arrogance. Always talking about how we're wasting money and shit, and look what she's doing. She has messed up millions on that dumb donkey shit. You know how much she spends on Kush?"

Michelle gave Bree a dismal look.

"Hell no!" He held the 'L' as if he was singing, "Hell to the muthafuckin no, goddammit. It's still with me, how those stick-in-the-ass fuckers tortured me about my weed headed mother."

"I don't blame Mom," said Michelle. "Those tenants, and especially the tourists, were noncompliant, belligerent, and dirty. Instead of all that Kush, she needta smoke they asses."

"Oh, that's your answer? Mow they asses down with a Thompson?" Kenneth turned slowly while clapping to an imaginary audience. "Future business head, current business head." He clapped louder. "Fucking A."

Michelle held her head up.

Bree gasped. "Kenneth!"

"We know what the fuck she is and how she do."

"You can't talk about anybody in this bitch, little brother. How many goddamn children is it now, fuckboy?"

Bree blocked Kenneth's swipe.

"Deadbeat!" Michelle said.

"What IS your devil-horse lookin' ass doing here?" Kenneth quipped.

"I'm here to be our mom's voice." Michelle retorted.

Bree mouthed, "It's alright" while holding Kenneth back.

Three stretch limousines pulled to the estate's entrance. "That's gotta be Dad in one of those," said Kenneth. He rubbed his hands together. "I can't wait until he hears the whole story."

Electronic house music drowned out Kenneth's voice. When the driver of the second limousine opened the doors, a cloud of Dominican smoke curled to the roof of the car. Michelle and Bree complained about the strong stench of scotch, hurricane cocktails, and seafood.

One of Joseph's personal assistants handed Kenneth two medium-sized boxes.

"Samantha, what the hell is this?"

"Seafood po-boys, dressed. Distribute to the peacemakers at the meeting, po-boy," she exploded in paradoxical laughter, "there are hundreds more boxes coming."

Kenneth looked at the limousines. "Where the damn boxes?"

"Being flown in." She spoke disapprovingly. "Today, one of your glorious jobs is to help the caterers."

Kenneth held his arms out and looked down at his suit. "What the hell I look like, a goddamn waiter?"

"A very expensive waiter. Seriously, that message is from your father." Samantha looked at Kenneth's suit. "I suggest you go to the main house and change clothes."

"I haven't been to this equestrian estate in fourteen goddamn years. I have NO clothes up there that will fit."

"You can find some in the guest wing."

Kenneth joked with a snickering bodyguard, "Okay, but if someone touches my diamond suit..."

The bodyguard could barely contain his laughter. "I know you ain't fucked up about a suit, Kenneth."

16

"I'm not, but whoever touches it will be."

"Enough!" Samantha said. She signaled to the bodyguard, and told Kenneth to go to the guest wing.

Kenneth uttered, "Old crow lookin' ass." He hopped in his silver sports car and drove to the main house while Michelle and Bree snapped pictures with their camera phones.

"There's Dad," said Bree.

Joseph waved at his daughters as soon as he stepped out of the limousine. He looked around, thought about the last time he had been to the equestrian estate. "Le cavalier de Satan. This is where Mom told me about her wild childhood, and how Grandma Ginger addressed her as Satan's Rider."

The blackness that served as a trippy movie screen dissolved in a liquid lightshow. Splotches took on trippy patterns—paisley, psychedelic, and bulbous, danced with backwards lyrics and melded with present time's sepia.

"Sir? Mr. Charlemagne, sir." The security agent put his hand on Joseph's shoulder. "All scheduled to appear have arrived. They're waiting in the conference hall." When he received no response, the agent signaled for the three emergency physicians and three psychoanalysts huddled outside the medi-spa and clinic. Their feet struck the ground like horses' hooves, ushering Joseph back to coherency. "No, Nukey. I visited the mobile clinic at the hangar house."

Nukey shooed the doctors away. "Mr. Charlemagne, I heard about the episode on the corporate jet." He put his hand on Joseph's shoulder. "We all want to make sure your health hasn't gotten any worse."

"It hasn't." Joseph pulled a Dominican cigar out of his inside pocket. "I haven't been to this place in a very long time. I'm afraid I've forgotten the way."

Nukey gave Joseph a triple torch diamond and brass cigar lighter adorned with skulls and roses, and a matching cutter. "This is for you, Mr. Charlemagne."

Joseph was impressed, until Nukey lit a doobie with an immodest lighter: one of a woman sliding up and down an erotic pole.

"Thank you, Nukey. This is my go to company."

"It's an anniversary gift. I remember the last time you were here. Fourteen years ago today. 1992." He ghost inhaled, blew smoke tornadoes

17

and rings while Joseph looked in wonderment. "Please," he finished up rather quickly, "follow me, Mr. Charlemagne." Nukey signaled area security personnel—four bumbling security guards dressed in black and red camouflage to follow them.

"This place has changed. The colors: red, black, gold, the blue and red wildflowers, the vineyards... antique opulence!" Joseph spoke in Nukey's ear, "Are the extra guards necessary?" The smell of marijuana on Nukey's clothes was overwhelming. Joseph massaged his forehead.

Nukey masked his voice. "Yes. There have been many attempts at theft and kidnapping." He smiled at area security personnel. "The Golden Lobby is basically the same."

Pictures of Joseph's mother and grandfather at the stables, candid childhood shots, pictures and paintings of his childhood pet, Mr. Horse Head, decorated the wall behind the front desk. Pictures of his grandmother, circa 1922, her records, scenes from her jazz performances in Italy, the jazz funerals in New Orleans, and many pictures of the musically inclined Charlemagne family lined the music hall.

"Nukey, do children under 18 get free lessons for music and sports," Joseph said.

"Yes, they do."

Joseph looked at the massive computers in the Sci-Fi office. The computers were 'talking,' spitting out cards, and making phone calls.

A woman overseeing the smaller computer robots blindly put her clipboard on the table when she saw Joseph. She squealed. "I haven't seen you in soooo many years!" Other employees flocked to Joseph's company.

Joseph said, "I know. It's good to see you, Mallory."

Mallory bit her lip. "Will I see your son, Mr. Charlemagne? I have seen his entire portfolio." She fanned herself with a little hand fan she yanked out of another employee's pocket.

Joseph looked at the ceiling, rolled his eyes around to Mallory's eager face. "Yes, Kenneth will be here."

Mallory gave Joseph a hug and kissed him on the cheek before skipping back to the Sci-Fi office.

"In addition to all sports and musical instruments, there is still a waiting list for free horse and pony riding lessons," said Nukey.

"Those things are handled by Bree, right?"

"Most of them." Nukey's eyes met the floor. "She was going to discuss her progress with you at the next big meeting, which as it turns out, is today."

"I'm looking forward to seeing more of this place, I've neglected it for far too long, but I'm not happy about what's been going on at Blueberry Manor while I've been away. I suppose that's what the meeting is about."

"We understand your apprehension, Mr. Charlemagne."

Joseph nodded, unsure what to think of the cheesy grin on Nukey's face.

"Your daughter, Bree, has left a lasting impression on me. With the pet therapy program, the new petting zoo, pet boarding," he turned around, "that's the pet hotel. She put the pet training and summer camp in place. She has hired many new people."

Joseph said, "What the hell are they responsible for?" unable to get the stars in Nukey's eyes out of his wit.

"I am most familiar with the concierge service. And there are many weddings, parties, funerals, sports events, veterinarian conventions, all kinds of things held out here. The jobs became too big for Bree to handle alone, though she practically lives here at the sports complex."

"So, you've been helping her?"

Nukey nodded.

"My Bree has been an athlete and trainer ever since childhood. She has been a professional swimming instructor for three years, a veterinarian for two. I'm proud of her. In fact, she met her fiancé at one of the football games out here." He blew a huge cloud of smoke in the air.

Nukey pulled in the corner of his mouth, exposing his boyish dimple. "Excusez-moi, Monsieur Charlemagne. Je ne devrais pas trop parler... I should not talk so much."

Joseph tapped Nukey's shoulder blade while mouthing, "It's alright. Now you be careful, Nukey. You never know when I'll show up."

"I understand, Mr. Charlemagne."

"Talk to your boss. Big Theon could have a more suited position available for you."

"But—" Nukey smashed his open palm against his forehead.

"That is, unless you want to be a veterinarian or get into athleticism."

"No, of course not, Mr. Charlemagne."

A guard opened the doors to the conference hall. The rich, familiar smell of wood welcomed Joseph; however, the buzz of people darting around, developing a tight strategy for damage control annoyed him. He tapped his cane on the wall, hitting one of the light switches by accident.

Everyone scrambled to a seat, but not before a silver disco ball came shimmering out of the ceiling.

"What's the purpose of this meeting?" Joseph looked at his grandmother's and mother's pictures, ribbons, and trophies in the trophy cases, their eyes sparkling due to the disco ball's rounds.

BJ Valenteen, a short man of Middle Eastern heritage raised his hand. "Mr. Charlemagne, BJ Valenteen here."

"Yes, I see you, BJ." Joseph sat at his usual table. Kenneth along with several business associates snuck in the meeting via the back door.

"My eyes went blurry after receiving that court order from your wife."

There was light groaning among several of the board members. "Fuckin' great... HER again!"

"That should never have happened," Joseph said.

BJ attempted to loud talk the crowd. "Many of us received eviction notices from Mrs. Christel. For the past six months, she has driven almost every tenant away from the estate. Many of our companies have lost valuable executives because of her antics."

Joseph banged his gavel on the table. "Silence, everybody! Go on BJ."

"I interrupted Ms. McDaniel, the senior event coordinator and told her to set this meeting."

Joseph looked around. "Where is Ms. McDaniel?"

"Vacationing with her mother in Hawaii."

Joseph looked at his mother's pictures. "What incident did you witness?"

20

BLUEBERRY MANOR

"I witnessed an extremely heated argument between Christel and Rosswell S. Reinhart. Mrs. Christel cursed at him, spat and insulted his mother."

The room gasped.

Another board member chimed in. "And keep in mind that his mother died three days ago. That's probably why he snapped, grabbed Mrs. Christel's throat and threw her on the ground. The incident is all over the local and worldwide news, the 'normal' internet and there are uncut versions on the dark parts of the web. You know, the parts you have to pay a satellite company to see." He addressed Joseph, "Mr. Charlemagne, sir, have you seen the incident between Christel and Mr. Reinhart?"

"My doctors wouldn't let me see it on the jet, or in the limo," said Joseph, "but I did get a call from Kenneth." Thick wafts of smoke circled his head.

"Mrs. Christel helped run people away using amped-up stories of Suntilian Devils; the amphibian and reptile hybrids that live underneath the Suntilian Isle Cul-de-Sac," said BJ.

Joseph smiled. "I know about Suntilian Devils."

"Well, for us it's just a story, but others swear it's the golden truth. Christel likes to play on other people's fears."

A board member said, "Like Satan." Others shook their heads and mumbled in agreement.

"She's a beautiful disaster," said one of the new board members. His gaze fixed on Michelle, 5'6" 135 pounds with tan skin, platinum blonde hair, brown roots, and hazelnut eyes.

Michelle spoke softly. "Bree, that creep-ass new board member has loud thoughts."

"You'll never know he's been married ten months. His wife just gave birth to triplets last week." Bree slowly cocked her head, widened her eyes at the board member, and flicked her tongue.

Michelle also stuck out her tongue, not realizing she'd just piqued his interest further.

BJ continued. "She also brought about absurd hikes in rent, phony court orders, and unwanted media attention." BJ ruffled his papers.

The room gasped.

Members of the board broke off in little conversations...

An elderly man shook his fist in the air. "She should be ashamed of her vile, degraded self!"

"Mr. Reinhart has a ruthless lawyer. He will press for a lawsuit," said BJ, "and then it's over for us."

Joseph stood, banging his gavel on the table. Dominican smoke circled his entire being. "For the new guys," everybody looked at the young bodyguards, "Rosswell is one of my best friends, the COO of Charlemagne, Khoury & Greco, a multinational law and engineering conglomerate I started up in 1978. That's for those who failed to do homework before getting hired. Rosswell is the husband of another longtime friend and business partner of mine, Cortina Khoury-Reinhart. That my wife and my best friend are at odds is a big, costly, scandal-seething deal. And you," Joseph pointed his gavel at Cahlus-Azari.

There were gasps and muttering. "Must be serious. He never calls 'em out by name."

Joseph banged his gavel on the table. "I didn't want to call you out in front of everyone, but—" Kenneth rubbed his hands together. The wide grin on his face would have been disturbing if he weren't so refined. "I know Big Theon has already punished you. I agree with his decision of demoting you instead of firing you."

Uproar!

"You have excellent references; however, important information slipped past your executives, things I realize aren't your fault. It has also come to my attention that you weren't briefed accordingly before taking this job, so..." Joseph rounded his shoulders.

Kenneth yelled, "That's all it is to it?"

Joseph said nothing.

BJ tried to speak over the nonsense. "Mr. Charlemagne, I invited everyone here because many members of the Blueberry Manor Estate Board of Directors were vacationing in Paris with their mothers." Several board members loosened their ties. "Kenneth was modeling in Épernay."

"Where's Kenneth?"

Kenneth stood in a perfectly tailored, tighter than usual, charcoal gray suit, brown shirt, no tie, and brown loafers, no socks. Several women fanned themselves. Two others actually fainted. Embarrassed, Kenneth buttoned two spacey buttons on his shirt and unbuttoned his jacket. He couldn't hide his ankles.

Joseph's voice softened. "You look so nice."

Kenneth shook his head, a slow no.

His voice dipped to a snappish, cranky low. "I thought I told you to

22

cut the shit?"

"I apologize, Dad; however, the photoshoots are infrequent. They don't now, nor will they ever interfere with my CEO-in-training duties."

"Good answer. And your image?"

"Impeccable."

Several women expressed their agreement.

Kenneth smiled at Michelle and Bree. He caught another young woman (the daughter of the COO of one of Joseph's restaurants) before she hit the floor.

Michelle spoke to Bree. "They some dumbass hoes. They know how many children Kenneth has, yet they still run after him. And because of the dumb bitch that fainted, that's why Dad doesn't allow girls who aren't a member of the board to attend these meetings."

"What about the first two who fainted? They've been on the board for fifteen years."

Michelle hunched her shoulders. "Some of these women have known Kenneth since birth." She hissed, "Shameful. What-in-the-hell do they see in him anyway?"

Bree wiped a speck of Michelle's spit off the side of her face.

The new board member drooled over several pictures he had snapped of Michelle.

"Look at him," Michelle said.

"Who," said Bree.

Michelle laughed. "The new board member. He's hella bold. I could get his ass fired for taking pictures of me. And tell Nukey's ass to keep his eyeballs off you or else he stands a chance of getting fired too."

"Nukey went to school to be a veterinarian but never became one. Guess he's living his dreams through me." Bree tried to cover her smile but was unsuccessful.

"You like that criminal!" Michelle exclaimed.

Bree shushed her. "As much as I can. If it weren't for Jon."

Michelle interrupted her. "Don't let Nukey hear you say that shit. The twisted motherfucker would kill Jon."

Bree waved her hands. "You're making something out of nothing, Michelle."

"Alright, 'making something out of nothing.' I know sicko motherfuckers like Nukey. Who do you think taught me how to stalk that fine Pika?"

"Do you mean the Hawaiian model?" asked Bree.

"Yes. A sicko like Nukey taught me the ins and outs of stalking. Keep fucking with him, Bree, and we'll find you on the side of the road in a torn nightgown and shit."

"You have a wild imagination. If anything, if Dad is concerned about Nukey's feelings for me, he'll move him to another location. Nukey is a hard worker. Dad doesn't want to lose him."

"Nukey is a criminal, dope head and liar is what he is." Michelle crossed her arms, squeezing her plastic chest. "I heard from a," she cleared her throat, "friend in the industry, that Nukey's ass went to jail for kidnapping women and forcing 'em to work in his adult films." She laughed. "He wanted the realistic effect. He's never been to goddamn college. He's a pot-face liar. A fuck up. He's gonna forget, light the Kush in front of Dad and it's curtains for him."

Bree's voice went up a few octaves. "Does Dad know Nukey's a criminal?" Michelle pursed her lips. "Then why'd they hire him?"

Michelle claimed, "Nukey's father, Mr. Whitehair, creepiest of all creep-ass fuckers, is a friend of Big Theon. So watch out, Bree, you're right, Nukey will be around for a long time…"

A male board member shushed Michelle and Bree. They both made wry expressions at him until someone caught the attention of Joseph, who waved his cane and told them all to listen to BJ.

BJ continued. "I knew that you, Mr. Charlemagne, and other business associates were on the way to Reims from the six-month long business trip to New Zealand." The entire crew, including Joseph, had guilty looks on their faces. "Yes, the rest of us thank you for your brave contributions. I hear that area is harsh. And a little R&R afterwards would not be unexpected."

Kenneth and the entire crew gave knowing glances at one another.

"Everyone could get to this conference hall at around the same time, much quicker than if we tried to meet at Blueberry Manor. Besides, I believe Christel and her band of reporters is expecting that."

"They're at Blueberry Manor now," Joseph said.

"Correct, Sir. Here we must break down what this means and how much she has cost the companies this time."

A board member screamed, "Not a-DAMN-gain! There was groaning and uproar. Joseph beat his gavel on the table.

BJ and the other board members' words faded in the background. Joseph thought about moving out of Blueberry Manor, in one of the

BLUEBERRY MANOR

cottages at Suntilian Isle Cul-De-Sac: a three-story casino complete with antique muscle cars, Italian cooks, gourmet desserts, and delicious processed food. The gambling, cars and food helped Joseph deal with the triggers, the guilt and shame brought on by not witnessing his mother, father, sister, or brother's last death struggles.

He went on weird binging sprees and self-medication ruins shortly after each incident. He allowed family members, friends, and a few business associates to inhabit specific areas of the compound—the Suntilian Isle Cul-De-Sac, two hotels, a palace, manor houses, and the chapel for little or no rent. His actions angered Christel, especially when he let people inhabit the grounds for a song.

Just the thought of Christel driving even more people off the estate with her madness was overwhelming. His blackouts were frequent, but as of lately, they'd been escorted by sweet-smelling memories and pictures of the past.

Joseph didn't want to be at this meeting, at this sensitive place with its nostalgic manifestations. He grudgingly looked up, saw pictures of his mother and father's wedding in 1946. A yellowish-brown picture of Joseph's uncle, Augustine-Baptiste, jumped out of a shadowed corner, not one to miss the chance of showing out during this visit.

He massaged his temples, chipping away at wilder visions. His mother's illegal procedure, surrounded by dangerous herbal mixtures, animal parts, and Grandma Ginger's demonic verse:

She's a pale rider, riding her ashy horse; cutting us down with her scythe. SSS-SSS-Serpent Race!

He saw his birth in 1952, relived his parents' divorce in 1955, and the murder of his father's second wife, Madame Antoinette. He could see her lying dead in a bowl of poisonous chicken soup, her eyes totally white, mouth ajar.

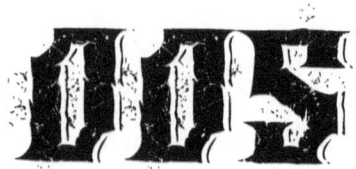

Christel threw two bottles of medicine in her empty brass waste basket. "The hell with medicine. What fucko needs this medicine?" She forced herself to the elevator, rubbed her eyes, kept walking until she fell at the feet of the staircase. She slurred, "They've moved the goddamn drawing room again."

"Lost? Do you need any help, My Lady?"

Christel ignored the help. She always ignored that kind of help. She only conversed with supervisors, which of course, weren't really help, though sometimes they had to do the same work as lower staff. Once she made it to the drawing room, she saw Joseph standing at the bay window. She switched to victim mode, going on about one of her friend's small-headed husband, new spa treatments, frozen hurricane cocktails, peach tea and vodka, and perhaps a little spiced rum for her coffee.

Joseph refused to speak. All he could think about was the barren estate and the urge to squeeze her fat ass head in a vise. *It's baffling how beautiful she is,* he thought, the same 33-years later. *Same waxy hair, slightly lighter than it was then, oval face, alien-like Nordic features, large almond shaped eyes lined with purple shimmer eyeliner, smoky eyeshadow, long brownish eyelashes and thick brownish eyebrows. Such a fucking shame. All that beauty and talent wasted on a monstrous whore.*

Joseph screamed internally, FUUUCK! SHUT YOUR FUCKING MOUTH, YOU EVIL BITCH.

"Can't stand mumbling," said Christel. "You're on my last goddamn nerve; blocking sunlight with your silent treatment head ass. And why the hell *are* you here? You wanna cry because of exile," she whimpered

26

BLUEBERRY MANOR

like a bratty teen. "Well, the restaurants and wine houses are always full of disgusting ass people, and if you think about rolling your eyes at me again, fatman, I'll stab a knife inside your big brown body fat."

"You're impossible." Joseph slid his left hand across his forehead. The burning at the back of his throat made him cough, an empty faux cough. He inhaled deeply, ending each breath with an awkward snort.

"You're turning me off my food, you asshole."

"You have no fucking food!" Joseph responded.

"I told you to cover your mouth when you cough, goddammit!" Joseph slammed his fist on a table, smashing it in chunks.

Christel shrieked, "What the hell is wrong with you?"

Joseph squeezed, "I can't hold it in any longer," through clinched teeth.

"I know that look, you dummy bastard. Well, per doctor's orders you can't say anything to me or your blood pressure will skyrocket again." She turned her back.

Joseph slipped his curved fingers around Christel's neck. "That's why I moved to Suntilian Isle."

She laughed. "Did you growl at me? I haven't seen you in over six goddamn months." When she turned around, Joseph's fingers were pressed against her thyroid. He shook her neck back and forth, swimming in her lifeless stare.

In his mind, he'd put Christel in a chokehold. Blood spewed out of her perfect nipples as he posed for his mugshot, one heel dug in her back, the tip of his toes planted firmly in her plastic split.

"What the hell you think you're doing, madman?" She could only manage three hollow swipes at Joseph's sleeve. His eyes went cloudy with aspiration to squeeze something until it popped. "What's wrong with your eyes!" After perceiving fast shadows on the other side of the drawing room door, she flailed her arms and legs while yelling, "You wanna strangle me?"

The head housekeeper, fifteen parlor maids, ladies' maids, and several butlers trampled each other. Some started fights of their own. The servants dedicated to Christel attacked the ones dedicated to serving Joseph, breaking several pieces of furniture on the way to the great house.

27

The head housekeeper called out to one of the butlers, "Mr. Placidus! Go back to your assigned station. Christel's servants have pocket knives this go round!"

"This *is* the chamber I assigned Placidus," said the house steward. "So uncouth." He screamed while ducking, "Mrs. Hermina!" She hurried to Mr. Cornelius, "I thought Sir Joseph moved in one of the cottages at Suntilian Isle as soon as he returned from New Zealand." His grin was tall and sly. "What's he doing here now?"

"He did move," Mrs. Hermina said. She caught a flying vase, "But he entered the manor house before sunrise." Mr. Cornelius shook his head. "Some folks saw him walking through the house, smiling, like a big fat madman."

Mr. Cornelius gasped. "Has he lost his mind?"

"All I know is he waited for sunrise in the very place My Lady has her morning cocktails." Mrs. Hermina ducked and screamed after a dish broke near her ear.

Mr. Cornelius narrowed his eyes. "The sorciére."

Mr. Shellcroft, a middle-aged butler with a fishtail bun leaped behind a sculpture after furniture smashed against the drawing room door. "Mr. Cornelius, they'll surely leave a bloody scene. The last scene was abominable; just thinking about it makes my stomach queasy."

"No queasy stomachs on my watch," said Mr. Cornelius, "you should go, and call for several vans of emergency help on the way out."

"What if My Lady notices my absence?" Mr. Shellcroft protected his head from flying teacups.

Mr. Cornelius laughed. "That's easy. If the sorciére asks about you, I'll say the noise agitated her rabbit farm." A small piece of wood flew into Mr. Cornelius' mouth. "I hate her 'vomit is a sign of the devil' speech. Now go!" He looked around at the broken furniture.

The thought of Mr. Cornelius calling Christel a witch made Mr. Shellcroft laugh aloud. He held his jiggly belly, shaking as if he'd created a new dance.

"I'll surely need emergency care," said Mr. Cornelius, "but I should clean this place before My Lady sees it." He swallowed. "I'm appalled. This is NOT part of my job description."

Joseph screamed, "Oh my fucking Christ in the goddamned crux!" Christel's hurricane glass slipped out of her hand.

BLUEBERRY MANOR

"Look at this fucking shit!"

"Let me go! It's your fault I dropped it." She searched a cabinet for her color changing highball glass, "Screaming like a goddamn loon!"

"If you weren't so fucking annoying," Joseph said.

"Fuck you, dummy bastard!" Christel snarled. "You don't know fucking annoying." She spiked her peach tea with vodka. "Such a soft butter-brown cookie."

"Why are you bringing race into this?"

She bickered, "Butter-brown has nothing to do with race, you stupid, ignorant, illiterate ass Guinea. Who gives a fuck about your punk race anyway? Guinea nig—"

Joseph struck Christel's mouth with the back of his hand, causing her to fall face down in a puddle of hot tea.

She bragged, "You didn't break me. See what the hell you done did with that weak ass pimp slap, you idiot. You made me spill goddamn tea on the rug. Lick it up!" She twitched. Blood from her mouth rolled off her teeth. "Bald, where the fucking hell are you?"

"The Green has gone barren." Joseph raised his hands as if he could restore its splendor.

"Look at you, you big baby," she laughed, "with your head up, crying like I stole your last bottle."

He yelled, "I'm not the alcoholic."

"Fuck you!" Christel walked to a mirror, cleaned the blood in her mouth with an old linen napkin on the floor.

"Because of you my land has been trash for six goddamn months. Chasing tenants away, closing the compound... What the hell is wrong with you, Christel?"

She bellowed in the intercom, "Hey! Where the hell are you parlor maids?" She whispered. "Want something done right 'round here..."

Joseph followed her to the kitchen. "Look, you wench, father and I raised a hotel on this land to house family, friends, friends of friends." He apologized to the lower staff.

"I'm not here for them, Joseph." Christel screamed at the kitchen and laundry maids in French. "Move! And where the hell is the head housekeeper? I should clean house."

"You knew!"

"Knew what?"

"The dignitaries were to pay little to no rent."

29

Christel laughed. "Dignitaries?"

"How could you do this to our family's businesses? Look at it." His attempts to grab Christel's face were unsuccessful. He fell on the sharpened tip of an oyster knife.

Christel laughed hysterically. "You're so fucking dumb."

Joseph's vision went red. He choked on the mere thought of drowning in thick, red liquid. As he coughed up blood, Christel's laughter took on a slow, barbarous pitch.

Several servants rushed to Joseph's side. He carried on while rejecting their efforts to dress his wound. "Look at my weeping land. It longs for lots of familiar trampling feet."

Christel raced up to the servants and took the dishtowels out of their hands. "You stupid or what? These are my best dishtowels, goddammit. Look at the embroidery here!" She clapped a towel on Joseph's wound. He winced.

Christel mocked him. "And I didn't do anything to the family's fucking businesses!"

"You chased tenants away with your drunken ramblings, hike in rent, bogus court orders." Joseph started to tremble.

"And what the hell's wrong with you?"

Joseph said, "I looked over the past. No, I was there, seeing it as it happened, in real time."

"Like a goddamn ghost?" Christel fluttered her fingers as if she were summoning a spirit.

"Maybe. It was definitely an OBE experience."

Christel rolled her eyes. "Liar."

"I saw the purple orbs. They brought me here. I floated over the whole compound, remembering its conception, the growth and the peak of its success. And now I remember what happened just three days ago."

Christel searched the floor's crevasses with her eyes. "You mean to tell me, you've been on a blackout this entire time?" She laughed. "You're a stupid, dumb Guinea. Go on to the goddamn doctor, Madman."

"I've already been to several."

"You're crazy, Joseph. You need to see all he doctors you can."

Anger made Joseph's eyesight fade to red again. "I saw Grandma Ginger. I felt her pain giving birth to a baby who looked like the people who killed her entire family."

Christel's cheeks inflated. She popped out a horrible wheeze,

30

coughing, holding her chest, rolling on the floor as if she had demented fluid in her lungs. She fell short of breath, but still managed to say, "Why the hell," and "KKK!"

Joseph could only imagine Christel's mocking: of Grandma Ginger's fear of the archaic nemesis, of her minor and the major breakdowns, and when she killed herself because his mother looked like a white girl. Joseph slid his fingers across his forehead. Christel's horrible wheeze had started to echo throughout his reality. He cocked his head and continued. "My Momma." He poured himself a cup of coffee spiked with spiced rum. "Mother Denzi. I saw her, felt the pain of the medium. I saw her and Dad's meeting, their marriage, and the breakdown."

"What goddamn breakdown? All the goddamn Charlemagnes are fucking head cases," said Christel.

"I'm not talking about ALL the Charlemagnes, just my uncle, Augustine-Baptiste."

Christel went into an immediate daze, grabbing onto several pieces of broken furniture in an attempt to stand.

"I saw him threaten Mother Denzi. I saw her procedure. I saw my grandfather force Mother Denzi and Dad on this land-Blueberry Manor, inhospitable countryside, an abandoned castle because of her mixed heritage. Through hard work, extremely hard work, they made this land what it is today."

Christel walked toward Joseph.

"No, don't come near me, Christel!"

"Why?"

"Because I'll surely kill you."

She cackled. "Whatever, Madman. And I'll haunt you every second. I'll make you crazier."

"Everything goes back to mixed heritage." Joseph slammed the now empty coffee cup on a table. "Generations of racism. I want Blueberry Manor, Blueberry Village, Blueberry Hills Compound, whatever they wanna call it, to be a place anybody can come." He waved his hands in the air. "I want this entire compound filled with all shades. You knew that from day one." He raised his voice, "you know racism rode my Grandma Ginger senseless! it turned my mother into a murderer!"

"You're not making sense, you doddering old bastard. No... you know what? Fuck your vision! I'm tired of family and friends freeloading. And the tourists were fucking criminals."

"There's no such thing as freeloading. Even if we didn't have more than we could use in one damn lifetime, to keep all this to ourselves is blasphemous. I don't understand your way of thinking. What's wrong with opening our home?"

Christel shook her head in victory. "Shut your ugly mouth." She clasped her fingers. "Nobody wants to hear about that dumbass, boring ass, donkey ass shit." She grabbed Joseph by the elbow. "You know what? Just leave!"

Joseph rolled his eyes, allowing Christel to believe in her strong grip. "No surprise you want me to leave." He broke away from her manhandling.

"Hell, yeah I want you to leave." She followed him to the great hall, "So what? So what if I did away with the little shits, so fucking what?" She poked Joseph's nose with her long, iridescent nail claw. "And this time, I'm gonna invite the judge in to make it a permanent stick."

"It figures. Who'll help you pull the boring shit off, huh?"

"I don't need anyone's help!"

"Who is it? Clarence the goddamn Priest!"

Christel took an unnatural gasp, then bellowed, "So what if he does goddamn help me?" She raised her voice to a screech. "You won't goddamn help, goddammit!"

"Clarence pretended to be me on several occasions. I should put his ass in jail."

"Joseph! You bush viper!"

"What is it with you and that fly motherfucker? You're old enough to be his fuck-king mother!"

"If I had him at fifteen!"

Joseph attempted to talk over her but Christel made it impossible.

"I don't give a damn about tenants and digni-fucking-taries. So what? The fuckers were making up lies to the media so's I had to kick 'em to the fucking curb. So fucking what? The people did nothing but peek through the fucking bars and use the um, the fucking spray cans on the front damn gate. You and your father raised a circus. How dare you smear this elephant shit all over my head! I'm no ringleader, goddammit!"

"They were peeking through the bars to see you, you whore," said Joseph.

"Did you say whore?"

"I said, w-h-o-r-e, whore."

Christel bumped Joseph with her chest. "You calling me a whore with your big bad ass?"

"You're a violet eyed, platinum-haired whore. Get outta my face, Christel!"

"Now wait one minute you Guinea bastard. You big fat jack of an ass. Don't go brand new, putting all this shit on my head."

Joseph walked toward the front doors with his ears plugged. He accidently kicked her ankle on the way out.

"That was no accident you." She struggled to keep her balance. "Damn right I did what I did!" She fell on the floor, her back to the front doors. "I'm glad they're fucking gone, you," she twitched, "Bald... Bald Balderson!"

nknown voices cleared their throats.

Christel looked up. "What the hell are you people doing here? I didn't call for emergency goddamn help."

"My Lady, I'm Monsieur Moreau," he introduced his wife and a few other emergency medical technicians, "we all have instructions to take you to L'Hôpital Mont Olympus."

"I don't... if anything, drag the madman's ass to the goddamn madhouse this time."

The emergency help looked confused. Monsieur Moreau said, "My Lady, are you referring to Mr. Charlemagne?"

"Who the hell else?"

"We did not see him when we walked in. Only you on the floor," Madame Moreau said. "Is this another breakdown?"

"No!" Christel spoke to Monsieur Moreau. "That's not possible. You're all some blind motherfuckers is what you are." She looked around, still rubbing her ankle.

"Do you need us to look at your ankle," said Monsieur Moreau. He reached down.

"No," Christel swatted. "Get the hell away from me. How long have I been on the floor?" One of the emergency medical technicians took notes. "You! What the hell are you writing? Stop that writing. I need no help from you or anyone else. And you can't make me."

Some of the emergency medical technicians looked at each other and raised their eyebrows.

"How could you not see him when you strolled in, goddammit?" Christel struggled to get off the floor by herself.

"We don't know how long you were on the floor," said Monsieur Moreau. "If he was here at all, perhaps he slipped out one of the other doors or windows." Monsieur Moreau examined the windows and doors.

34

BLUEBERRY MANOR

"There's gotta be at least twenty in this room alone." He grabbed Christel's arm.

Christel jerked away. "Leave me the fuck alone! What do you mean 'if'? If I said he was here, then he was here."

"Whatever you say, My Lady, but we still have to follow our instructions."

"Who gave you your instructions?"

"Your brother."

"Tell him to go to hell."

"My Lady, we have specific instructions. We are not to leave here without you."

"Well I guess you guys will be here all fucking night."

"That's a very tempting offer, but—" A woman cleared her throat, "Excusez moi, mademoiselle."

Christel smiled. "You can stay too. I don't discriminate."

"We have no choice but to take you willingly," Madame Moreau pulled out a pair of handcuffs, "or by force."

Christel's eyes lit. "What kind of force?"

While walking the grounds in "Forest of the Blind Monk" territory, Joseph felt heavy breathing on the back of his neck. He pawed around, ending his movement with a karate pose. "Just what kind of spirit are you," he demanded. After asking that particular question, Joseph could feel his lips wither. His eyes felt small and red, knees buckled, teeth chattered, and cold liquid beaded across his forehead.

Joseph covered his mouth. All he could smell was foul breath. A heavy buzzing knocked him off his feet. He fell on the ground, put flowers in his ears and covered his head with his arms.

Everything had gone black; however, he was consciously aware of his surroundings. He could see a gang of brown goosebumps out of his third eye. His body ached with painfully numb needles that stabbed his internal organs. He opened his eyes to a blurry scene. Three mysterious monks: dark skinned, long bay colored robes, sackcloth, with black points like Mr. Horse Head's coat, and a tonsure.

Joseph said internally, *I shouldn't have eaten seven blueberry muffin cupcakes. They weren't vegetarian or vegan.* His eyes focused on a dark red demon in a short sackcloth robe. He loosened his white rope belt, removed his hood, revealing a tonsure. The unshaved hair was a curly afro. He had a black mustache, pointed goatee, and black misshapen hooves.

"Why under God's sun are you sitting up here arguing with that devil's assed hoe-bitch? Look, she does what-the-fuck-ever, so you do what-the-fuck-ever."

"And how am I supposed to do that?" Joseph asked the demon. "She's stronger than me. I don't like all that cursing. The doctor advised against it."

"Motherfucker is you slow?"

"No."

"Do I have to teach you how to tie your damn shoes?"

"No."

The demon laughed.

"It's not THAT funny." The demon laughed louder. Joseph's face twitched, reminding him of Christel's horrible wheeze. "Please, stop laughing!"

The demon stopped laughing as loud. There was a look in his eyes that could have been mistaken for genuine concern. He laughed. "Get'cho ass off the ground." He extended his hoof. "But you don't like all that cursing, tho?"

Joseph hunched his shoulders with a smile. "Doctors advised against it."

"Shii'iit, you better know right now, you don't need Christel's permission to do a'one goddamn thang." He poked Joseph's side.

"Ouch!"

"You needa get that looked at."

"What?"

"Nothing. Like I said before, you the man. You don't have to do all that cursing to be the man either. Be nice and clever to her bitchass needs."

"I don't follow."

"My man...my man, Joseph." The demon fully materialized and put his arm around Joseph's neck. "This what you do, build your world-renowned cousin a bakery. One free to the public. Make this whole brown area right here available for the touring. And did I say free to the public? You'll make a killing from that million dollar 'free' bakery."

"What? Do tell. What do Christel's uncanny abilities to draw and drive everyone away from this place have to do with building my cousin a bakery?"

BLUEBERRY MANOR

"Christel, that greedy bitch will hate you for giving away her million dollar muffins." He muttered, "Simple bitch."

Joseph's eyes lit. "That's the ultimate payback. I'm like that's what her ass gets for being so damn gluttonous." A wild, open-mouthed ripple swept across Joseph's new found essence, producing a weird light that only the demon could see.

The demon winced.

"What happened?" The demon hunched his shoulders. "Christel loves my cousin's muffins, eats the vegan ones continuously. She hates paying for 'em."

"Cheapass wants 'em fofree."

"Yep!"

"Am I preaching or what, Joseph?"

"Making my cousin's pastries, especially her blueberry muffins, free to the public will piss Christel off something awful." Joseph laughed. "She'll hate it!"

"And you gotta make 'em with the plain and vegetarian recipe so Christel can't eat any nor sue your cousin."

Joseph laughed. "Heeeyyy... You're right. What's your name?"

"Call me Dee-Mown."

"Yeah, that is the ultimate payback, Dee-Mown!"

"My man!" Dee-Mown high-fived Joseph then disappeared.

Joseph laughed hysterically. "That's so simple. Why didn't I think of that petty shit myself?" He put his pointer finger to the corner of his mouth. "Since Christel is vegan, and claims sole ownership of the vegan recipe," he snickered, "she won't be able to eat the free muffins. That's a slap in her bones." Joseph skipped through the forest singing, "Genius!"

Utterly absorbed with serving his bitch of a wife, Joseph decided to do what Dee-Mown suggested. In order to pull it off without Christel or their children knowing, he made arrangements to send them, along with several servants, to their private island in Canada. *Three months is more than enough time*, he thought. *It's perfect timing. Christel has been working very hard on her jewelry and art collections, Michelle has been helping Christel, Kenneth has been modeling and I doubled up on his CEO-in-training duties, Bree has been up for four days with her sick children and fiancé, and Pearlie has been training for a beauty pageant and doing commercials. They all need unplugged R&R.*

Joseph made arrangements to take them to the airport hangar-home where they boarded the jet for Canada. As soon as his family's jet disappeared, Joseph rubbed his hands together and pulled out the yellow bullhorn, the one his employees hated. "Time to do some serious work. Quickly!" Several people sunk to the ground while plugging their ears. He slapped a long nosed woman on the butt, "Hey you, go down to the deli, grab a few of your people. I need all the help I can get. We needa get this done. I'll pay triple exxxtra."

The employees' scattering made the ground shake.

November, 2006
Charlemagne Island
(Canada) Victoria, British Columbia

Christel looked down the indoor balcony as if she'd never seen the entrance hall before, eyes bigger, glassier, and scarier than usual. There was a massive 32-year-old oil painting behind her. She was the mirror image of that painting. Her books lined the bookshelves on either side of it. Newspaper clippings, magazine centerfolds, and action shots at her crystal and diamond mines decorated the round foyer table. Her jewelry studio had a live video of her showings in Rome, Italy. A terribly obsessed fan who calls himself "the projectionist" ran her performances (musicals and cinema) 24/7 in the movie room. Gold albums decorated the walls of her music studio. Her paintings and ceramics cluttered the creative art studios, and lined every hall in the mansion.

This island was Christel Charlemagne's island. She (the birth personality) had more control over countless alter identities. She did not have as many non-human switches, hallucinations, or hysterical conversions. Christel could hear the Beings of the Light clearer. She knew their mission, to squeeze important messages through unbalanced chakras and personalities, but something (or someone) inside refused to accept their messages as truth.

A gold dot hovering over the second staircase divided into four powerful spirits of Light (Unconditional Love, Unconditional Friendship, Peace, Brutal Honesty). She followed the spirits to the pink and white guest chamber, unsure if this was another lucid dream.

Unconditional Friendship droned, "You have always been baffled by our protection." Christel plugged her ears with the silicone earplugs she grabbed off a table. "We will give you the knowledge you need in order to overcome the—"

"Why the hell are you bothering me?" Another entity, one hidden deep inside Christel's psyche found a way out through violent spasms. A strange grin crept across her face. The squishy voice of a toddler shot forth. "Dis guess wing is my purrrsinal sanctuary for today." She shrieked. "What sweetness! It smells like curly flowers and long burning incense." She opened the double doors. "My mommy's in here." She found a large u-shaped sofa and twelve pillows in the middle of the room. "Cést sympa... It's nice." She sat in lotus position, closed her eyes and focused on each breath.

The Voice of Brutal Honesty spoke. "The problem with religion: they talk too much. What's left unsaid is the journey. If they say, 'my way is the only way,' there is no personal journey; no personal connection to the Source Creator of All. Be wary of those who tell you how to develop a personal connection. They're robbing you of your Free Will. Your will to find God the Creator."

Christel opened her eyes prematurely, hoping to catch a glimpse of Brutal Honesty. She checked behind seat cushions and pillows. She poked out her lip. "I want to see more than gold dots and beams." Tired of coming up empty, she fell back on the pillows, engaging in a short restful nap.

The door burst open.

Christel opened her eyes to three irate servants: the middle aged Thomasson, thirty-three-year-old Maylah, and Maylah's pubescent sister, Nella.

"My Lady! We've been looking everywhere," said Thomasson. His flared nostrils screamed disgusting.

"In all these years, you've never entered the guest chamber," said Nella. "Somebody left the faucets running in the scullery. There's water everywhere."

"There *was* water everywhere," Thomasson and Maylah said in unison. Thomasson continued. "We lowered ourselves on dreaded hands and knees."

Maylah said, "And we cleaned it all up."

Christel looked at the servants, their wet shoes, Thomasson's wet pant legs, the girls' wet stockings, their wrinkled hands, broken nails, and shiny brown skin. "How dare you look like that when you're supposed to be on the job."

All three servants gasped.

Christel laughed like a baby. "I'm just kidding, Lilies." The servants laughed in staggered mode.

Christel crawled off the floor, brushed her hair back, and skipped down the hallway. "Whup! There's water everywhere."

Nella snapped her small fingers at the lady's maids. Christel hit a puddle of water after jumping off the last curved step. "What the serenated hell!"

"Oh! You've splashed water all over your face," said Nella. "let me…"

Christel jerked away. "Get your grimy hands off me, you simp. There's no need to help because all three of you lazy ass bitches are fired."

There was silence, then faux fainting spells from all three of the servants. While on the floor, they asked each other about Christel's mental state.

"Just who the hell do you think you are disturbing my meditation and… donkey shit!" The servants wailed. Christel silenced them with quickened craze. Her eyes darted from the floor to the ceiling, voice husky. "Shut up! Don't you know you're scaring the rabbits and birdies? Get off the goddamn floor!"

The servants stood at attention. They looked at each other in horror. Nella said, "Has My Lady taken her meds today," in Maylah's ear.

"My Lady, we're not scullery maids," said Thomasson, "all the cleaning we did isn't in our job description."

"I don't wanna hear your lame ass incompetence," Christel said.

Kenneth and Michelle came bursting out of the elevator. "This some bullshit," hollered Kenneth.

Thomasson yelled, "Master Kenneth!"

Christel waved her finger in Thomasson's face. "Shut up, you!" She turned her attention to Kenneth and Michelle, "What the hell are you two going on about?"

"All of our clothes are missing," said Michelle, "and another hidden possession of mine." She opened the walk-in shoe closet in the cloakroom.

"If your lying sister isn't in there, check the tearoom," screamed Kenneth, "check in that box of feathered boas."

"That's what I'm doing, punk ass! And she's your sister too."

"So?"

BLUEBERRY MANOR

"So *you* check!" Michelle slid out of the cloakroom covered in shiny flecks. "You're her favorite sibling."

Christel said, "You're not making any goddamn sense."

"Pearlie's up to her old shit," said Kenneth.

Michelle pursed her lips.

Christel sighed. "What prank has Pearlie pulled now?"

"I saw something in the flower bed before we noticed the full blastedness of the faucets." After sniffing, Maylah wiped her nose with her handkerchief.

"Well, you should have got the something out of the bushes, you idiot," Christel said, "and what the hell are you three doing here? I thought I just fired all youse."

Michelle said, "Mom, how could you?"

"You know how Pearlie gets when she's bored," said Kenneth, "how is that Thomas, Nella, and Maylah's fault?"

"Who's Thomas, Nella, and Maylah?" Christel pointed at Nella. "And what's she staring at? Is she ill?"

Nella's thoughts were loud. They cut through Kenneth's aura like an arrow. She whispered, "Kenneth and I will have five children with tanned skin slightly darker than Kenneth's, caramel blonde and auburn colored hair, hazel eyes, and extra shiny teeth. The oldest child, Kenneth II, will have thick brown eyebrows. He'll be a tall, musically inclined, production artist. The girl will be a production artist as well, and the triplets—two girls, one boy—will be reality stars."

Kenneth lived Nella's vision for a few seconds, until Christel's clapping and finger snapping brought them back to the present.

hristel cupped her hands across each other, creating a deep echo that made the room quiver. She snapped her fingers loudly. "Hey! Come back to goddamn earth, will ya? Hey!" She kept snapping her fingers until Nella blinked. "Wipe that cheese and wine grin off your fucking face."

Nella cut an embarrassed glance at Maylah who was elbowing Kenneth. "The jig is up," she drawled. Burgundy sweat traced Nella's hairline and dropped on the floor. She wiped up the speck of sweat with her bright white handkerchief.

"Christel, calm down." Kenneth smiled at Nella. "You can't fire them. You need all the help you can get," he covered his mouth with the handkerchief he took from Nella, "with that badass devil baby you call yourself raising." Nella laughed like a greedy warthog, then took her handkerchief from Kenneth and covered her nose with it. Her eyes fluttered while taking in the smell of Kenneth's sweet-minty breath.

Christel said, "Kenneth!" She cut an evil eye at Nella.

He mouthed, "What?"

"I hate mumbling, you twerp!" Christel turned to Michelle. "Did you check Pearlie's wing?"

"Whaddaya think? It's full of water traps," said Kenneth, "that's why I'm all wet."

Nella blushed.

"I didn't ask you, Kenneth," Christel said. She snapped her fingers at Michelle. "What about the gym?"

Kenneth laughed. "What the hell do you think?"

Christel screamed, "I've had enough of you, little boy!"

Kenneth looked behind him. He said, "I don't see a little boy."

Nella dropped her head. "Me neither."

Christel swirled around, "What's that?"

BLUEBERRY MANOR

Nella said, "I saw Ms. Pearlie in the pantry, My Lady."

"I saw her destroying food in the pantry too," said Michelle, "Thomasson had just come back from the grocer."

"Why not stop your sister, you fool," said Christel.

"I couldn't get through all the food and boxes piled on the floor. I yelled, but Pearlie had those big headphones on. She was—"

"Turning spicy gelatin and whipped cream into some drinks?" Kenneth said. He held his throat. "She did that shit in Spain."

Michelle reached for a bag of chips. When she opened them, she found crunchy vegetables inside. "Look at this...she replaced my hot chips with celery and carrots. Pearlie has gone too goddamn far with these pranks!" She threw the bag across the room.

Nella cleaned the mess.

Christel laughed. "You need those vegetables, Jiggle What."

Michelle pouted. "You calling me fat?"

Christel ignored her. She reached in her pastry box to find a tray of cherry tomatoes. She whispered, "I need a motherfucking drink." She went to the cocktail lounge and found that her black vodka bottles and unusual wine decanters were broken. "Pearlie!"

Kenneth said, "Now she's done it."

Christel and Michelle slipped on fake milk while sobbing. Kenneth freaked out when he put his hand in a big brown pile of crap (chocolate sauce and slime). "I'm gonna whip her little ass for wasting my good shit," said Kenneth.

Christel bawled. "You're not whipping anybody, you spider!"

"Mom! I can't spend any more days off the grid in this log cabin," said Michelle, "it's killing my spirit, and my tailbone."

Twenty-four-year-old Bree climbed in her carriage shaped pod and plunged on the bed face down. She sunk deeper in the mattress and turned to her side, looking like she'd fallen in a vessel of quicksand. Dark blonde curls covered her dimples; short, muscular legs pointed upward. "This is the life," she yawned.

Seconds after she'd drifted to sleep, her phone buzzed. The tone looped around sixteen times before she could muster enough strength to answer it. "Hello... How are the children?"

A deep voice said, "Who the hell is this?"

"Jon, is this you," Bree yawned, "stop playing games."

"Who the hell do you think it is, hoe?"

"You've never called me that, Jon. I'm surprised at..."

The voice interrupted her. "I said, who the hell is this?"

"Jon! I have no time for your donkey-bullcrap."

The voice went deeper. "I have noooo fucks left."

Bree spoke a little clearer. "Look, whoever this is..."

"Who the hell is this?"

"I'm too tired for your..." Bree fell asleep while holding the phone. The phone fell out of her hand and rolled underneath her queen-sized bed.

"You wanna know who this is so bad? Check the ID next time, you lazy—" Bree started snoring. The deep voice echoed, "Wake up, you bitch!"

Sport psychologist and celebrity fitness trainer, Jonathan Jones II, had taken his and Bree's two children, Tres and Sharmona, and Michelle's daughter, Nicole, to Haiti to visit his mother, Mrs. Tennolyne Jones, a dark-skinned woman with burnt orange hair and caked-on makeup. After Jon read about Joseph's plan to reopen the compound in France, he called Bree's phone but kept getting a crazy signal.

"What the hell. Ain't this a bitch? I've never heard of this shit before," Jon whined.

"What's wrong, son? What has that Bree Charlemagne done to you this time?"

"No, Ma, it's not like that. I'm trying to get through, but I'm getting a weird signal."

"Have you paid the phone bill this month?"

Jon pursed his lips.

"Well, it could have slipped your mind." Mrs. Tennolyne cut her eyes at the children. "You have more responsibilities these days."

"I enjoy taking care of the children."

"I don't give a damn, Jon. Bree should be ashamed of herself." She crossed her arms. "A mother of two children, you should be able to reach her at all times."

Jon scrolled through his phone. "We're raising three children."

"Jon, I don't understand why you're raising Michelle's child on the low. You have two children of your own. You don't have time for another one."

BLUEBERRY MANOR

"We're making time, Ma. Michelle is under severe emotional strain. We're helping her out."

Mrs. Tennolyne raised her voice. "Emotional strain? I don't give a good goddamn! She's under another nigga, that's what she's under... the hoe."

"Ma!" Jon checked on the children. "That's a sensitive area."

"I'm sure it is."

"I don't mean it like that. Michelle's in no condition to raise a child right now. Not like Bree and me."

"What did I say, boy? I said, I don't give a damn."

Jon said, "Maybe Bree fell asleep holding the phone again. She's at the log cabin mansion in Canada. The one with a pod chamber in her wing. It's cool. The only way to get in is if you have a smartcard. She only gave out three. One for her, one for me, and one for the head housekeeper."

"Is that something to be proud of?"

"No, Ma. I didn't mean to brag."

"Since she's at the private island," Mrs. Tennolyne sighed, "why not take the children with her?"

"Bree needed a good massage and some rest. She was up four whole days with all three children." Jon smiled. "And with me."

"Why? If she needed help, I was available."

Jon wiped sweat from his forehead. "You asked, why was she up for four whole days with us?" Mrs. Tennolyne bucked her eyes. "Because she took care of us."

"That's what nurses are for! For dealing with sick people." Mrs. Tennolyne waved her hands around. "Bree's no goddamn nurse."

"She's hands-on, Ma. Dealing with four sick people is—"

"Nope! That ain't no excuse. She's somewhere traipsing with that whore mother and sister of hers is what."

"Ma! Christel is still the children's grandmother." Jon pointed at his kids. "Michelle is their aunt. She's Nicole's mother. I don't want the children to hear you talking like that about any of the family members."

Mrs. Tennolyne snaked her neck several times. "I don't give a good goddamn if they hear me or not. Especially that Nicole. She needs to know what kind of a mother she has."

"What do you mean? She's only five years old!"

"If you ask me, all the Charlemagnes should be ashamed. Lying and running round the streets like some wild and loose harlots. Even that

45

model fuckboy."

"Ma! I've never heard you use that word. What do you about that word?"

Mrs. Tennolyne raised her head up high. "I know a lot of words you've never heard me use."

"Are you talking about Kenneth?" Jon laughed. "Kenneth is cooler than a fridge. He's super smart and one of the best friends I've ever had."

"Your friend, ha! He's an immature punk is what he is. I'm tired of seeing them damn Charlemagnes in the news."

"Stop it, Ma, you don't know their real personalities."

"Well *you* should!"

Mrs. Tennolyne handed Jon the number of a private detective and gave him the 'you're not married to her yet' speech.

Jon put his head on the desk and pretended to listen.

Christel found five-year-old Claire Denise-Renée Patricia Charlemagne a.k.a. Pearlie making fake urine in the art studio. "Pearlie!" Christel heard a deep voice coming from under the counter. "What the hell is that?" She felt around until she found a phone. "Where'd you get a cell phone? Only Bree is allowed to have a cell phone in this cabin."

Pearlie stuttered, "I found it outside in-in the flowerbed."

Christel slapped Pearlie several times and dragged her down the hallway. A few maids lined the hallway, putting their heads down as Pearlie kicked. "Maids! Get back to work!" Christel yelled.

Michelle came out of her bedroom. "What's with all the commotion?" When she saw Christel dragging Pearlie, she said, "Mom! What are you doing? You're irrational!"

Pearlie screamed, "Not my face," while kicking and knocking expensive artifacts to the floor. "Help me, Michelle!"

Christel raised her hand when Michelle tried to save Pearlie. Michelle blocked her face. Christel threw Pearlie in the television room. "Stay in here! I've had enough of your madcap antics, young lady."

Pearlie screamed, beat, and kicked the door for a good twenty-five seconds.

"You said the television room was off limits on this trip," Michelle said. She screamed, "Hear me? You said..."

"Shut up, Michelle!" Christel shook Michelle's shoulders and threw her across the room. "Tell me! Where's Melanee?"

Michelle rubbed her head. "Why would I know anything about a fourteen year old? What can she do for me?"

"She's Pearlie's nurse isn't she?"

"Pearlie's nurse? I need a nurse." Michelle struggled to get off the floor. "Why'd you throw me against the wall?"

Michelle plugged her ears with her fingers, trying to mute the sound of Christel's sardonic laughter.

Christel said, "And if anybody asks, you just happened to hit the wall."

"Mom!"

"You know I can't talk to you when you're all...when you're so unbelievably goddamn hysterical, Michelle."

"Melanee's a child," Michelle said, "she's gonna let Pearlie watch all the television she wants."

Christel smirked. "You jealous?"

"No, I... You won't even let me watch the television shows I'm on in this godforsaken cabin." Michelle looked around at the extravagant art on the walls.

"I give no fuck about your television shows." Christel waved her finger in Michelle's face. "This is an artist's dream and you'd better remember that shit." She screamed for Melanee through the intercom.

"For all we know, Pearlie hid all the sweets in the television room. She did that shit in Spain."

"I give no damn about some goddamn sweets in Spain, Michelle! I have no fucking alcohol and I'm motherfucking..." Christel broke out in tears. "It's not fair! It's just not fair. I don't have time to be fucked up 'bout no goddamn fucking sweet Spain shit. You know you're scaring the Birdies of Burdopia with your loud ass mouth!"

Michelle mumbled. "You're an angry alcoholic."

"Stop mumbling. I hate mumbling!" Christel raised her hand. "How dare you pick on me?"

Michelle winced. Her voice shook at the notion of Christel's wrath. "You should send the servants out for more liquor."

"Already been done," Christel plopped on the couch, "Melanee! Fall-in, goddammit!"

hristel felt like she could tame all the wild birds on the island. *These birds are angels from the planet Burdopia, she thought. If they eat plain birdseed from my hand, they can sense my angelic presence.* She wondered, *Could I be a bird, an angel from the planet Burdopia?*

After three hours, Christel threw the plain birdseed on the ground and marched in the house. "Why the hell won't they fine-feathered-friend-looking asses eat from my hand?" She plopped on the couch, depressed, looking at blue jays on the wrought iron window box.

A big cardinal stared inside the house. Christel grabbed her ceramic pen and a notebook, sensing that the cardinal would relay a message to her through his small, curt chirps.

"Hello Christel, my name is Mr. Big Cardinal." He was a plump red-orange bird with gray streaks on his wings and tail feathers. He had dark brown eyes, a black mask around his orange colored bill and a tall bright crest.

"Hello, Mr. Big Cardinal. Are you from planet Burdopia?" Mr. Big Cardinal angled his head. He relayed a question mark to Christel's mind. She continued. "What do you want me to know, Mr. Big Cardinal?" She showed him her pen and notebook, both had birds drawn on them. She also grabbed a box of facial tissues from the end table.

"If you want us birds to eat from your hand, send your son Kenneth, along with a couple of servants, to the wild bird store on the mainland to pick up special bags of bird feed. Get the ones with black oil sunflower seeds, cranberries, cherries, blackberries, acorns, whole peanuts, and suet. And be sure to pick up a fresh bag of heroin."

Christel said, "Heroin? But I don't use heroin. I don't know where to find any on this island, Mr. Big Cardinal."

"You don't use it, but another aspect does. Send your head footman,

BLUEBERRY MANOR

Patrizio along with the men. Take Patrizio to the side and explain the situation to him. He'll know what to do." Mr. Big Cardinal flew towards the lake. Christel waved goodbye while wiping her tears with facial tissues.

Christel was puzzled, but attempted to force Kenneth, along with Thomasson, Patrizio, the gamekeeper, land steward, and two bodyguards to the wild bird store.

"You expect me to get on a fucking boat, travel to the fucking mainland, and ride in the same fucking car with Patrizio for untold hours for some goddamn birdseed? Hell no," Kenneth said. "I'm not going anywhere with that self-absorbed fool for all those hours. I told you what he tried to do last time. I'm not with that shit. The only reason I didn't shatter the fucker's jawbone is because his brother is trigger happy as hell. And you already have birdseed!"

Christel yelled, "Stop mumbling. I hate mumbling!"

"I'm not mumbling, you half-baked hoe!"

"You're going to the goddamn store with the goddamn fool for however long it goddamn takes, goddammit! Mr. Big Cardinal wants special birdseed."

Kenneth rolled his eyes. "Then send *his* ass."

"Don't play. You know birds can't go to the store." Christel erupted in laughter.

"They can't talk either!" Kenneth erupted in false laughter, slapping his knee in jest.

"I'll be damned if I disobey an angel from planet Burdopia for your ungrateful ass."

"Don't start that shit with me, woman." Kenneth side-eyed Christel. "Have you taken your meds today? You do know by the time we get back, the 'birdies' will be gone."

"So!"

"So?" Kenneth pointed at Christel. "Have YOU taken your MEDS today? You're usually not this unhinged on the island."

"What does it matter? The birdie told me—"

"Keep telling me what to do, bitch!"

"Did you call me, your own mother, a bitch?"

"B-I-T-C-H! And you're not my mother. I don't know who the fuck you are right now."

"I'll have you arrested for using that language with me! You always call me names."

Kenneth's voice waved. "How the hell can you do that, Christel?"

Christel whined like a toddler. "Stop calling me Christel. Call me Mom! This is supposed to be a retreat. This is supposed to be a nice off the grid, family trip that your father planned for us. Don't you care?"

"How can anything be a nice trip with you and your alters? I don't know who the fuck I'm talking to."

"How dare you!" Christel broke out in tears. "All I want is (distorted mumbling)."

"I thought you hated mumbling." As Christel cried, Kenneth walked towards the door. "You know what? Getting off this island is good. I'll go get your damn bird seed." He went to a hidden bar on the island with the land steward. After venting about their troubles, the two of them and a young bartender left the island with Thomasson, Patrizio, the gamekeeper, and the bodyguards in search of the special birdseed.

Christel screamed, "Bree won't wake up! I need her to babysit Pearlie, and take care of the rabbits at the rabbit farm, and, and I just need her."

Michelle picked at her fingernails. "Where's Melanee?"

"I don't fucking know. I think I locked her in the television room with Pearlie."

"Where's the gamekeeper?"

"I sent him with the others yesterday evening. I have a hazy remembrance of sending them for special birdseed on the mainland. I don't remember."

"Why'd you do that?"

"Oh." She threw her pointer finger in the air as if she was a student at school. "I'm gonna call Patrizio. Since they're going to buy birdseed, they should get something for my rabbits and the other small mammals to eat. Do you know everybody's numbers?"

"No, I don't know the numbers, Mom."

Christel interrupted. "That's alright, I'll find them."

"What's wrong with you? Have you," Michelle looked disturbed.

"Yeah, yeah, 'have you taken your meds today?' Is that what you want to ask me, Michelle? Well the answer is no. I don't need those motherfucking pills. I feel fine."

"Then why'd you send everybody out to the mainland?"

"I don't fucking know, and why do you care? Do you care that my precious rabbits have nobody in the gamekeeper's cottage? The little bitty rabbits with the cute little noses are left all alone with a robotic caretaker."

Michelle said, "Then they're not alone. The robotic caretaker is almost as good. He was programmed by the gamekeeper."

"Yes, they *are* alone! They're probably scared. I can't bear the thought of their fright."

"Then you go in there with them."

Christel cried. "I'll keep crying, and I'll disown you for taking that type of tone with me."

"What the hell did I do?"

"You know I can't go in there like this. They'll surely pick up on my anxiety."

"I don't know what to tell you, Mom."

Christel screamed, "And I'll disown Bree if she doesn't come out of that fucking chamber! She's in that goddamn pod. Yep, she knows I can't get in there without a goddamn smartcard. How'd she get to be so selfish?"

"Bree took care of three sick babies and Jon over a span of four days. She didn't get much sleep," said Michelle, "which is why she wanted to come up here in the first place."

Christel started pacing the floor. "Stop mumbling. I hate mumbling!"

"Bree took sleeping pills an hour ago, locked herself in that huge pod bed, so I don't think we'll be seeing her for the next few weeks." Michelle looked at the ceiling. "Wish I had a pod chamber in my wing."

"Didn't I say I hate mumbling!" Christel burst out in tears again. "I don't know what to do. I just don't know what to do. You know I hate pods, and mumbling, and..."

"Mom! There is a man standing outside the television room."

"Have you lost your damn mind again, Michelle?"

"Mom, I'm serious. What if he attacks Pearlie?"

"She's locked in the room, so even if there was a man standing there, he can't do anything to Pearlie."

Michelle screamed, "What do you mean if? Can't you see? The man could be an alien, or a Spirit, or a Suntilian hybrid thing. He can probably go through the goddamn door."

"I can't have you cracking up on me right now." Christel picked up the phone, ordered Perez Carter, the former footman, and those at the facility behind the mansion (Serenated Fool Insane Asylum), to come and sedate Michelle.

When Michelle saw the white coats through the window, she screamed, "Nooo...not Serenated Fool! Not again! Why do I have to go when there's nothing wrong with me?" She tried to escape the room, but every door and window she tried was locked.

"You're seeing the imaginary man again. Whenever that happens it's time for resty-rest at Serenated Fool."

As the white coats took Michelle away, Christel called Dr. Clark, Dr. Abram, and hypnotherapist Dr. Walker at a private institution in Florida, and made arrangements for them to come to the island.

ichelle's x-rays and tests turned up nothing.

While restrained to a fancy hospital bed, Michelle looked around the room, a pink Victorian room that resembled one of her old condominiums. She thought about small children. When some of them had imaginary friends, they were thought of as perfectly normal, but whenever she mentioned her imaginary friend, Christel would have her committed.

She whispered. "Mom said she only calls them whenever I threaten to hurt myself, but I only do that because the slow speaking doctors medicate me when there's nothing wrong. The antipsychotics are supposed to reduce my hallucinations and delusions." She laughed. "They think my imaginary friend is a delusion. They think I cannot take good care of myself."

Michelle looked at one of her bodyguards. "You know I don't need to be here. Mom is the one having a psychotic episode, not me. She's on that Burdopia trip. I want you to go find all three doctors. I'm signing myself out."

When the bodyguard left, Michelle snuck out of a back door in the bathroom. She went to the boathouse, hopped on a boat and sped to the mainland where she will look for a car and drive 45-minutes to one of her friend's mediocre department stores for a good internet connection. And a few good times on the beach.

Patrizio hung up the phone in Kenneth's limousine. "Well ain't that fucking 'A'."

"What's your problem now?" said Kenneth. He jumped several red checkers on the board then yelled, "King me, motherfucker."

A young bartender poured more Canadian whisky in Kenneth's shot glass.

Patrizio said, "That was Christel on the phone."

Kenneth took a sip of whisky. "What the hell's she doing calling the limo?"

"She wants us to go to a small animal store and get some fresh fruit and vegetables for her pet rabbits after we leave the bird place."

"Wonderful," said a bodyguard.

"What the hell, Patrizio," screamed Kenneth. Patrizio smacked his lips. "The small animal store is an hour away from the wild bird store. We won't get back to the island until tomorrow." His cellphone rang.

"Actually, it's a two hour thirty-five minute drive from the wild bird place," said Patrizio, "and I plan on stopping to get myself some breakfast and freshen up quite a bit."

The young bartender poured himself drink.

"Guess I'm stuck with you men for many, many, many more hours." Patrizio looked at Kenneth. "You know, you remind me too much of Vittore Yantorno." He demanded that one of the bodyguards call the wild bird place and give them an estimated arrival time. "I call him Turry."

Kenneth smiled awkwardly. "Yeah," then answered his phone. "What's going on?"

"Kenneth! I saw Mom through the window," Michelle said.

"What window?"

"I'm on the mainland. I guess she came here looking for me. I saw her get attacked by a drove of birds on the beach. She laughed about it then got in a boat and left."

"Where are you now, Michelle?"

"Don't worry about it. I just told you I'm on the mainland."

"How'd you get there?"

"Don't worry about me, worry about Mom and go back to the island. Perez Carter told me she's going to some nightclub."

"What nightclub," said Kenneth, "I don't know of a nightclub on the island."

"Well, there is one. Please come. Mom's clothes are all ripped because of the birds. She'll get attacked by some sleaze ball at the club and—just come back and drag Mom out of that nightclub."

"Calm down." Kenneth signaled to the others to stop talking so loudly. "We're on our way to get the fucking bird seed her stupid ass demanded us to get."

"You have to turn around right now. She told me that she doesn't

54

remember sending you for birdseed."

"Doesn't remember? She called the limo! Told Patrizio to stop at the small animal store after the wild bird store. I'm tired of this shit, Michelle. What does she want us to do?"

"I don't know, just come back." Michelle began to cry. "Mom's on the Burdopia trip and it's really confusing for me when she acts like this. I feel like I'm losing my mind."

"Be cool. We're on the way." Kenneth terminated the call. He turned to Patrizio. "We're turning around, heading back to the island."

"Why," said Patrizio.

"To find Christel's wild-loose ass. She's on the Burdopia trip."

Michelle charmed one of the eployees in exchange for use of his computer. After Michelle jumped on the internet, she noticed one of the trending topics was *Joseph Charlemagne to Open the Compound Once Again.* She screamed, "What the hell is this about?" Her strawberry and banana smoothie and a big bottle of cheap perfume fell to the floor. The splashing angered and shocked several attendees.

"You must pay for this," said Burda. "I shouldn't have let you in here. I knew you was a fuck up. Now clean it up! And pay for every wasted drop with your tongue."

Michelle was embarrassed, not because she made a mess in the store, but because it seemed as if nobody recognized her without the heavy makeup and designer gear.

"Hey, stupid girl, say something." Michelle stared at a painting as Burda snapped her fingers. "Hello! You must pay, you trifling assed bum, hoe-bitch!"

Michelle said, "I...I needa see the manager."

"Like me, the manager will make you clean!"

Michelle stared at one of the stunning employees while whispering, "She's a model in Asia named Lotus. I know she knows who I am." Michelle's deep stare excited Lotus. They made crazy loud eye contact with one another.

"Lotus, what's this?" Lotus hunched her shoulders and raised her arms. Burda poked her with a stiletto fingernail, moving her head from side to side. "What is this eye contact between you and that bum?" She turned to Michelle. "Stop goofing off! Clean up this mess, you worthless bum. Clean it up and pay for it or else I'm calling the manager *and* the police. Some lockdown in jail will teach your trifling ass."

François, Lotus's fiancé, noticed the eye contact and ran off to tell Mr. Calvin Cash, the manager.

"Mr. Cash!"

The flinging door startled Calvin, but not enough to make him stop doing his private business. "What is it this time, François?"

"Mr. Cash, somebody's causing trouble in the foyer."

"What the hell? You are such a goddamn tattletale."

"This time's different."

"If you weren't my sister's best guy friend, I swear I would... Look, let me finish up. I'm just about to come." When François went in to give Mr. Cash a hug and shake his hand, he noticed an inappropriate film of Michelle on the laptop computer.

"Hey! That's the girl causing trouble in the foyer. Who is she, some kind of porno star? And what are you doing watching that stuff? You're married to Burda—"

Calvin blurted, "Get the hell out of here, François, wi'cho sweet ass. Tell 'em na cool it out there."

François strained his neck. "Hey. What's that? What are you doing with that? Is that all you?"

"None of your goddamn business!" Calvin said.

With two big hearts in his eyes, François slowly backed out of Calvin's office. He bumped into Burda. "What the hell's wrong with you, François?"

"Burda, Mr. Cash said cool out on Michelle."

"Michelle? Who the hell is this Michelle? I'm telling this worthless bum to clean up the mess she made. This is expensive perfume." She looked at Michelle. "Look at her. She probably can't pay for the perfume or the smoothie."

"This girl you call yourself castigating is Michelle Charlemagne."

Calvin shot out of his office. "Burda! That girl is Michelle Charlemagne, the daughter of Joseph and Christel Charlemagne."

Burda was shocked. "The uh, our superiors?"

Calvin glowered at Burda.

"I apologize, Mr. Cal—" Calvin gave Burda a stern look, "I'm sorry, Mr. Cash."

Lotus and Michelle's crazy eyes intrigued Calvin. He went into a lecherous daydream, snapping out of it as soon as Burda's heavy breathing grew louder. Her shiny eyes and sharp facial expressions offended his ego.

BLUEBERRY MANOR

Why is this bitch straining her face, he thought, *she knows I'm not for that front street bullshit in public.* He whispered. "I don't give a damn if it is our anniversary today."

"What did you say, husband?" Burda's tongue scraped the side of Calvin's neck.

Calvin slapped his neck, turned completely around, forcing himself to stare deep in Burda's eyes.

Yesss, thought Burda, *look deep into my eyes cuz today is our thirteenth wedding anniversary.*" She whispered to Calvin. "I'm so excited. Where we going later?"

"Burda! Fool, what the hell is you thinking?" Calvin said.

"Huuuh?" Burda sounded like a dying animal. She tried to grab Calvin's arm.

Calvin snatched away. "Keep it professional." He brushed his hair with a small brush he kept in his back pocket.

"Oh!" Burda pulled back, shoulders stooped, mouth stretched.

"You should apologize to Michelle," said Calvin, "not to me, and um, clean up this mess, you bean bag."

"Yes, honey, right away." Burda tried to give Calvin a hug and a little peck on the cheek.

"Hold up, wait. Hold up...hold up, dammit!" He ended his rant with a slick about the hair. François, Lotus, and Michelle laughed hysterically. "What the hell you call me?"

Burda looked confused. "Yasss—"

"Do you have a nasal condition?" asked Calvin. Michelle laughed louder than everyone else.

"Yes, Mr. Cash, sir." Burda cut a shameful eye at Michelle. "Um, no I don't have a condition."

"That's what I thought. Now clean up this mess."

"What about—"

"Aaaat-tat." Calvin closed one eye and lifted his finger.

Burda asked, "Will, um, Michelle pay for it at least?"

Calvin raised his hand, "Aaaa'tat!" When Burda didn't respond he raised his hands higher as if he was going to hit her. "I said aaaa-to the motherfucking-tat! Burda recoiled. "You pay for this shit. How bout thaaaa-tat?"

"But I can't."

"Aaaa'tat! It's coming out of your pay." Burda put an argumentative scowl on her face. "Don't think about it! I dare you to say a-fucking-word." Calvin turned his back. "Lotus, Michelle, François, I want you in my office. Now!"

Michelle whispered in Calvin's ear, "Thanks, Calvin." She cut a shaded look at Burda.

As they slithered in the office, Calvin rubbed his hands while smiling lecherously. "I'm living out my sweetest, freshest, most fabulous dream." He beckoned another model, two nerdy girls, and three chubby guys while singing Marilyn Manson's rendition of "Sweet Dreams" under his breath.

ichelle took to the streets with the speed of a Thomson's Gazelle. Her shoulder-length hair extensions flew rearward like a kite, enabling her to sail through time like a platinum and black fighter jet.

Perez Carter saw Michelle wandering around the city's park. He said, "Michelle! I thought you and Kenneth were going to join me for this modeling session."

"I've been, wait a minute, has it been?" Michelle bit her bottom lip and leaned forward. Perez Carter caught her before she could hit the ground. "No, Perez, we have no time for modeling gigs."

Perez Carter furrowed his brows. "Are you okay? Are you on that stuff again? Patrizio told me about purchasing illegal—"

"Never mind that goddamn fucking shit." Michelle covered Perez Carter's mouth.

"You act just like someone is following you." His voice was deep and distorted.

"I need you to take me back to Christel Island."

Perez Carter moved Michelle's hand. "Christel Island?"

"Shhh!" Michelle jumped up and down; sprayed Perez Carter's face with sweet smelling spit. "I mean Charlemagne Island. You know what the fuck I mean."

"No problem." Perez Carter looked at his cell phone, "but my session's almost over and I can't—"

She spoke in a loud whisper. "It's an emergency, goddammit!"

"Do you know how long it took me to get this session?"

"You know better than to argue with me, Perez Carter."

He threw his hands in the air. "Okay. Anything, Miss Michelle. Tell me what you need me to do."

As soon as Michelle smelled walls of citrus fruit, she knew they were minutes away from the island. When they arrived, she ordered Perez Carter to escort her to a small corner in the courtyard before joining the family.

She had to think about how she'd break the news. *Mom's outside with the birds, Kenneth's sunbathing or resting. How the hell am I going to tell them?* She stuck out her chest. "I'll just blurt it out. "Mother!" Michelle's screaming upset a nestling of starlings. Their flapping wings, droplets, or her hard fall to the ground did not deter her speech. "Dad and Georgette are giving away free pastries."

"Where the hell did you come from Michelle," said Christel, "and you've scared all the bluebirds and cardinals away. Lurking in the shadows and shit."

"But, Mom." For some unknown reason she looked at the bathroom window and saw Clarence the Priest, completely nude, except for a white bath towel wrapped around his big blonde head. "What the hell is he doing here?"

"Who?" Christel looked around.

"Clarence the Priest."

"That's none of your goddamn business, Michelle. And get off the ground. You look stupid." She waved her hand under her nose. "Go shower! Who brought you here?"

"Perez Carter."

"Perez Carter? You left this island to be with Perez Carter?" Christel looked in the distance. "Who the hell is Perez Carter, and where is he now?" She scanned the bushes.

"That's not important, Mom. What is important is that Dad and Georgette are giving away your million—"

"Aaaa'tat-tat-tat-tat, Michelle. I'm not trying to hear your drunken ramblings."

"I'm not drunk!"

"The hell you're not. I haven't seen you in three goddamn weeks. And Dr. Malone told me about your escapades on the mainland."

"Who the hell is Dr. Malone?"

Christel looked at Kenneth's XL eco-friendly hammock. An embarrassing episode flashed before her: Kenneth and Patrizio grabbed her right arm; Dr. Malone grabbed her left arm on an overcrowded dance floor. She came out of her daydream when Michelle groused in frustration.

BLUEBERRY MANOR

"Why the hell are you yelling at me, Michelle?"

"I'm not yelling at you! You don't understand what I'm talking."

"What the hell *are* you talking?"

Kenneth rose up from the hammock with a bizarre European accent. "I say..."

Michelle screamed, "What the hell! Put on some goddamn clothes!"

"What's all the noise about?" said Kenneth. "A beautiful man like me shall not bear these most discourteous situations. You all should be ashamed for disturbing my peaceful slumber like so." He put on a pair of burgundy silk boxer shorts and the matching bathrobe.

Michelle said, "I'm trying to tell you."

Bree came outside. "What's all the hubbub?"

"Now she shows up," said Christel, "I should beat your fucking ass." Bree hunched her shoulders. "Jon's nosey ass mammy called a million times."

"You shouldn't say that word," Bree said.

"Don't tell me what to say!"

Michelle screamed, "Liiisteeen! I'm trying to tell you, you, and all of you." Michelle bent over to catch her breath. "Dad is going to reopen the compound to tourists." After Christel didn't respond, Michelle shouted, "Mom, you don't understand! He's giving away your blueberry muffins to the public for, for complimentary!"

"What?" Kenneth and Bree said in unison.

"He and Georgette are going to specialize in those blueberry muffins Mom likes to eat so much, but they'll be vegetarian, not vegan, and they'll give away all the pastries for free."

"Free?" Kenneth, Bree, and Christel said in unison.

"Free *vegetarian* muffins! That fuck shit fucker did that shit to piss me the hell off." Christel said.

"There's not that big of a difference between vegetarian and vegan," said Kenneth, "you're making it a big deal."

"There is a difference," said Michelle, "if you didn't eat, drink, and smoke like a goddamn slave you'd know it."

"You shouldn't say things like that, Michelle." Bree said.

Kenneth said, "Eat, drink, and smoke like a slave? Look who's talking! Michelle, you smoke like a goddamn smokestack."

Bree laughed. "Hey! But Michelle, he is right."

Christel screamed. "The hell he will!" She stood up and threw the whole bag of breadcrumbs on the ground. A drove of birds descended. "The hell they are! That's a recipe Georgette created for Joseph and me. The fuck they ain't! I'll be damned if they do some-uh-dat fuck shit behind my back."

Clarence the Priest came outside in all his nudeness. "What's going on?" he asked in French.

Bree said, "Mother, what the hell?"

Kenneth went temporarily blind.

Christel continued, "The hell if we funding some type of motherfucking soup kitchen! I ain't no ringleader! You know the fucking sacrifices we've made for this family?"

"Who's we?" Bree said.

"Are we leaving now," said Michelle.

"Hell yeah, we're leaving," said Christel.

"Yes!" Bree and Michelle said in unison.

"I'm bringing two of my bodyguards on the jet," said Kenneth.

Christel screamed. "Somebody go get Pearlie out the goddamn television room."

"She still in there?" asked Kenneth.

Clarence the Priest spoke entirely in French. "What's going on? Where are we going?"

Michelle rolled her eyes. "Uh, no not you. Stay your ass right fucking here."

Bree said, "That's right, Clarence the Beast." She raised her voice. "You're staying your turkey tail right friggen here!"

"Bree!" said Michelle. She turned to Clarence the Priest. "And what's up with the old ass two-way, Clarence? Don't you have a cell phone?"

Clarence the Priest struggled to find the right words, "In case I receive the, how do you say, messages." He rolled his long, tight torso. Little beads of sweat formed on his nose.

"You gotta work too hard," said Michelle.

Kenneth, still covering his eyes, mumbled, "Somebody point my perfectly tanned ass to the promised land." He stretched his arms out and grabbed Clarence the Priest's extended man part.

Clarence smiled. "Whoo! D'accord... Okay!"

Michelle giggled.

Kenneth screamed. "Whaaa'thuh!"

Bree grabbed Kenneth's arm and yelled, "It ends here, Clarence, you

BLUEBERRY MANOR

stupid goddamn freak!"

Clarence the Priest hunched his shoulders. "I'm only standing here." His mouth was long and pointed. "I should sue Kenneth because he touched me first."

"Ewww," Michelle and Bree squealed in unison.

"Stop shaking your manliness around like that, Clarence," Michelle said.

Kenneth screamed like a scalded animal. "Done-keh shiiit! Oh, gaaat-to the motherfucking-dammit you all to hell! Point me to the washroom a.s.a. motherfucking p—"

"Shut up, Kenneth. I'm sure it wasn't all bad for you." Michelle giggled. "But youse a dinge queen, so."

"Fuck you, Michelle," Kenneth said.

"Shut up, you prejudiced, racist witch," said Bree.

"Racist?"

"What you're implying is sooo uncalled for." Bree laughed. "You know Kenneth hates it when people refer to him as a white man." She patted Kenneth on the back and whispered, "It's okay."

Michelle said, "When did I refer to Kenneth as a white man."

Bree pursed her lips. "Isn't 'dinge queen' a white man who likes the company of black men?"

Michelle laughed. "Oh, Kenneth hates being called a white man, but he doesn't mind it when people refer to him as a fucking gay man." She screamed, "I told you he's gay!"

"There's nothing wrong with being gay," said Clarence the Priest.

"Stay out of this," Michelle, Bree, and Kenneth said in unison.

Bree raised her voice. "Nobody's studying you, Michelle! There's nothing wrong with being that way."

Michelle laughed. "You can't say it, Bree."

"Because it's offensive when you use those words to talk negatively about someone."

Michelle smiled. "So as long as I don't intend on being negative."

Bree folded her arms. "Forget you!"

"What?" said Michelle. "Gay means happy. Allz I'm saying is our brother's a happy boy. You outta know with all the chocolate effeminates in your fiancé Jon's family. And with all our carpet munching friends."

"Shut up," said Bree, "and Jon is not my fiancé."

"Why not? You guys are raising two children together."

63

Bree screamed, "Three!"

Almost instantly, Michelle's eyes teared. She lowered her voice so Kenneth (who was busy whining) and Clarence the Priest (who was busy doing muscle moves) could not hear her. "I guess I didn't count her as a child you and Jon are raising together." She kicked loose dirt around. "And I'm doing it again, aren't I?"

Bree gave Michelle a quick hug. She spoke softly. "I'll always love my niece, and that's how I raise her, as my niece. You'll always be her mother in my house." She raised her head. "A mother of respect."

Michelle mouthed, 'Thank you.' She grabbed both of Bree's hands. "Thank you so very, very much."

Bree raised her voice. "And Kenneth, stop whining. You'll wash Clarence the Beast's pissassidness off of your hand soon enough."

Kenneth said, "I feel violated. I have to take a quick shower."

Clarence the Priest laughed. "No need. I'm fresh and clean."

Bree, Michelle, and Kenneth had a distant conversation. They went inside, leaving Clarence the Priest outside.

"What? What did I miss?" said Clarence the Priest, "Hey, why's everybody leaving me? Is it because I'm white and nude?" He sat on a wrought iron bench and spoke French to all the birdies until his two-way chimed.

64

At Paris-Le Bourget, a private airport in Paris, France, big bulky cameras, strange looking microphones, screaming journalists, and hyped up police officers ran out to the tarmac at the sight of the Charlemagne jet.

Michelle threw her phone against the table, breaking it into four unusually clean pieces.

Christel daydreamed about all the lovely art she could make with the phone's fragmented parts.

Michelle said, "Mom! Snap out of it."

Christel jumped. "What the hell is wrong with you, Michelle? You're always throwing shit around, breaking shit and shit."

"I just a got a call that hundreds of journalists are at the airport waiting on us. Dad gave Grim Goresman permission to do an exclusive interview with you."

"I knew it. I've already made the call."

Michelle picked at her fingernails. "What call?"

Christel looked out of the window of the jet. "I've got the clones on standby. I knew those journalists would be out there waiting to get the tea. Even the rain wouldn't stop their crazy asses."

Pearlie's binoculars tumbled out of her hands. Two black circles adorned her violet eyes. "What's them doing out there, Mommy? Are we back in France? 'Cuz I miss Daddy smiling at me and tickling me and throwing me on the bed. And I'm tired of being on this jet." She jumped up and down on the couch.

"Sit down, Pearlie," said Christel, "you're acting wild." Christel took Pearlie's binoculars. "Look at their asses... hyped as fuck."

"Who? Who, Mommy, who? Are we back in France?" Pearlie sniveled. "Where's my daddy? I don't hear his laugh."

"I'm talking about the wild journalists that will meet the clones."

Pearlie hid behind Christel's pant leg.

"Are we clones, Mommy?"

"No, Pearlie, dear. The clones are people who look like us. They're in that ugly ass Boeing on the other tarmac. We're in the Airbus. We're going to the hangar home."

"What about Grim Goresman," said Michelle, "his big ass motorhome is parked at the hangar home right now."

Christel asked, "How do you know?"

"A friend told me."

She growled like a rabid dog. "Joseph! I'll kill that big fat jack of an ass! He has lots of explaining to do this fucking time, telling Grim Goresman about our private hangar…"

Pearlie ran to Michelle's arms, the way she always does when Christel uses the 'growling dog' voice.

Michelle laughed. "You sound a little like Ricky this time… Luuucy, I'm home!"

Michelle and Christel broke out in high-pitched laugher. Their falsetto shattered the teacup Pearlie held. After the pop, she felt a sting, looked down and noticed a small cut on her palm. After sweeping some of the broken pieces behind a couch, Pearlie crawled in the bar lounge and hid behind the curved bar. She panicked after noticing a small colony of ants next to a container of sugar. She pulled herself up and scooted along the countertop as if she'd lost her senses. She wheezed. "I can't find the door. Why can't I find the door!" She shook a shelf lined with liquor bottles, knocking a heavy jug of candy-infused vodka to the floor.

Michelle and Christel stopped laughing. Michelle said, "What was that breaking sound?" She and Christel searched the room. When they did not see anything out of the ordinary, they continued laughing, cracking stale Lucy and Desi Arnaz jokes.

Pearlie slipped in the spilled vodka, falling hand first on sharp pieces of glass. The glass cut through to her palm, turning her small cut into a gash. She hyperventilated, shook at the sight of so much bright red blood. She grabbed at her throat, wiped sweat off her forehead and gasped for air. She heard a high-pitched utterance from behind.

"Let me dress that nasty cut on your hand."

BLUEBERRY MANOR

She closed her eyes, hoping the pale thing would disappear, but he didn't. He just stood there, a blindingly white thing that looked oddly familiar about the eye area. He took Pearlie's hand and licked all of the blood. "There," he giggled, "I've had my fill of little girlie blood for today." He put a bandage on her hand, wiped the blood off her neck and gave her a green rubber ducky. "Now go to your mother." His voice raised to a dizzier pitch. "She will not notice the missing floral teacup." He disappeared in a vicious clap of powder smelling fog.

Pearlie was confused, but looking at the fresh beige bandage, she knew this particular episode was real.

Christel said, "Joseph's big bad ass wanna fucking play with me, huh? They wanna see Hizzle's goddamn show, huh?"

Oh no, thought Michelle, *Hizzle's one of Mom's most self-destructive alters.*

"What are you thinking?" Christel startled Michelle. "Why'd you jerk like that?"

"What? I'm not thinking anything."

Christel grabbed a bottle of vodka, threw the top on the floor, and guzzled it so fast that huge streams splashed on the carpet. "I'm gonna give 'em a grand production." Her voice changed. She pulled Michelle close and confided in her.

Bree sported a blank expression on her face. "When Michelle and Mom talk about Dad, I tune it all out. Mom has deeper riddles. With all those alters, I don't know who's talking anymore. I think I heard Mom say something about Hizzle."

"I don't give a fuck about Hizzle," Kenneth said.

Bree looked around frantically. "Kenneth! Where's Pearlie? Where'd the broken pieces of Chinese Porcelain come from?"

"I don't know where Pearlie is." Kenneth fashioned small headphones on his ears, bobbed his head to hip-hop music.

"Kenneth, listen!" Bree removed Kenneth's headphones. "They're trying to turn Pearlie against Dad."

"It'll never happen," said Kenneth, "stop acting paranoid."

"How can you be so blasé?"

"About?"

"About Pearlie, Hizzle, and Dad re-opening the compound. Hizzle is one of Mom's most dangerous alters. What if Hizzle hurts Mom?"

67

"Sorry, Bree. I know you love her and all but I can't stand that bitch Christel Charlemagne. Fuck her in both ears."

"You mean our mother?" Bree laughed. "Kenneth, why don't you try calling her 'Mom' from time to time?"

"Maybe when she starts acting like one I'll do that. Besides, Dad did this re-opening the compound behind our backs and shit because of Christel's trifling ass. It's the ultimate payback." He mumbled, "Thin bitch."

"How could you possibly know it's the ultimate payback?" Bree gave Kenneth his headphones back.

He put his hand on Bree's shoulder. "Dad told me something before we left, what, almost five months ago. Dad said, 'I have the ultimate payback in mind.' Re-opening the compound has to be what he meant."

"See," Bree folded her arms like a scorned little girl, "you and Dad are always keeping secrets and crap from me."

Kenneth laughed. "Easy."

"What do you mean by easy?"

"Whenever we tell you anything, you always go back and tell Christel, Michelle or Pearlie."

"So you're saying I'm a tattletale?"

"Tommy the Tattletale looking ass." Kenneth laughed. "So what if Dad's re-opening the compound to tourists. I think it's goddamn funny."

"Opening the area to tourists does not bother me either. I'm excited about it." Bree looked out of the window. "It's what Dad needs, after Mom chased the tenants away and all; however, I can see it from both sides."

"What do you mean?"

"Even before the tourists were getting free things from us, they were vandalizing and causing all kinds of trouble."

"They did that shit because of Christel's nasty ass."

"You can't put everything off on her."

"Christel," Kenneth scoffed. He popped two tropical punch candy cubes in his mouth, "that bitch went and hit Dad where it hurt most. I'd never seen Dad so depressed after she did what she did to him. Chasing everybody off the compound and closing Blueberry Manor. Dad started to eat weirder foods, unhealthier things, a lot of gummy-ass cheese. We have to watch him."

Bree held out both of her hands. "Don't you see my hands here? I'm holding them out for a reason."

68

Kenneth slapped her hands. "Low five."

"Give me some candy, you punk. Hurry before Pearlie brings her hyper little self over here. You know she's not allowed to have candy. It makes her hallucinate."

"Christel gives it to her."

"Dad doesn't like when Mom does that."

Kenneth said, "I thought the candy got stuck in your braces."

Bree crooked her neck. "I know you playing. I got those big silver braces removed over three years ago."

Kenneth looked up, head tilted to the side, "Exactly how old are you, little sister?"

Bree rolled her eyes. "Are you kidding me or what?"

Kenneth shook his head. "No."

"I'm twenty-four." Bree raised her voice. "I have two kids, dammit! Bananigans!"

"I'm telling Dad about your foul mouth." Kenneth held his fingers up in a cross. "Great Horned Owl, we got a blasphemer in this bitch!"

Bree said, "Who's the tattletale now?" Bree and Kenneth laughed while lightly boxing and checking each other.

Michelle and Pearlie appeared behind Kenneth. He jumped. "What'thuh? Where the hell did you two come from? Looking like a couple of creep-ass hanks."

"We're on a jet, goddammit! And put your fucking teeth back in your fucking mouths you two," said Michelle, "kee-hee-heeing your asses off. We're gonna be landing soon." She rubbed her hands together. "We're gonna give the journalists a show."

Pearlie shouted, "I smell candy. Give me candy!"

Christel yelled at Kenneth and Bree. "Youse people play too goddamn much. You're too loud. I could hear some of your conversation from the goddamn bathroom."

Kenneth ribbed, "You needa flush yourself down the toilet!"

Christel spun around. "What was that?"

Kenneth hid behind Bree.

Christel raised her head in victory. "That's what I thought."

Bree asked Pearlie about the green duck she held in her hands. "What's up with the bandage...and," she sniffed the air, "it smells like someone's been in my box. Pearlie, have you been in the bar lounge again?" Pearlie looked at the floor. "You know that area's off limits to you."

Pearlie jumped in Kenneth's lap. He leaned into Bree, "Michelle and Christel are jealous because we're having more fun than they are. Sour asses."

Bree's soft laughter turned into a peculiar grin after she examined Pearlie's bandage and the green duck closer. She looked at Michelle.

"Don't give me that angry look, Bree," said Michelle, "you know she's always playing doctor, wrapping herself in bandages."

Bree said, "Where'd she get the green duck, Michelle?"

Michelle ignored her. "Yeah, get ready for the show." She skipped to the other side of the jet. Bree told Kenneth to send his bodyguards to the bar lounge.

Pearlie spoke to herself internally…

Powder Man's hiding under the bar in the bar lounge. Powder Man's been sippin' Bree's liquid candy but I can't tell anyone about him or I'll get in trouble for being in the bar lounge and braking Mom's favorite Chinese Porcelain. Pearlie rubbed her eyes. *So I'm not gonna say nuthin' to nobody 'bout Powder Man on the jet.* She gave Kenneth a tight hug.

"Pearlie!" Kenneth forced Pearlie to look in his face. "What's wrong? Why are you shaking?"

svaldo Grimaldi-Gorosito a.k.a. Grim Goresman, was one of the photojournalists waiting for the Charlemagne family's arrival at Paris-Le Borget Airport. Dressed in a black and red silk suit and Italian dress shoes, he paced from one side of the lot to the other, stopping every few seconds to scan the pinkish-blue distance.

After settling in the executive business lounge, he heard commotion on the tarmac, and looked up to see lights descending on the airstrip. *Wha'thuh. I thought they were using the Airbus this go-round.* People were pouring out of the airport's museum, tearing past fixed base operators, crawling on what they thought was Kenneth Charlemagne's SUV limo. "Look at those fools," Grim gloated, "there's no way I'm getting this suit wet. If a speck of rain gets to me, I'll sue." He laughed. "If they're so smart, why not smell the set up?"

He looked at his watch. "Right on time." He pulled his camera operator, Desiderio Hunter, away from the window. "You check the flight plan, Desi?"

"Don't worry. My cousin is the driver of the Charlemagne Airbus."

"Why is the Boeing out there?"

"That's just a distraction."

"I know, but... Who are the people getting off the Boeing? Is that Christel posing for pictures and talking to random journalists."

"Those are clones and look-a-likes, Grim."

"You expect me to interview another one of those human-cyborg robot things?" He folded his arms across his chest. "No. Effing no! Don't push me. I'll go on strike again. I refuse to interview another one of those creepy fake Charlemagnes."

"Calm down. Everything's real this time. We've already cleared the interview with the real Joseph Charlemagne, and remember, the real Charlemagnes are on the Airbus."

"Good." Grim paced the floor. "Guess I'm nervous."

"Those people out there didn't do what we did. That's why they're talking to some fake ass Charlemagnes who'll give them some fake ass news."

Grim hiked his head to the left. "This is new for me, being kept in the dark about how the interview came about."

"You're in a different game."

"What do you mean?"

"You're not into shock journalism anymore. The sensationalism, fake alien stories, bloody hoaxes, and creating mass hysteria. Nope, not like your brother, Chrimm."

"My brother, Chrimm spoke to a *real* alien."

"Everyone knows aliens don't exist."

Grim burst out in misplaced laughter. "And you? Your kind shouldn't exist. You're another whore."

Desiderio laughed. "Where the hell did that come from?"

Grim bleated like a sheep, "Baaa-baaa-baaa. Wake up!"

Desiderio yowled like a wolf.

"I report the truth. It just so happens many of the things I report are weird. Shocking things other guys won't touch. That's why they moved me to the deep web."

Desiderio scoffed. "You report the truth?" Grim shook his head in agreement. "Oh, like when you spoke about the Spirit Children Community?" Desiderio cackled like a big hen. "You went outside your damn mind with that one."

"I saw the children with my own eyes." He could barely talk over Desiderio's laughing. "A community of blue babies and children that had been miscarried and aborted."

"You don't realize how many Christian women you offended, do you, Grim?" Desiderio rolled his eyes. "My wife included. I caught hell for your story."

"How many times do I have to tell this shitty world, you included, I saw 'em out of my own eyes? The children came to me. I didn't go searching for them."

"Hypothetically, if they did come to you, they were demons pretending to be of the Light. You were doing the devil's work simply by passing it off as real news." Desiderio pulled a cross out of his jacket and held it up to Grim.

"I've had it with your Christian doubt, false messiah, and hypocrisy." Grim pushed Desiderio's cross away.

Desiderio gasped and screamed in slow motion as his twirling cross crashed on the ground.

Grim said, "That's right. Devout Christians are the absolute worst, the most dishonest creatures I've ever run across."

"What's your beef?" said Desiderio.

"My number one beef is some of these stick in the butt Christians are conditioned to believe all psychic powers are bad. You blind guys can't see those particular teachings nullify your God given strengths, making it impossible to detect energy."

"So? I don't have to detect energy. My foundation of rock, Jesus the Christ, does it for me."

"Exactly! Christianity makes you weak. You Christians have no choice but to run to your preacher, pastor, priest, or some go-between to tell you the difference between Spirits."

"All Spirits are deceitful. I don't need a go-between to tell me that." Desiderio climbed on a chair. "You can't touch me, Grim, I'm way too high."

"Hell, yeah, you're high, clown."

Desiderio hit the ground like a cat. "Fu...fuuuget you."

"Not all Spirits are deceitful. It's that all the Spirits you've come across are deceitful."

"Jesus Christ said—"

"You depend on a fake Jesus to do what God gave us the power to do when He created us."

"So now you hate Jesus Christ?" Desiderio scolded. "Evil, sssinful SSSatan worshipper. I knew it. I knew it when I saw your pet snake."

"Don't be crazy. I don't hate the *real* Jesus Christ and I don't worship Satan."

Desiderio twirled his finger next to his temple.

"No, you're the crazy one. You're stuck in that little box, where all you Christians make excuses as to why you're oppressed. Can't you see God and Satan are the same?"

Desiderio put his hand over his heart. "You blaspheme too much!" He walked into a large plexiglass window. "It's impossible to explain anything to a stubborn nonbeliever like you."

"And it's impossible to explain the Spiritual to a person deeply rooted in Earth Religion." Grim laughed. "Face it. You're a mindless Christian solider. You're unconscious. You've been stripped of all your senses. All you know how to do is *baaa* like a goddamn sheep."

"Whatever, Man," Desiderio's face grew red, pupils widened, bottom lip bled.

"What's wrong with you, Desi? Are you worried about the lizard accounts?"

"No. I know nothing about lizard accounts, and I couldn't find anyone else who knows anything about them, either. Are you sure the lizard accounts really exist? Maybe it's a conspiracy theory, that the Charlemagnes force their servants into adult entertainment at around fourteen years old and sacrifice the ones that refuse to do it. Maybe they're not a part of the Illuminati's weird agenda. Perhaps there's no such thing as the Illuminati at all."

"Bullshit. I know for a fact they run a porno ring and they're a huge part of the Illuminati. I only have to prove it." Grim said.

Desi gave Grim a hard pat on the back. "Get ready to go under and up in luxury. Don't talk. Just walk in this extravagance."

Grim coughed. "If you weren't so good at your job, or my sister's brother-in-law, I swear I'd fire your hypocritical ass a million times."

Desiderio smiled. "Isn't job security great?"

A team of black bodyguards helped Grim and his crew go through an underground tunnel and up to the Charlemagne family's private hangar.

Grim was amazed. "Now this is what I call a Grim Goresman exclusive. Look at the magnificence! Get ready, Desi. As soon as I finish interviewing Christel, I'm gonna upload it to the video magazine."

"I thought we were going live on the deep web."

"Oh yeah. Great idea. We'll go with the live broadcast on the deep web, then cut out or dub over the obscenities before we upload it to the video magazine."

Desiderio flashed his teeth. "Cool."

"I've already written and uploaded the article. Christel Charlemagne is a predictable bitch. How much do you want to bet that my article will be 100% even though we haven't shot the interview yet?"

"Oh no," Desiderio said, "I don't doubt your skills or the drunkass bitch and her antics."

"Look at this! The whole Charlemagne family is a real jackpot. Just look at this. I've seen luxury, but not like this. I can't believe it."

"You should know," laughed Desi, "I heard tell about you and Christel back in the day."

"How do you know it wasn't a clone or a weird look-alike? She's got 'em running all around town."

"Because she's the one who bought you those incredibly expensive $40,000.00 shoes. Your broke ass can't afford that shit."

Grim looked around the corner, put both of his hands over Desiderio's mouth. "Shhh," he looked around, "for one thing, I'm not broke. For another, I was a freshman in college."

Desiderio moved Grim's hands and replied, "Why the hell are we whispering? Everyone else has moved ahead."

"We don't want anyone thinking it's a conflict of interest now do we? I'm not going back to jail because of her. I don't want anything to go wrong with this interview. I've already been accused of reporting fake news stories, dating clones, and getting involved in strange cooking rituals. I don't want my probation officer up my ass again."

Another camera operator came around the corner. "We're ready, Mr. Goresman," he yelled.

"Thank you." Grim patted Desiderio on the back. "Let's go. Do you job, Desi."

Desiderio checked all of the cameras. "Camera operator mode! C'mon guys, get ready. C'mon guys, we're on in five, four, three, two..."

LIVE ON THE DEEP WEB:

European multi-billionaire Joseph Charlemagne, owner of the impressive Blueberry Manor Estate, has plans to whet the public's appetite with gourmet food and fine wine.

While his château already boasts two gourmet restaurants, two wine houses, a cul-de-sac, hotels, a reconstructed castle, and several other personalized gems, he and his cousin, master pastry chef Georgette Milan, will open The Blueberry Queen Café, a complimentary vegetarian boulangerie funded by several wealthy businessmen and corporations. Starting tomorrow, not only will tourists have longer hours in which they can circuit the grounds, but also, guards will allow more people through the main gates. Not all are happy about the complimentary café. Many think it will become a magnet for corruption, despite countless security officers, police, and other emergency personnel at Blueberry Village. One of those naysayers was Joseph Charlemagne's wife, Paulina Denise-Renée Christel Broussard-Garcia Charlemagne a.k.a. Christel Charlemagne, former beauty queen, model, artist, co-CEO of a crystal and diamond mine, and the CEO of Automatique. I managed to catch up with Christel Charlemagne, and she and Joseph Charlemagne's son, twenty-seven-year-old Kenneth at Paris-Le Borget Airport. Christel and Joseph's daughters: Michelle and Bree refused to be on camera. We do not have permission to speak with Christel and Joseph's five-year-old daughter that they call Pearlie.

"The French Guinea jack-bastard's jack of an ass is so motherfucking gad'damn stupid in the ass. He's stupid, stupid right up there in the motherfucking ass in there." Christel took a sip of vodka straight out of the bottle. "You know he into some stuff with men who look like—"

Kenneth dropped his phone. "Christel!" He laughed nervously. "You're extra funny today. Joking around." While side eyeing her, he changed his tone to scary-sweet. "There's no need to lie on Dad." He thought his voice was off-camera. "Keep on... I'mma shake the shit out you."

Christel jerked away, "Fuck off, Kenneth." Her words were barely audible. "Who's the lie? Who's the lie, huh?" She turned her attention back to Grim. "You know how many extra'uh millions we're losing?" She grabbed Kenneth's collar. "Well, do you? You know what the fuck I've sacrificed?" Kenneth threw his hands in the air. "Hay'yale. Why not charge dem asses for pastries?" She took a sip of vodka straight out of the bottle then stared directly into Grim's eyes. "Look'ah me. I have to pay full price for the shit and I'm a family member for shit's sake and Geeeooo created the muffins fur me." She beat her chest and took another big swallow of vodka. "Fur me goddammit! Chef Milan a five star chef!" What in the hell to the motherfucking nawl!" Christel eased closer to Grim. He waved his hand under his nose. "Why in the hell you up in there smelling, Grim?"

"Oh, this," Grim waved his hand under his nose a little faster. "This is nothing." He giggled.

She butchered Grim's name. "You know, Grrrr-Grrr-Grim? Joseph's ass," she giggled and hiccupped, "is into some unnatural stuff wif manses. That shits unnatural."

Kenneth screamed in the background, "C'mon."

"With men..ses!" Christel bucked her eyes. "I know his ass is queer. What the hell is wrong with him, huh?" Christel sounded as if a demon had stolen her soul midsentence. "What the fuck is wrong with the muthafuckas, huh?"

Grim Goresman turned to face the camera. "As you can tell, Christel Charlemagne does not like the idea of a free bakery on the compound."

There was mad laughing in the background.

Christel hijacked the microphone. "I hate the fucking fact that my, my fucking gad'damn Joseph and Miss'sess Mi-fucking-lan giving away my shit for fucking free! The public getting free gourmet, gaddammit! I can't believe the shit! I ain't no fucking soup kitchen! They don't even respect our," she burped, "they don't even respect our prahhh-purrr-tee."

Someone handed Grim a microphone. Christel continued. "And another goddamn thing, goddammit, they don't deserve the shit."

Grim gestured, "Thank you," and then turned to Christel. "Just who are you referring to?" At this point, he was trying very hard to keep a straight face.

"Who in the hell you think? Them damn tourists! Just who in the hell you think?" Christel put her finger in Grim's nostril. "Hey, it's so real and so smooth and clean in here. It's so cleeen." Grim looked embarrassed but said nothing.

Christel continued with the previous conversation. "Them damn tourists. Even before he opened the castle grounds, they were looting and all that super dumb shit. We had to get guards, police, and, and, and emergency peep living on the...why play savior to the dizzressspeck?" Christel drank every drop, "And a gatdam chapel cuz they asses kept getting' kilt!" She threw the empty vodka bottle on the ground and some of the glass popped in Kenneth's face.

"Chill the fuck out," Kenneth yelled.

Somebody passed her a bottle of what appeared to be red moonshine. Kenneth and Grim attempted to pry the big bottle out of her hand.

"What in the hell are you doing? This is some of that red shit," said Kenneth, "bitch, you wanna die?" He signaled for one of the bodyguards.

"Wha'thuh the fuck, huh?" Christel's voice was slow and broken. "Da bodyguard took my shiii. Give... me myyyy shhhiii——" She tried to fight the bodyguard.

Grim asked, "Christel, what's this I hear about kicking family and friends off the grounds."

Christel crooked her neck. "So? What the hell you try'na say, huh? Yeah, I kicked dem off."

"Many of them said some awful things about you. Are you concerned?" asked Grim.

"I don't give a fuck. We have a hotel next to the castle and call it Parkrose of Blueberry Village. Joseph opened it up to a few folks and they got on my goddamn nerves. Drunk off champagne, high off drugs, full on gourmet. Fuck."

Kenneth attempted to take over the conversation. "There was a time when we had hundreds of paying customers. It was like a little village." He cut an evil eye at Christel. "They named it Blueberry Village. Most of them went to other parts of the world so Dad opened the hotel to family and—"

"Whores of Babylon!" Christel babbled.

Kenneth and Grim looked at each other in horror.

"Joseph has a soft spot. He likes playing savior to all them underage chicken dinners... Whores!"

Kenneth said, "Hoes like you," under his breath.

Christel had mistaken Kenneth's voice for Grim's voice. "Are you're being a smart ass, Grim?"

"No, I didn't say any—"

"Are you being a smart ass, Grim?"

"No, please believe me. I didn't—"

Christel pointed her wobbly finger at Grim. "I said, are you being a goddamn smart ass?"

"No, Mrs. Charlemagne."

"Zitto e lasciami... parlare!" Grim threw his hands in the air and mouthed, "Fine."

Somebody whispered in Grim's ear, asking him what Christel said. "She said 'shut up and let me talk' in Italian," Grim translated.

Christel screamed, "Lies!" Grim and Kenneth jumped. "They threw they own hobo asses in tall grass. I don't give a fuck, and Joseph, and Joseph, Joseph did the shit right hurrr to piss me off." She fell to the ground on purpose and slammed her fist on the concrete. "And I'm gonna beat the blubber off all the fat fuck's big ole fat asses!" She stared vacantly then rolled to her feet. "That's a lot of beating, but I'm damn good."

Kenneth cackled. "Well, yeah, my, she's way over the top at times." Christel rolled her eyes while reaching for the bottle of red moonshine in the bodyguard's hand. She lunged at the bodyguard, knocking the red moonshine out of his hand and onto the ground. "No!" She flew to the ground and began slurping the moonshine.

Kenneth snatched her by the hair, tried to speak softly but Grim could still hear the conversation. "Look, you platinum haired whore. You're not making this situation any better. I hate your fucking ass." There was mad laughter and knee slapping off camera.

Christel kept repeating, "Ain't done shit."

"Excuse me, Grim, we have to go," Kenneth said, "our car is waiting." He pulled Christel to the limo.

Christel fought Kenneth and struggled to get back to Grim.

"You got one more time to hit me, you bitch," Kenneth warned. "You hit me again and I'll stomp your plastic ass. I'm here, platinum-haired hoe. I wanna be all the way in the right when I pile drive yo ass, you wench."

"Let me go, Kenneth! I'm not plastic!"

"Fuck you."

Christel screamed, "I'd rather go with Grim. Hey! Grrr-Grimmm! I see you work, Grim, wit'cho—"

Grim blushed then told his crew, "I don't know what she's talking about."

"Shut the fuck up!" Kenneth told Christel.

"Let me go," Christel shouted, "Grim, hey Grim. I know how to break you. You know I know how to break you real good. Remember the last time?"

Once at the car, Kenneth pushed Christel's head down.

"Bald!"

"Your damn ass cat ain't here!"

"Baldness of Fatterson!"

"Get your dumb ass in the car."

About an hour after Christel's embarrassing interview, Michelle and Bree attempted to go inside the hangar home and relax before the two hour drive to Reims. As Michelle and Bree walked up the driveway, twenty bodyguards surrounded them. Michelle said, "What the hell is this?"

Bree pointed at the crowd, "Where'd they come from!" She shouted at one of the bodyguards. "They're climbing over the privacy fence. Do something!"

Ten bodyguards warded journalists. Seven were involved in bloody fights with fans. The crowd trampled three undercover police officers unconscious.

Kenneth watched the fiasco through the limousine's window. "What'thuh hell? How'd that happen?" Kenneth saw crowds of people climb over the privacy fence and dart across the grassy field. "They're trespassing! This is a private hangar home. How the hell did they even find this place?" He punched a tiny table, "Motherfucking Grim! I'm kicking his ass the next time I see him." He grabbed two hidden guns then burst out of the limo. "Not on my goddamn watch!" Kenneth threw his raincoat back and grabbed at his guns but several personal assistants pulled him back in the limo. "What's up with this motion? It isn't your job to stop me," he pointed at the unruly crowd, "Stop them! They're the ones trespassing."

"Calm down, Mr. Charlemagne, we're on it," said one of the Personal Protection Specialists.

"You're not on anything, PPS!" He looked at the other Personal Protection Specialists and Personal Assistants. "Those people are going to maul my sisters to death!"

"Do you want a murder charge, Mr. Charlemagne," said one of his assistants. The assistant took Kenneth's guns away. "It's our job to keep

80

you safe and in line. Right now, you're not in your element."

"The hell I'm not in my goddamn element," Kenneth said. "This is our private hangar home. I want every one of those wild child bastards arrested." Kenneth made a bodyguard call for several police vans. "I'm firing all of you people if Michelle and Bree aren't in here in the next few minutes. Unharmed." A bodyguard handed Kenneth a laptop computer. Kenneth frowned. "What the hell is this?"

"Read the article, Boss," the man said, "there are several articles out there already, but this one is the funniest."

"I do know Grim's show is on the deep web. How'd so many people see the interview already... uncut and uncensored? It's unbelievable."

"Thousands have access to Grim's interviews before they cut the good stuff out and sell it to a tabloid or something."

Kenneth shook his head. He read the article entitled *'Christel and Kenneth Charlemagne's Bloody Fight.'* "There was no fight," he said, "that's not blood. That's when Christel's nasty ass slurped red moonshine off the ground." He looked at a now passed out Christel, "like the slurp-ass bitch she is. How can she sleep through all the chaos outside? I can't be positive 'round these fucking idiots."

Kenneth heard the sound of Styrofoam boxes rubbing together. He screamed, "How the hell can you bodyguards eat!" He looked at the traveling grill and chefs outside. "Where'd they come from? This ain't no picnic!"

The bodyguards slowly closed their containers.

A Personal Protection Specialist said, "Kenneth, Sir, the chefs were already here, waiting for you and your family. They thought everybody, including your employees, would like a good meal after the flight from Canada."

"Under normal circumstances that would have been cool," he raised his voice, "but this isn't normal! Bodyguards, do your goddamn job! What the hell you think I pay you for... to chill in the goddamn Caddy all goddamn day eatin' goddamn barbecued cheeseburgers and chicken-goddamn-wings! Get'cho..." Kenneth tried to pimp slap a member of the flight crew. "What are you doing in here? Get back on the jet."

A member of the flight crew said, "but there's food out here. We don't have any food," he pointed to the jet, safely parked in the hangar, "in there."

Kenneth screamed, "Shut the fuck up!" He turned to the bodyguards.

"This ain't no utopian metropolis. This is war! Get the seasoned chicken legs out your goddamn mouth before I—" He turned to face the bodyguards' manager, Officer Quennell. "These greedy motherfuckers ain't following script. I should kick some ass myself 'cuz you're not doing your job."

Officer Quennell mouthed 'okay,' tried to calm Kenneth by patting him on the chest and back.

"No, don't touch me! What the hell's the matter with you. It's your job to make them follow script, not mine."

"Don't worry. We've got the right people on the right jobs this time, Mr. Charlemagne," said Officer Quennell. He eyed the bodyguards.

"I want it to be a fucking bed of roses this time. If not, I'm firing your ass for goddamn good. I will not tolerate so many fuck-ups in one damn day." He looked at everyone inside the limo and those outside by the traveling grill. "Keep playing around and none of you will be able to find work anywhere in France. Not even cleaning porta potties!"

Despite Kenneth's fussing, his Personal Assistants succeeded in getting the Charlemagne family and a few bodyguards to make the trip to Reims on a two-story party bus, while other bodyguards and employees followed in SUV limousines. Kenneth folded his arms, "Damn that Grim Goresman. It's his fault. He gave those mad fans the location of our hangar home. Everything's his goddamn fault. I should sue."

Bree held her stomach.

"What's wrong with you," said Kenneth.

"Don't you hear that? Mom and Michelle are talking about Dad again. Whenever that happens, I get nauseous."

"I'm not studying their asses. But I am concerned about this so-called porno ring."

Bree got her laptop from the coffee table. "There are reports, pictures, and some claim to have video of you being at several orgies."

Kenneth laughed. "That's probably the clone. Besides, plenty of my friends work in the adult industry. Hell, Michelle is an adult film actress."

Bree lowered her voice, "That's Mom's fault. She turned Michelle into an adult film actress."

"Michelle is a grown ass woman." Kenneth looked at Bree's laptop. "What are you doing entertaining that smut? The people Grim talked about during his interview are not slaves. There is no porno ring. They wanna do the fuck shit they do."

"Are you talking about our servants?"

"Yes."

"Is it really a coincidence that ALL of our servants work in the adult industry," asked Bree. "Is it? Because I don't believe in coincidences."

"Not all of them are involved in the adult industry. Some of 'em are old as hell."

"I'm not talking about the old ones." Bree giggled.

"All of our businesses are legal. We have licenses, but we can't control what our employees do in their free time. If they wanna work with adult stuff, that's them."

"That doesn't make the fact that most all of our servants are involved in the adult industry go away. We've been the butt of conspiracy theories for years." Bree pulled up articles about the family's scatterbrained shenanigans on her laptop. She showed them to Kenneth.

"I'm surprised at you, Bree," said Kenneth, "keeping up with lies like that. They lie on us, modify pictures, we have clones, look-alikes, and stalker fans that imitate us running around. We're always the butt of fake ass conspiracy theories."

Bree raised her eyebrows. "Like the ones about the Illuminati."

"What about the Illuminati?"

"This one is true, that our parents throw wild, creepy parties because they are down with the Illuminati's agenda."

"What," Kenneth raised up in his seat, "you mean to tell me that for years I've been preaching against the one world government and 'depopulate the world' crap and my own parents are down with the fucking agenda?" He licked his tongue out in disgust. "The fucking agenda... literally."

"In a way. At first, they were forced to host those parties. Later on they liked it."

"How do you know?"

Bree pointed at her ears. "I got ears, Kenneth. I hear things and I know things. Another thing I know is they're gonna get Pearlie's young nurse next. They recruit at around the age of thirteen or fourteen."

"Melanee," Kenneth shrieked. Bree shook her head slowly. "I can't believe it. Who's recruiting?"

"Take the wool off your eyes, Kenneth. There IS a porno ring and Mom IS the ring leader."

83

Kenneth slid back in his seat. "I'm worried about that Meyer Johnston. And he's sniffing around Michelle."

Bree looked at the wall, trying to keep a neutral face. "What's the problem?"

"Even though Dad and Meyer are close friends, Meyer's involved in something Dad's against. I can feel it."

She smiled. "I don't think it's serious. I think it's because they use Meyer to recruit other slave beaus, he's heavy with the initiation crap and he's an extremely fluid *adult* actor."

"What the hell is a fluid adult actor?" asked Kenneth.

"You know," Bree elbowed Kenneth, "He's spilling."

Kenneth gasped. "Stop fucking with me. You speak in too many riddles at times." Kenneth grabbed Bree's laptop, looked up articles about Meyer Johnston. "I never really thought about Meyer's dumb ass orientation. I figured the only person he was interested in was Michelle."

"I don't think he's interested in the people he works with," said Bree. "Well, there was one time when he hooked up with some older dude in one of his movies."

Kenneth glared out the window. "No surprise."

Michelle walked down the little steps, slid behind Bree, and threw ice-cold water on her head. "What'thuh hell, Michelle! Why'd you throw cold water on me? You know it gives me an anxiety attack!"

"Stop lying, Bree," said Michelle, "you're not having an attack right now."

"Oh, I have to die before you believe me?"

Some of the water splashed on Kenneth. He screamed, "What the hell! Where'd you even come from, Michelle? Go back to the second floor with Christel's drunk ass."

"I tried to sleep, but couldn't because of your loud mouths. I could hear your conversation on the second floor."

"So," said Kenneth.

"So, don't discuss that shit."

"Discuss what," asked Bree.

Michelle said, "The porno-ring."

"Oh, 'cuz of Meyer Johnston?" said Kenneth. "He was the number one slave beau up until a few years ago. They called him peacock," he laughed, "looking motherfucker."

84

"I don't give a fuck about his status," said Michelle.

"Yeah, Michelle, you won't say a thing about his aaasssss," Bree spoke in slow motion.

Michelle side-eyed Bree. "Shut yo' ass up. I don't give a damn. I don't care about his movies."

Stop fucking around," said Kenneth. "You love Meyer's mawn'kass like that barbecued ribeye, you platinum haired whore."

An assistant named Candie brought Bree some towels and escorted her to the dressing room. Candie told another assistant to clean up the water and dispose of Bree's wet clothes once she changed them.

Michelle noticed the traveling grill behind one of the limousines. "You know how much money you're wasting with that big ass barbeque grill, two personal chefs, and the party busses for all the bodyguards and shit? And they dumb asses driving slow as hell, constipating the streets."

"At least my bodyguards protect the whole goddamn family. You nor Bree have bodyguards. Y'all rely on mine. So be grateful, bitch," Kenneth retorted.

"I don't give a damn," said Michelle, "too much extravagance."

"What about the limobike you got to impress ya boy, Meyer?" Kenneth whispered, "Stupid ass. Both of y'all stupid as fuck."

Bree stuck her head out of the dressing room. "What about you and Christel's party buses, Michelle? You're the one who demanded that we leave Kenneth's limo and ride on this one."

Kenneth smiled and shook his head. "Right."

Michelle lit a doobie. "It's not about that. Discuss no-such'a-thang, get it? You don't know who's listening. That's how they get in."

"Believe that. That's how they found out about your nudie pictures and my hidey-holes," said Kenneth.

Michelle and Kenneth could hear Bree laughing in the dressing room.

"I'm serious, Kenneth. When you gonna learn to shut your fucking mouths? That's the problem. Playful sons of bitches."

Kenneth, Michelle, and Bree heard Christel screaming from upstairs. She woke up hitting her fist against the wall. "Fuck you mean you can't? Try me, bitches!"

Kenneth giggled. "What the hell's wrong with that bitch."

Michelle said, "Fuck you think? She's tired."

"She's drunk is what she is." Kenneth looked around. "Where's Pearlie?"

"Sleep. She finally told us about her little imaginary friend named Powder Man. That's what was bothering her on the jet."

"Christel should look into that shit. Pearlie's probably not lying."

Bree joined them. "Wouldn't be surprised if the demons on the estate is actually the Illuminati's aliens, and they've mind controlled Mom to in-friggen-sanity."

"She hollering about some damn clones and she acts like a cyborg at times." Kenneth turned his attention to Michelle. "Where'd you get that blunt? You got enough weed for me?"

As Michelle walked away, Bree elbowed Kenneth in the ribs. "Bree! Wha'chu do that for? Sharpass bow."

"I don't think you want any of that."

"Why the hell not?"

Bree laughed. "You like it with crack?"

"Depends on whose."

"The drug, stupid man. That's a 3750. Marijuana and crack."

"I tried that shit. I'm sticking with Purple Kush."

Speaking of crack, you seen the picture circulating around social media and everywhere else?"

Kenneth frowned, "Of Michelle? Hell no."

"Good. You don't wanna see it."

"My partners take they pick. I don't have shit to do with Michelle's butt-ass, but how the hell you know about it, Bree?"

"Somebody sent the picture of her and Lotus to my phone. It shocked the crap out of me. I didn't bother watching the movie with Calvin and François."

"Hold up. There's another movie floating around?"

"Yes."

"I'll be damned."

"She's got another short film 'servicing' some department store employee." Bree frowned. "I'm not here for that."

"You said she hooked up with Lotus?"

Bree shook her head *yes*.

Kenneth looked disappointed. "My dreams are shot."

"Why?"

"Ain't no way I'll ever hook up with a girl who's had anything to do with that nasty sister or my...or Christel."

Bree gasped.

86

BLUEBERRY MANOR

"What the hell's wrong with you!" Kenneth checked under some of the seats.

"You almost called Mom your mother."

As soon as the family arrived at the compound, Christel stormed in the main ballroom at Blueberry Manor. "Where the goddamn hell is Joseph?" The rest of the family followed her. Pearlie was holding onto Bree while Michelle and Kenneth were trying to calm Christel, trying to stop her from bashing several banquet tables with a hand carved cane. Christel hit Kenneth, knocking him to the floor and threatened to bash Bunny Hopson's— maîtresse—brains in next.

Christel screamed, "I know what the fuck you do at these banquets." She smashed several glasses. "Joseph and I used to host these together!" She checked behind every curtain, underneath tables, the huge bouquets, debris, and the round stage. "Where the fuck is he? I'll kill him in cold motherfucking blood. I'll teach him to re-open the compound behind my back, and sell my goddamn muffins at a soup kitchen. Those are *my* muffins, goddammit. You know how long it took Chef-fucking-Milan to perfect the pot? She looked at the ceiling. "Joseph is probably hiding in a goddamn chandelier. Come out, asshead! Shit eater! *Je serais damné si les idiots piétinent ma merde sep dans matin jusqu'*à minuit 24 heures 7 jours par semaine! Putain! *I'll be damned if the idiots trample my shit twenty-four hours a day, seven days a week! The whores!*" She climbed on ladders, screaming, smashing chandeliers as the guests left. Once the family helped Kenneth off the floor, they called Mario and a few nurses in order to apprehend Christel; however, once they arrived on the scene she had gone.

The guards, juiced up on hot coffee, orange juice, and buttery croissants, sported uniforms of yore, ready to go to war with millions of tourists who claimed Blueberry Manor Castle & Carnival, the restaurants and wine houses as their own from seven in the morning until midnight, 24 hours 7 days a week. Although the restaurants and wine houses now boasted the same longer visiting hours as the castle, tourists at one of the restaurants and both of the wine houses were only seen by appointments and reservations. Blueberry Hills Compound, the part of the estate which consisted of all private residences visible from the skytrain, was open to tourists from quinze heures (15 hours or 3:00PM) until dix-huit heures (18 hours or 6:00PM). The residences were closed to visitors on Sundays.

Joseph, who'd been celebrating the re-opening of the compound for three days and nights, had gone into blackout mode in one of his offices at Parkrose. He heard his personal secretary, Madame Perret, ringing him, but he did not know how to respond. He could not speak properly, and so he paced the floor in confusion, going over alphabets and numbers in his head.

Madame Perret had been ringing Joseph to no avail. She glanced at the mailroom supervisor. She said, "Excusez-moi," and then switched to the old school intercom buzzer.
ANT-ANT-AAAAAANT!
"Bonjour, Monsieur Charlemagne!" Even though the electrifying buzz jump-scared him, he could not think in a coherent fashion. Falling back on the couch, he thought, *all I wanna know is where I am. I feel that I should know this place, but I don't.* He blank stared at the cold white ceiling, taking in an air of depression and loss. His eyes darted, trying to find the

source of jamais vu.

To him, it seemed as if he'd just closed his eyes when he heard a loud whisper. "Bonjour, sorry to wake you, Monsieur Charlemagne," said Madame Perret, "but there is someone here." Joseph forced his eyebrow muscles to work. "Mr. Charlemagne!"

Through his blurry eye slits, he saw dark skin. *I remember complementing smooth dark skin*, he thought. *I remember dark-skinned curves, jet-black braid-out, long purple cape dress.* He paused inside his mind, "Long purple cape dress." Joseph griped, "do you think those clothes are appropriate, Madame Perret?" His eyes drooled at the very thought of her designer platform pumps. "You're draped in diamonds!"

"You don't remember?" Madame Perret said. Her thick French accent was a powerful trigger.

"No," Joseph replied.

"Someone pulled me away from a dinner party last night; told me to come in and check on you."

Joseph popped into himself. "Oh my God, Madame Perret, where am I?"

"You're at the Parkrose office."

"And I've been here, at the Parkrose office all night?"

"You've been in here ever since I arrived."

"When did you arrive?"

"At about eleven-thirty last night. She glanced at her diamond watch. "It's now five twenty-five in the morning."

"I remember." Joseph pressed his fingers against his temples.

Madame Perret's voice went up a few octaves. "You remember what?"

"I remember that we're hiring a new secretary today. Is the new girl here?"

Madame Perret dropped her head. "Oui, elle est... Yes she is."

"Does she know I'm in here?"

"Yes, but she doesn't know you're in here sleeping."

Joseph laughed and cut an embarrassed eye at Madame Perret. "Thank you for not asking about last night." Thoughts of inappropriateness flooded his conscious.

She stroked his hair. "Was it not a memorable event?"

Joseph cleared his throat. "Who's here?"

"There is the mailroom supervisor, Drystan Fortier."

"Okay." Joseph jumped up, spruced himself, and straightened his desk. "Send him in. And thank you."

Madame Perret held the door open as Drystan rolled a big wire utility cart into the office then returned to her desk.

"What's with all the boxes?" asked Joseph.

"These boxes are filled with notepads, Mr. Charlemagne."

"Filled with notepads?" ·

Drystan laughed. "Ouai. These are messages from the switchboard operators. But Madame Turcotte wants me to make sure you read this morning's reports about Kenneth and Michelle and Christel's arrests before you look at any of these messages."

Joseph muttered, "So much bad publicity. I'm tired of it. And I know so many others are tired of it as well." He looked down to see 'R.I.P. Birdie, Susan, Sid, and Roxie' then screamed, "Who killed my son's dogs?"

"Aaa-aaa, nope, I saw you, Mr. Charlemagne. You cheated. *Je vous raconte*! I'm telling." Drystan laughed.

"Hey now! Just don't tell Lydia." Joseph's laugh irritated his windpipe. "She'll get at me. Aaaa-aaageee-again."

Drystan's knees shook. "Are you alright, Mr. Charlemagne?"

Joseph waved his hands. "I'm fine."

Madame Perret also buzzed and spoke softly in the intercom. "Are you alright, Mr. Charlemagne? Can I bring you something?"

Joseph spoke into the intercom as best as he could. "Yes, I'm alright. Can you bring me a glass of water, a picture of orange juice and a breakfast platter from the castle?"

"Yes... Oui, Monsieur Charlemagne."

Joseph looked at Drystan. "Thank you for bringing the mail to me personally, and shut the door behind you."

"Will do, Mr. Charlemagne. Oh, and Madame Emma LaChapelle has been calling nonstop."

"Ma tante?"

"Si, yes, your aunt."

"What does she want?"

"I don't know. She does nothing but cry. The operators can't get anything out of her but sniffles."

"Thank you, Drystan."

"Anytime, Mr. Charlemagne."

BLUEBERRY MANOR

Joseph spoke to himself, "What the hell's going on in this morning's news? The switchboard operators have given me thousands of messages, and it's only ten after six!" He cupped his chin with his right hand. "Well, I think there was a full moon last night. Must've triggered my family's mental issues big time. Guess I should hire extra security. The media will be all over this place soon, if they aren't already."

Friday, December 29, 2006

He looked around for a pitcher of plain coconut water, but only found a bowl of blueberry oatmeal, miso soup, and a jar of brass monkey with peanut butter and crab salted around its rim. Joseph rubbed his forehead. "Who the hell is responsible for all this?" He opened three windows, hoping to whisk away the odd smell of sheep's head, ostrich egg omelet, and a banana and bacon Bloody Mary cocktail.

Lingering cigar smoke and thick citrus air freshener made him nauseous. While massaging the cramps in his stomach area, his eyes fixed on Christel's air purifier and a bottle of the lower staff's vinegar and baking soda concoction. *Maybe I have an attack of the flu*, he thought, until the bumbling sound of tiptoes on the hardwood floor dredged up memories of last night. He remembered rum punch, long island iced tea, bourbon, and a scantily clad Madame Perret in the wine cellar. He remembered smoking countless cigars, smoking too much blueberry Kush, but eating no food.

He thought he'd feel much better about himself if he was to revisit the promise of burning a few calories a day. He forced himself out of bed, combed his hair, and slipped on a black and white workout suit. He hydrated himself during the cardio, stretching, and weight training, showered, and then went into the steam room for twenty minutes. After the schvitz, he took another shower then slipped on the triple-XL blue and white tracksuit Kenneth bought him last year. *Now it fits.*

The old Victorian conservatory and opera house proposed a camouflaged method of peering at tourists. The belligerent ones seemed to bring comfort, especially today. He didn't know if it was because they irritated Christel, disguised paranormal activities, masked the burning in his chest, or maybe it was because they reminded him of an odd childhood.

He hid behind the Gothic fountain, kept surveillance for hours, looking

91

AMINA CAPRICE ANDOLINI

for Nasira Pang, a ghostly hybrid like his beloved blueberry strain. She was a Saudi Arabian goddess; a mixture of every goddess known to man-of every significance, every color, every dimension—a brown skinned, dark haired, 5"7' work of art, 23 years his junior. Joseph had her once, for about five years, but now, he could only dream of its lifelong transience.

An unsurpassed, mysterious tie. One he and his wife could never go in for, even without Christel's multiple personalities lurking behind the gatekeeper, daydreaming of living life through her strange shenanigans. Even without Joseph's love for brooding; the way he hid behind alcohol, blueberry, "poor people food," and all manners of "poor people things," agonizing over the deaths of his family members.

He plopped on the couch, feeling the psychedelic thoughts of every guest. The thick smell of blueberry filled the glass house with faux aspiration and faux anticipation of feeling his Twin Flame's jade.

He wanted cannabis-infused blueberry muffins, wine, unhealthy foods, something to take his mind off the pain. He shot up, remembering that today was Fried Chicken Friday, and returned to his bedroom yelling, "I've gotta call Jeeves." He shook, barely missing the sharp edge of Christel's fancy letter opener while feeling for the intercom button. "The bitch will kill me one way or another."

Jeeves Belvedere, one of the so-called Blind Monks of the Light and one of Joseph's butlers picked up the call, catching only the distorted end of Joseph's voice. "Sir? Is this you?"

"Oh, I didn't know. This thing is on, huh... um, Curt, I mean Jeeves, bring me the usual."

"But your health, Sir."

"I don't care about my health!" His thunderous tone scared every servant in the vicinity. In a more appropriate way he said, "Look, I'm stressed. Just do what I ask of you."

"But—"

"I'm giving you ten minutes, Jeeves. Today is the *holiday* edition of Fried Chicken Friday, so I know about the millions of greasy fried goodness already prepared."

"Christel and the Blind Monks say you must."

"FUCK Christel, and FUCK the FUCKING monks!"

"Joseph!" Jeeves put his hand over his heart. "I'm trying to give you a channeled message from—"

Joseph ended the call, but apologized after Jeeves brought the usual

92

up to his bedroom roughly five minutes later. "I apologize, Jeeves. I didn't mean to go ballistic, to talk about your religion and shit."

"My religion?"

"The Blind Monks is your religion, isn't it?"

Jeeves dusted his pant leg with a small broom he kept in his inside pocket. "We're not a religion." He laughed, "We call ourselves Blind Monks because humans cannot see us. We have the ability to hide behind the Veil. We come from all over. Third Dimension, Fourth Dimension, Fifth Dimension, from all over the Universe. We are Of the Light and Of the False-Light Syndrome."

A weird shiver shot up Joseph's spine. His knees buckled, teeth chattered, and cold liquid beaded across his forehead. A loving Energy chilled the room, Energy so strange and so loving, it was scary. Flashes of the neutral Squid Beast similar to the one responsible for his sister's death, but Joseph's parasite had thick patches of carpet-like hair and hooks on its tentacles, played before him.

"The ones who allow themselves to be seen help transport Spirits to the Underworld. Some counsel the living if they have a troubled soul," said Jeeves.

"So I don't understand the creepy rituals."

"It's okay, Mr. Charlemagne, sir."

Joseph flashed back to possession in Forest of the Blind Monk Territory, in the area between Haunted Garden, near the Musician Tarot portal and Mad Trees Isle where many trespassers went to commit suicide. Paisley splotches danced before Joseph's eyes.

"Quite alright, Sir."

Joseph rubbed his eyes. "So what if they're demonic?"

Jeeves loud talked Joseph, "Quite alright, Sir." His voice returned to a softer tone. "I understand wholeheartedly. You must know we only look out for you. You are my employer and a very good friend. I don't want anything to happen to you." Jeeves sighed heavily, as if he wanted to say something important but he didn't know how to wrap the words in silk. "Have you taken your afternoon medicines?"

Joseph darted his eyes to the left. "Yeah...Yeah. I take my medicines the way I'm supposed to take them." Joseph laughed awkwardly. "Of course," he slapped his knee in jest, "Zeeland makes sure I take the meds."

"Zeeland? I've never heard of a Zeeland."

Joseph cut him off with an ugly cough.

"Very well then." Jeeves popped a smile on his face. "Good day, Sir." He turned sharply towards the door.

"On that note, I'm out. I'll see you tomorrow." Jeeves' voice took on an air of sadness. "I'm leaving you to enjoy your uh, greasy fried goodies." He looked around at bunches of cigars, smoking devices, and empty liquor bottles strolled carelessly.

"What's wrong, Cousin? You've never been so pale."

Jeeves mouthed, "I feel your pain."

Joseph realized the wetness that surrounded him was sweat rather than water from a swimming pool. It took human form, gently waking him from a cool, summery pipe dream. Like a blind man, he touched the side of his face. The impression of a wooden gargoyle made it somewhat sore and multicolored. As flaming hot teeth chewed at his abdomen, he wondered how long he had been at the foot of his bedstead.

He remembered nothing after feasting on fried foods and washing it down with 'Bloody Fuck' wine and 'Hell Naw' beer. At 6:00 in the morning, he slinked to the kitchen for coconut milk. "Coconut milk stops the burning," he said to Christel as he passed her in the hallway, waving his hand toward the kitchen.

Christel gasped. "You don't look so good, Joe. Yes, coconut milk... I'll meet you in the kitchen."

The heat that rose from Joseph's navel fashioned itself into a hallucination of his late parents, and siblings, before he made it to the refrigerator.

While chanting it's time in Italian slang, his thickset mom served yummy greasy foods alongside giant bottles of painkillers on a bronze pushcart. Its sharp wheels scraped along cobblestone road creating foul smelling smoke. In between puffs on a Cuban cigar, his dad ate wild blueberries while coddling bottles of 'Dizzda Shit' and 'Psychedelic Reel' wine like fragile newborn babies. Through purple teeth and black gums, he laughed as Black Moor goldfish devoured the flesh of their counterparts in oddly shaped ponds of 'Redass' cooking oil and 'Blackass' hot sauce. His siblings popped out of the ponds in three-second intervals, flailing and splashing as if they were gasping for air.

Joseph came around with three short shakes of the head. To his surprise, he was already sitting at the kitchen table with his right cupped, ready to grab a glass of cool milk.

"Here," said Christel. "Here's your fucking milk." She plopped the glass on the table. The clink and splash made Joseph cower. "I know that yesterday was Fried Chicken Friday, Joe. So do I have to stand up over you with a fucking stick? Huh? I told you not to eat that fried junk. It's bad for your goddamn health, you know." She said, "Fucking shame."

"You're bad for my health! And when did you start caring about my health, huh?"

Christel took an American magazine off the kitchen counter. She looked at the dumb look on Joseph's face. "And what the hell is wrong with your ass?"

He said, "My mind is stuck."

"On fucking what?"

"On my mom and dad's message."

"So fucking what?"

"Je pense que je suis à demi mort," Joseph said.

Christel's laugh distracted him. "And what the fuck does that really mean, dummy?"

Joseph said nothing.

"Youse an illiterate fuck, you know? Half dead my ass."

Joseph rose from the table and headed toward the door.

"Where the fuck you going? Aren't you going to finish the rest of your goddamn milk? You told me coconut milk is the only thing that stops the burning."

Joseph saw a black drape cover his third eye. *Oh well*, he thought, *we all have to go sometime*. There was a strange mix of anticipation and fear. As he turned the doorknob, he gave Christel a look that sent hate waves through the back of her platinum colored head.

"I asked you a goddamn question, you big water headed asshole!"

"I'm not studying you, Christel."

"Bald...Baldness of Fat!"

"You know that cat is a ghost, right?"

Christel ignored him. "Bald!"

He shouted, "Well fuck you then. And fuck your fucking ghost-cat. Fuck this fucking fuckery."

"Clusterfuck it then!"

Joseph put his hand over his heart.

"Where the fuck you going?" Christel screamed.

He tore out of the door.

"What about the rest of your goddamn milk?" She forced her head out of the door, but Joseph had completely vanished. She slammed the door closed, shaking all the pictures and utensils on the wall. "Asshole."

Michelle stuck her head out of her bedroom door. "Mom! What's wrong? Est-ce un tremblement de terre? Is it an earthquake or are you and Dad fighting again?" She gave Meyer (who had spent the night in Michelle's bedroom) a peck on the lips before rushing him out of the back door.

"Ain't no earthquake this part of France, and I can smell the shitbag you've been hiding in your room," Christel told her.

Michelle pressed her trembling fingers against her mouth.

"Besides, I'm reading style magazines in the kitchen." She slammed the magazine on the table. "No, I'm going to the tearoom with the others. I have no time for your foolishness!"

"I had to get away from that bitch," said Joseph, "je ne suis pas d'humeur à pelleter la merde. Je ne peux pas. I'm not in the mood to shovel the shit. I cannot…" He saw his friend, Meyer Johnston, leaving the manor house. "What's he doing loafing behind the manor? Better not be what I think."

Discomfort started at the breastbone, traveled upward to the jaw, and down through Joseph's left arm as he walked. He wiped sweat from his forehead. I have to make it up this hill, he thought. He put his hand to his heart once he reached the top, catching the eye of an American tourist.

"Oh," the tourist said. "It looks like the fat Frenchman is reciting the Pledge of Allegiance to us. Look!"

Debilitating pain took the form of a wrestler, wringing Joseph's body like a face towel. Pain as splitting as the spit from a BAR made his knees buckle. Gasping for air, he managed to produce a choking motion before tumbling down the hill; cutting through grapevines as if he was a chainsaw killer.

A Spanish tourist saw him, grabbed her rented cell phone, and called for emergency help.

ookie Davis, the daughter of Jessica and Bernard Davis stopped drinking her peppermint tea when she heard the sirens blaring outdoors. She turned to her best friends, Pearlie Charlemagne, and a giant stuffed lion that went by the name of Delroy Davis. "Hey guys, you hear da ambalambs?" She turned to her mother, "Bahhbuh, I wonder where dey goin'?"

"Probably coming this way," Bernard said. "You know how pesky the tourists can get this time of year."

Meyer came in the tearoom through the back door. "Whoo-weee! I told Joseph to get a court order so these people'la stay off the lawn. He too kind-hearted, always trying to satisfy errbody. That's why his tail gettin' sued like forty goin' north. He's gettin' fucked over!" Looking over his shoulder, Meyer shouted, "Ain't that right, Christel? You know all about fuckin' ova Joseph."

Christel gave Meyer a cold look.

"Bananigans!" Meyer thought back to just last week, when he caught Christel and the actor Arturo Salva in the attic, right above Joseph's game room. "I don't understand y'all Charlemagnes. Y'alls is crazy as some damn road lizards ridin' on thuh storm and thuh highway looking asses."

"UUUP!" Bernard laughed like a retarded hyena.

Jessica nudged Bernard in the ribs. "Laughing is very inappropriate, Ben. Christel has a real medical problem. You know all about that."

Bernard raised his shirt to check for a mark. "I'm trippin' off City Boy here. No screet light lookin' ass." He mocked Meyer. "Y'alls is crazy as some damn road lizards."

Jessica said, "That's enough, Bernard."

Bernard continued. "The fucker from the boondocks, middle of nowhere lookin' ass; stupid dog lookin' ass, crazy as some damn road lizards lookin' ass. Ay Jessica," Bernard took on a Southern accent, "I ain't never heard no shit like that a'fore in my life lookin' ass."

"You stupid or what?" Jessica put a fake smile on her face and then turned her attention to Cookie. "Um, Cookie, you and Pearlie can go over to Mrs. Reinhart's house now. C'mon, go on with Mrs. Milan."

Cookie whined, "But Bahbuh? What about Delroy?" She pointed her stubby little finger in the stuffed lion's direction. "And what about our tea party? The one them syreens interrubbded?"

Jessica laughed. "Well, you girls can take Delroy and the tea set to Mrs. Reinhart's. Go on now. Mrs. Milan will walk with you." The girls grabbed Delroy and the tea set and escaped out the back way with Mrs. Milan.

"Fuck you, Meyer," Christel said unenthusiastically. Turning her attention to the outside frenzy, she said, "Fuck, we're gonna be facing another damned lawsuit. I can't stand those greedy tourists. I'm so tired of this fucking shit. I'm tired of those people faking injuries on our property. When the sneaky sons of bastards get good lawyers, they can leave their day jobs. C'mon guys. Help me deal with this shit."

The Charlemagnes, along with a few tenants fluttered to the lawn like bitter butterflies. Christel, already frustrated, pushed and kicked several tourists on the way to the accident scene. As a protective measure, two bodyguards jumped in front of Christel, making their weapons visible, gazing at the crowd like ruffians. Several other bodyguards positioned themselves next to a fleet of luxury vehicles, displaying grim seriousness.

Once Christel arrived at the accident scene, flocks of tourists and medical help parted like the Red Sea. Uninterested family and friends dropped behind her, not offering much support; however, they stood alert when the metal stretcher, the object of their aversion became visible.

"Oh my God, that's Joseph," screamed a disoriented tourist, "that's not an intoxicated day-tripper."

"Berries and goddamn Christ," screamed Chef Martina, "that's my boss's cousin." She threw her head back in an overly dramatic fashion. She grimaced, "Who dem boys done sacrificed?" She looked around for an answer, but everyone was engaged to their own shock. "They like some hooongry spiiiduhs, and my Joseph, he the motherfucking repast." After removing her apron, she broke out in a holy dance that silenced the crowd even further.

Christel tore through the silence with an animalistic squeal. She

BLUEBERRY MANOR

clawed at her face, froze for a few seconds and then flew about the grounds in a deceitful, spaced-out urgency.

Christel forced her way in the ambulance. Bree put her hand on her forehead as if she was about to faint. Once able to talk, she demanded to ride with Jessica and Bernard in one of the family's cars. An old friend, Luigi Mosserelow, also jumped in one of the family's cars. Kenneth, Michelle, and other family and friends stayed behind.

Meyer slapped his knee while laughing. "Aw, what's ever'one so worked up about? What's that? That's no big biggie. Joseph'll be back in time for the annual poker game tonight." He said, "I think he done had a lil'ole heat stroke attack on dat hill is all." He looked around for confirmation but did not find any.

Kenneth and Michelle gave Meyer sorrowful looks behind his back.

Kenneth sighed, "Michelle, did you check Dad's color? I've never seen him look like that."

"I keep seeing it, like a never-ending movie. I don't wanna own that horrific image of D-Dad." The shaking in her knees caused her to stutter. "I've-I've been so m-mean to Dad lately. I just don't know what to do..."

Kenneth grabbed Michelle's shoulders. "Don't worry about that right now! It's not about you."

Michelle slithered away from Kenneth's grasp. "What Meyer doesn't know is Dad has had several heat strokes in the past, but he never looked like that. Meyer needs to be watched. Whenever something traumatic happens, he goes back to witnessing the deaths of Aunt Willow and RainBeau, and Uncle Blaze's breakdown. Meyer was so young. He was only fifteen years old at the time."

"I don't care about Meyer." Kenneth picked pine needles off a tree branch. "You mean Dad's little sister?" Michelle nodded her head while wiping tears. "How does Meyer know Aunt Willow again?"

"Aunt Willow and Meyer were zoolinguists."

"What's that?"

"Animal telepathy. People who can talk to animals." Michelle took a deep breath. "After Aunt Willow and Uncle Blaze changed their names and moved to San Francisco, they met up with Meyer and his cousin, RainBeau RiverStone. Aunt Willow married RainBeau within months, so I guess you can say Meyer and Aunt Willow were cousins." She also picked pine needles off a tree branch. "I guess we're all cousins."

"And Dad brought Meyer to France after RainBeau's suicide and Uncle

99

Blaze's breakdown," Kenneth emphasized.

"Yes. RainBeau's suicide was so bizarre. Meyer told me all about it."

Kenneth was unimpressed. "Oh, really?" He gave Michelle a look of suspicion.

"Meyer and some others tried to get in RainBeau's locked room, but he turned up the stereo and told them all to go away. After a few minutes, Meyer broke the door down and found RainBeau's slumped over corpse in Aunt Willow's favorite chair. There was a rock song with 'rhapsody' in its title playing."

Kenneth pursed his lips. "Meyer told you that stuff?" Michelle nodded her head. "What was the significance of his going out music?"

"How could you be so mean, Kenneth?"

"Well, that's what it was."

"Besides being RainBeau and Aunt Willow's favorite song, I guess the thought of dying was euphoria. The thought of being without Aunt Willow was hell. The thought of being with her was rhapsody." Michelle moaned, "RainBeau was such a romantic."

Kenneth scoffed. "If you say so."

Michelle cried loudly. "Oh, Kenneth! Meyer's gonna have a panic attack. What am I gonna do?" Kenneth gave her a hug.

Meyer sneaked a peek at Michelle and Kenneth from behind an Austrian pine tree. While churning dirt with his heel, he said, "Boy oh boy. I wish I was the one giving Michelle a hug like dat Kenneth ova dere." He sighed. "He's a lucky damn dawg." He searched the sky, searching for spiritual comfort, but was only able to bring a recurring nightmare to fruition.

Normally, fifteen-year-old Meyer couldn't see in the water, or perhaps he never noticed after twilight. On the evening of Sunday, July 3, 1977, he saw Willow Worth-RiverStone in the water, in a horror-struck daze, paying homage to an amazing sea creature.

He understood Willow's awe. With its guise of a multicolored alien, its huge head, massive tentacles spreading out and curling inward, he was under the same spell as she. Splotches of red provoked hysteria, while the white streaks on its tentacles rooted them back to another melodramatic world: one with rose-colored romanticisms, purple proses, and beige undertones. In the new world, there was no danger.

100

BLUEBERRY MANOR

The creature had an otherworldly glow. Pastel colors: pinks, purples, and blues. They were close enough to its eyes, big white slits and huge black centers. There was a telepathic signal, one both Willow and Meyer followed. They felt as if the creature was gentle, and childlike, and all it wanted to do was play around.

Willow wanted to play around, to flow in and out what looked like a graceful chiffon nightgown; however, the creature was so huge, that one slap could send her plummeting in whatever direction it preferred. That was her only fear.

The creature was electric pink, and wild, and painful to Willow's lungs. Euphoria and fear stopped her heart. Perhaps, this was something the sea creature sensed. Enraged, it slapped the water, probably an attempt to restore Willow's life.

Willow's limpness came barreling to the creature. Frightened, its beak sliced through her torso, an ugly, raggedy break. The superior half drifted away, as if it was on a mission. Willow's husband, RainBeau RiverStone felt that mission. He got out of bed, staggered to the bow, and nearly jumped in the ocean when he saw Willow's corpse rocking the hull. He shook and slapped Meyer in an attempt to shake the dead psychotic stare off his mug.

"Meyer! What the hell happened," said RainBeau, "why is my wife in the ocean?"

When Willow's brother, Blaze peeked over the railings, his sister appeared to be sleeping, smiling, in perfect peace with the melodramatic world, which was now her eternity. "Come out of that water, Willow! It's too late for that shit," Blaze screamed. His mind would not allow him to believe that his little sister was dead.

RainBeau fished Willow out of the water, ribcage crushed, torso deflated, clumps of blood swung from meaty tendons as organs continued to drop in the ocean.

The creature let out a horrible screech. People from distant places: the shore, the lighthouse, and other Fairey Amira boats scuttled to the scene with nets, harpoons, and guns in tow. They managed to catch the sea creature, pulled it to shore in a huge net where it died a few seconds later. Its tentacle was wrapped around Willow's inferior half.

RainBeau attempted suicide several times; however, on Tuesday, July 5, 1977, Meyer found him sitting in Willow's favorite chair. Lifeless. There were drug cocktails and several liquid concoctions on the coffee table. His

AMINA CAPRICE ANDOLINI

cryptic death note—words written with a dull black marker on a piece of white cardboard—rested on his disembowelment... FUCK PAIN NO FEAR IN HELL—RHAPSODY.

Kenneth stopped himself from expressing genuine sympathy toward Michelle. He said, "There's nothing you can do about Meyer's fake ass panic attack."

Michelle stared blankly. "Meyer was only fifteen years old when Dad brought him to this estate. He'd already seen the disturbing, watery, drugged-out faces of Death." She whimpered inaudibly.

Kenneth talked over Michelle's whimpers. "This is ridiculous. You're way too invested in Meyer's feelings."

"What are you talking about?"

Kenneth pointed his finger. "Oh, so you wanna be in Meyer's company right now? We're your family, not him!"

Michelle puffed her cheeks and covered her mouth so the words *Meyer is Nicole's father* could not slip out.

"Why are you covering your mouth?"

Michelle slung her arms around her body like a playful child. "Your anger is misplaced. And you're making a big deal out of nothing, you, you pig."

"For the record, I like pigs. That's why I don't do the pork anymore." Kenneth said, "I told Dad about all the weird-gargoyle meat and he still ate the shit."

"That has nothing to do with this."

"Yea it does. Especially the cute little pink ones and the cute little black ones."

"And all because he used to be a slave beau," grumbled Michelle. "You should be ashamed of yourself."

"Slave beau? No, Michelle, I'm not even talking about Meyer right now."

"My ears are hot," whined Meyer, his eye was dangerously close to a pine needle. "Lemme just see what they're talking now." Meyer eased closer and closer.

"You hear that, Michelle?" asked Kenneth.

"What?"

"Sounded like a cat yowling."

"Yeah," Michelle laughed, "Mom's dead cat is yowling on the Other Side. The poor thing has had several names: Bald Balderson, Baldness of Fatterson and Baldness of Fat. Pretty traumatic when that giant bird swooped down and grabbed Bald out of Mom's arms. Its talons looked like claw cranes."

"Fuck you. I'm real, dammit."

"All I know is you need to leave Meyer alone, Kenneth. He has feelings about this too."

"Who gives a damn about Meyer's goddamn feelings? Dad should be your focus, not Meyer's ass. See, I knew you were in love with him." Kenneth raised his head. "I have occult knowledge about Cupid and his bow."

Michelle bucked her eyes. "Are *you* in love with him?"

"Hell, he's got enough love for all of us, goddammit!"

Michelle stomped her feet. "Stop talking about his infamous man part. You should be ashamed of yourself."

"What do you know about his infamous man part?"

"None of your goddamn business!"

"The hell it ain't. I saw Meyer tipping out the back of the manor. Look, I just wanna concentrate on," Kenneth saw Meyer staring at them. After Meyer noticed Kenneth's stare, he ran away. "Hell, naw. The stalker head ass bitch spying on us!" Kenneth ran after Meyer.

Michelle screamed, "Kenneth! Come back here!" She ran behind Kenneth and Meyer. "You're mixed up!" Michelle caught up just in time to see Kenneth push Meyer on the ground and punch him in the back.

Meyer screamed, "Dayum, Kenneth!" He protected his face. "Wha'thuh?"

After showering Meyer with blows and bites, Kenneth seemed to disappear via smoke like a vampire bat.

"Wha'thuh?" Meyer looked at Michelle. "Kenneth done disappeared 'way from dis bitch in a cloud of smoke. Where the hell did he go?"

"Meyer, Kenneth didn't disappear. The both of you kicked up a dirt cloud when fighting." She looked around, "It's odd... I don't know where he went, though."

BLUEBERRY MANOR

"Don't say no excuses, Michelle. Don't defend him. Your brother done assaulted me then disappeared. I'm convinced Sheriff Osco Pall's wife is right. That fucker's a Dracula!" Meyer tripped over a pile of rocks when he attempted to get off the ground. "Wha'thuh fuck? Michelle!"

Michelle screamed, "Meyer! Are you alright?"

"I got dirt in my eyes is all. And look at my clothes. And where the hell dat vampire go? You see him?"

"Your eyes are so red!"

"I just poked'em with a pine needle over yonder."

"Oh, so you're the yowling cat." Michelle laughed.

"What?"

Michelle helped Meyer off the ground. "Don't take it personal." She spat out dirt and small rocks. "He's my brother, so, yeah."

"What do you mean, don't take it personal? That so-and-so just punched me in the head!"

Michelle erupted in tears. "You weren't listening to me."

"Don't cry no more." Meyer wiped Michelle's face while staring at her long tanned neck. "I heard you." He gave her a warm hug. "If you think everyone done found out about us, why not announce it to the whole world out yonder?"

"No, Meyer. We were raised as cousins, you're so much older and uh, more experienced than me and..."

A tourist with a disposable camera walked up to Meyer and Michelle. Meyer pushed Michelle away from him.

Michelle stumbled... "What the hell?"

The tourist did not know English. She said, "Disculpe. Lo siento mucho, pero eres su hija?"

Meyer said, "I know you saw Kenneth sucker punch me, lady." He laughed, looked at Michelle, then at the tourist. "That snotty bastard needs to raise up off me cuz I ain't no dayum punching bag. I understand being angry, emotional, scared, whatever the hell they he is, but dayum, it's not that serious. Joseph just had a lil'ole heat stroke on," his voice deepened, "own de fucking hill. Big fucking deal. Now go away, pendejo." He spoke to Michelle. "Doesn't that mean stupid in Spanish?" Michelle shook her head yes. Meyer continued to speak to the tourist. "Now go away before I do something I ain't done in a few hours. You know I know you."

A visibly shaken Michelle spoke to the tourist. "No," she side-eyed

Meyer, "as you can imagine, everybody's grieving around here."

Meyer said, "What the hell did she say before, Michelle, dayum! I don't speak no Spanish."

Michelle rolled her eyes. "Don't worry, Meyer. I speak a little Spanish."

"Really? What language can't you speak?"

"The tourist said, 'excuse me' then asked am I his daughter." Michelle told the tourist that she is Joseph Charlemagne's daughter in Spanish then asked her name.

Meyer interrupted. He said, "excuse me," to the tourist then side-eyed Michelle. He turned the tourist around to face him.

"Meyer! What are you doing," said Michelle.

Meyer continued talking to the tourist. "What's your name? You sho look familiar." He put his arm around the tourist's shoulder.

The confused looking tourist turned to face Michelle. "Me llama es Manuela Morales." She continued to speak to Michelle in Spanish.

Meyer interrupted again. "Hey! She don't even not speak English, Michelle. How the hell she know what done happened? She don't even know a heat stroke from a heart attack."

"You don't even not speak English, Meyer. And what does not speaking English have to do with telling the difference between a heat stroke and a heart attack?" She lowered her voice. "You know Dad did not have a simple heat stroke on the hill."

"My, darlin' Michelle, a heat stroke ain't simple. Cousin Earl had a heat stroke and died."

"Meyer! Your Cousin Earl isn't dead." Michelle pointed to the other side of the compound. "Look, Cousin Earl's over there," she looked at the tourist and said, "eating a blueberry muffin" in Spanish. The tourist snickered.

Meyer exposed his teeth to the tourist, then spoke to Michelle. "Oh, *that* Cousin Earl. You mean the cousin me and Joseph share? I thought he had done died up in this bitch a long, long time ago."

"Does it matter," asked the tourist in Spanish.

"Hell, yeah, it matters. That fucker owes me twelve-damn-dollars in this camp! Immo go get my money."

"Bye, Meyer," said Michelle, "you're such a liar. I thought you didn't know any Spanish. You knew when the tourist asked *does it matter* in Spanish."

Meyer blathered, "You caught that? You wasn't sp'osed to catch dat, but no, it don't matter. I'm proud to be a country-born Texan." He pointed at himself. "Fuckin' A!"

Michelle said, "You're Puerto Rican."

"But I was born in Texas. Check the accent."

"Senorita Morales isn't blind. She said she saw Daddy have a heart attack and—"

Meyer interrupted with a cornfed smirk.

"What, Meyer? She's a goddamn nurse! She knows what a heart attack looks like?"

"Yeah, she played a nurse in my last movie. That's where I know her from." Ugly lines appeared on Michelle's face. Meyer pretended to cough. "You're off, Michelle, and you, you're the one in denial. Ms. Morales said she thinks Joseph had a heart attack. So this lady here don't even know for sure what he had." He crossed his arms and raised his head in victory. She's not a real nurse. Now top dat."

"Top that?"

"Top dat!" Meyer picked at his fingernails. "I know thangs. Me and Ms. Morales spoke to each other in another kind of language," his eyebrows rose and fell several times, "if'n you know what I mean, Michelle darling."

Michelle yelled, "There's no reasoning with you. It all comes around to your stupid movies, and... and that!" She grabbed Manuela's hand. They both stomped off to find Kenneth.

Kenneth made it to a secluded area of the compound, he thought to himself, *Yesterday was Fried Chicken Friday at the Manor. Dad's like an addict when it comes to fried foods. I knew I should have stuck around to monitor his health. Jeeves is so laidback when it comes to Dad, and I blame nobody but me.* He cried in an ugly, muffled way. "If only I had been there." He pounded his fist in the cold, rocky ground. "I blame me. I blame meeee!"

Blueberry Manor Estate looked like the red-smoldering rebirth of a city after a crucial war. Unidentified bodies lay dead on the grounds, hit by cars, trampled by paparazzi, photojournalists, business associates, and alleged family members. Before this day, no one could tell the difference between robotic security guards and its fleshly counterpart. The distractions: accidents, phone calls, and screaming journalists caused short circuits in the humanoid guards resulting in butchery and assault, turning the once benign creatures into neck-snapping monsters.

After an hour or so of answering prank calls at Parkrose's front desk, Kenneth took a walk about the grounds. He sat on a concrete slab, daydreaming of how he had been disgraced by his father. *Christel can fuck off*, he thought. *I'm in this situation because of her loose attitude toward bone-yarding*. He could hear his parent's famous words in his head, which sometimes reminded him of a dull double act.

"*This situation is a grave tragicomedy,*" *said Joseph,* "*I should put you on display at the castle. The girls would really like that.*"

"*THE GIRLS! I heard that, Joseph,*" *said Christel. Kenneth should be neutered, like the damn dog he is. He blames the shit on me, but I didn't tell the fucker to father all the goddamn children of the goddamn rainbow. Children he won't goddamn claim, goddammit!*"

Vivid hallucinations took human form, marshalling Kenneth into a pseudo convulsion. He saw his six children (Aqua, DeShawn, Marie, Mickie, Jaye, and Mercedes) materialize before him. Their mothers shook their fists in a huddle.

Kenneth held his ears, "Stop threatening me!" He reached for his children's gummy sweet innocence, not realizing the feeling that had taken him over was one of undeserving pride and shame. He looked at his red hands, covered in the blood of his own madness. He imagined four fiery women with fiery hooks in his heart. The women ripped Kenneth apart. They set him on fire while they danced and relished in his pain.

Kenneth saw Darie Despree, dark brown skin with brown eyes and long black hair, working in a posh hotel in New Hampshire, USA. She had on the blue jumpsuit that he bought her for her seventeenth birthday. The vision filled him with unspeakable joy, until their daughter came to Earth on his eighteenth birthday. He saw himself in the hospital, denying his part in Aqua's existence even though she looked eerily similar to Michelle. He didn't know why he denied her, perhaps he was too young, not able to handle the thought of creation.

Kenneth saw Tracee Mantega, tanned skin with brown eyes and long brown hair, on a beach in Puerto Rico. Tracee was a tarnished gemstone, the way Kenneth preferred. He was tired of the beauty contest looking, plastic filled, carbon copies of his mother and sister. At that time, Tracee wasn't a successful writer. She wasn't a sought after beauty or a fashion icon. She was a nineteen-year-old Gothic. She wore baggy clothes, black makeup, listened to rap music (gangster rap and reggaeton), lots of Nirvana, and had a round-the-way attitude.

He saw himself continuing to play on Darie's infatuation. After the birth of DeShawn, who also looked like Michelle, he continued to deny his part in Aqua's as well as DeShawn's existence. When Darie found out about Tracee Mantega, Kenneth's alleged fiancée, Darie wanted nothing to do with the Charlemagne name. She severed ties, only communicating with Joseph and Bree on birthdays and holidays.

Kenneth married Tracee shortly after Darie severed ties with him. To his disillusionment, after Tracee acquired some success with her writing, she gave herself a makeover. She had become one of the beauty contest looking, plastic filled, carbon copies that he claimed to dislike. Because of her makeover, he divorced Tracee before their daughter, Maria Inez Mantega-Charlemagne, came to Earth in 1998.

In 1999, Kenneth saw Moanie Mahonie on the set of one of Meyer's adult films. He immediately moved her in his wing, infatuated by her surgeon's curves, puffy plastic-ness, and fake tan, shocking Christel, Michelle, Bree, and Tracee beyond words. Three months after Moanie moved in the manor, Michelle's private investigator discovered that Moanie had been feeding information to the media. Kenneth put Moanie out of the manor a few months after their daughter, Mickie, was born.

He met Anadancia DuBois at one of his friend's bachelor parties.

She popped out of an eleven-foot-tall cake wearing nothing but a long diamond navel ring. Kenneth moved her in Suntilian Isle, and sometimes she'd share a wing with Bree, acting as her au pair.

After Kenneth and Moanie Mahonie's son (Jaye) was born in 2000, Bree discovered that Anadancia, the third cousin of Moanie Mahonie, was also reporting Charlemagne secrets to the media. Once Kenneth found out that Anadancia had collected $5 million as a spy, he threw her off the grounds but continued to see her. After their daughter, Mercedes, was born in 2004, Kenneth cut ties, denying both children and refusing to give them his last name.

He woke up crouched under a tree, protecting his head from the falling nuts. "Good God above, Bree was right. Until now, I never realized what a horrible person I am," said Kenneth, "I'm just like Christel as a parent. He cried, "I don't wanna be a fucking deadbeat anymore. I'll fight to get back in their lives."

Michelle put her hand on Kenneth's shoulder. "I've been looking all over for you. Are you alright?"

"No. I don't know what alright means anymore. And I won't be halfway there until I gather all of my children and their mothers under one roof."

Michelle bucked her eyes. "Kenneth! Are you insane! Do you remember how much trouble those women were?"

"Drive faster, Mane! Can't you see the EMTs are leaving us in the dust, Duke?" said Bernard, his voice shaky due to Jessica's cruel elbows.

The driver spoke in French. "I cannot understand! It is'a too much yelling and screaming in my ears."

Bernard said, "What the fuck you just call me, Mane?"

The driver signaled to one of the bodyguards. "Help me deal with this chaos, huh."

"Look, Bernie," the bodyguard was unusually calm, "we're moving as fast as time will allow, so sit back and shut up before I power drive that ass. Can't you see you're scaring the driver with your shit? You've been yelling the whole time."

Bernard slid back in the seat. "Do better, goddammit." He mocked Jessica. "And why in the hell you doing all this jerking beside me? You having a seizure too?"

She hit her forehead with her open palm. "Joseph didn't have a seizure."

Bernard arched his back and moved his head from side-to-side. "How do you know, woman?"

She rambled, "What about my best friend, I've gotta tell my best friend about Joseph."

"Why is it so important that Winter-Jem knows about Joseph?"

"Are you kidding me? She's Joseph's niece! She'll be devastated. I've gotta get to her before the paparazzi or some silly tourist does." Jessica shows Bernard her cellphone. "I'm trying to call Winter-Jem, but I can't stop the shaking."

Bernard poked out his bottom lip. "Give me the damn phone." After a few seconds, Bernard handed the phone back to Jessica. "It's ringing." Bernard screamed at the bodyguard. "Can't you get off your ass and send for a police escort? The driver eats shit."

Someone handed the bodyguard a large Styrofoam box.

Bernard smiled. "Hmmm... Ribs."

The bodyguard took a long ragged breath, as if he'd rather be anywhere besides in Bernard's company. "How do you know these are ribs, Bernie?"

"I recognize the box."

"The bodyguard began to eat.

"Well fuck you in both ears with your big ass," Bernard said, "and my name ain't Bernie!"

Jessica said, "Calm down, Bernard, I can barely hear on this phone."

"That's your own damn fault with that cheap ass phone." His bulged his eyes and stuck his neck out. Jessica could see veins throbbing on one side of his head. Bernard turned to face the bodyguard. "The least you can do is give me a goddamn blue plate special. Them ribs looking tasty as fuck."

The bodyguard said, "I got a blue plate special for that ass, Bernard."

"Yeah?" Bernard jumped up and swung his arms around.

The bodyguard poked Bernard's shoulder, forcing him back in the seat. "Yeah!"

"Well, we gone see what you got, muthafucka."

Jessica shushed Bernard, and then screamed into the phone. "Is somebody there?"

Suntilian Devils are fourth dimensional amphibian and reptilian hybrids that live deep beneath Blueberry Manor Estate. They worked with others of the Left, all of which claimed to come from the Suntilian race, naturally or otherwise. The Level One third dimensional creatures were humans held against their will—cloned, jailed, used for food, etcetera. Level Two fourth dimensional creatures were shapeless. They resembled brown blobs and had long hairs where their backside should have been. Higher levels were used for demonic orgies, nightmares, and hallucinations, alien and OBE abductions, black arts, mysticism, the Occult, and numerous others.

Suntilian Devils were negative entities that worked with fourth and fifth dimensional demons. Those demons reported directly to Lucifer. Lucifer reported to both the Dark, *Demonio-Claude*, and the Light, *Prince'El*. All creatures, no matter the level or dimension, could summon SOURCE HIGH, a dimension of Energy from which all Life originated.

Suntilian Devils came above ground at Suntilian Isle Cul-de-Sac, hence the hauntings, and caused havoc in Forest of the Blind Monk Territory, Haunted Garden, and Mad Trees Isle. Their agenda was to procreate with third dimensional humans on Earth, control the minds and bodies of the reputable, notorious, infamous, and influential in order to strengthen their underground race.

Sunteela, one of the queens of the fourth dimensional Suntilian Nation, had been banished from her daily trips above ground because she'd befriended a human. She heard a voice say, *"The lizards have a message. Don't play with your food,"* before her cage door swung open.

"Yes! Who's there?" Sunteela asked.

"This is Omar." Omar made himself materialize, first his yellow eyes, then his cartoonish black-tipped horns.

"What the hell do you want, Omar?"

"We have a new mission. Kenneth, Joseph Charlemagne's son, will be very weak, very soon. Just the right tenderness for wolfing." His forked tongue slid out of his mouth and wrapped around the place Sunteela's neck should be.

"How do you know this? You're not authorized to bring me these messages."

"I know Joseph will have a heart attack. Kenneth will grieve for a while, before stepping up to his CEO position. That's when he'll receive the news about his triplets. Do you think you're up for the task, Sunteela?" Omar asked.

"Why me?"

"Because you're the only one available who can download Dana-Lyn Martinelli's information and take on her flawless form. We'll take her tonight."

"What, this Kenneth has it bad for her or something?"

"Yes. Dana-Lyn is his current object of affection. You must get him hooked, and get in the family way as quickly as possible. We have big plans for those triplets."

"And I must do this in secret?" Sunteela asked.

Omar laughed. "Of course." He licked his fingers. "And I have a few plans for Kenneth myself. I mean it. Don't fuck around on this plan, Sunteela, or the lizards will send Troll Trollman and his Shadow Beasts after you again."

"Okay, I'm ready." Sunteela took Dana-Lyn's form. Omar was so happy that the saliva that flowed out of his mouth formed a deep puddle on the floor. "Bring her to me. Once I steal Dana-Lyn's memories, the transformation will be complete."

Omar shook with giddiness. "Take it easy, Sunteela. We'll get her tonight."

Sunteela answered, hoping that she remembered the person on the other end of the phone. "Yes. This is Dana-Lyn. Who's this?"

"This is Jessica...Jessica Davis. Where's Winter-Jem?"

"They've all gone to the manor house to find Joseph. Have you tried Winter-Jem's cell phone?"

"Yes, but she didn't answer. Why are they looking for Joseph? Have they heard?"

"Heard what?" Sunteela hoped that Jessica was not sensitive to the spiritual realm.

Jessica spoke in an inaudible tone. "I hope she didn't find out from a wacky, misinformed tourist." She raised her voice. "Nobody's at the manor house."

"Somebody's always at the manor house." Sunteela looked out of the patio door. "It looks like an abandoned castle from this angle. It's smoky. I can't see anything but bodyguards and the forest. It reminds me of the time when the Glenn man tried to hang himself with a grapevine and a snake." The thought brought her more joy than it should have.

"A tourist called for help and now we're on our way to," Jessica spoke with a bodyguard in French. "Yes, we are going to Mount Olympus Hospital."

"What happened?"

"I can barely hear you, Dana-Lyn." Jessica plugged her left ear and kicked Bernard. "When Jem returns, tell her to meet us at L'Hôpital Mont Olympus." She terminated the call.

A few seconds later, Winter-Jem, her stepbrother, Derrick Ortega, and his half-sister, Keisha Martinelli, all came through the front door of the apartment house. "Whew, I wonder what's going on," said Winter-Jem. "There isn't anybody at the manor, which is pretty odd. The main gates are attempting to close, journalists are running wild, tourists trampled, hit by cars. I wonder what that's all about? Maybe a tourist had another fake accident. Dana-Lyn," she put her purse in the closet, "remember the time when the Glenn man tried to hang himself?"

Sunteela looked straight ahead, as if she'd just had a revelation. "I know what the phone call was about."

"What are you talking about," said Winter-Jem. "Are you sick or something? You've been odd since this morning."

"I just got a phone call from Jessica. I couldn't hear well. There was commotion all around, but I know she said they were taking someone to L'Hôpital Mont Olympus."

Winter-Jem sat down, stared directly in Sunteela's face. "Taking who to the hospital?"

"I believe they're taking Joseph to the hospital." Sunteela felt as if her lips were stuck together.

Winter-Jem jumped up. "Parle moi!"

Sunteela said, "You know I don't understand your French."

"Comment puis-je sortir d'ici... putain!" Winter-Jem started smashing bottles of wine against the wall, and then she, Derrick, and Keisha rushed out of the door.

Kenneth went to a café in Parkrose called The Coffee Break Nook. He stared at the wallpaper; tripped outside of his right mind when Sunteela brought him a pitcher of icy pink lemonade.

"What took you so long to give me food and drink? I have been out here, in the wilderness, starving for years! I am too weak to fight in this war. What kind of soldier do you think I am? Do you think I am not worthy of nourishment?"

Sunteela played along. "I'm sorry, soldier. I came to your aid as soon as I heard your cries for help. Please accept this token, as this icy pink lemonade is a good source of hydration."

"For me?"

"Yes. This lemonade is for you."

"Thank you, Captain." Kenneth grabbed the pitcher. Sunteela thought inappropriate thoughts as streams of lemonade fell on Kenneth's shirt and splashed onto the floor. For the first time, Sunteela felt weak, as if she couldn't go through with the mission. She remembered the night before, when Omar, disguised as a small one-eyed incubus, appeared in Dana-Lyn's bedroom. He sodomized her, which was not a part of the plan, draining her strength as if he simply unplugged a cable. Sunteela was able to replicate her form and memories, becoming the "new" Dana-Lyn, while Omar carried the original deep into an underground tunnel, in the area next to Haunted Garden and Mad Trees Isle.

She pulled herself out of daydream mode, feeling ashamed for letting her mind wander to such a filthy place. "Would you like some more?" she asked Kenneth.

"That's all for now. Thank you, Captain," he said.

Look at those groupies over there, thought Sunteela, *swooning and flocking with their signs up. They're a big bunch of raggedy hoes. That's what they are. You know, I should snatch a piece of that iron fence outside and bust heads all over the fucking place but I can't. The real Dana-Lyn would never do such a thing, and Kenneth is too fragile right now. He may break if he witnesses such violence. The pathetic beast already thinks he's alone on some battlefield.* Sunteela felt strange, as if a piece of her soul loitered in the garden.

"What the hell," said Sunteela.

"What? Stop mumbling so much," said Kenneth. "I can't hear you. I hate mumbling!" He slapped himself. "Oh God, I'm starting to sound more like her." He hissed and booed.

"Excuse me, Kenneth. I'll be back as soon as I take care of the fucker in the garden."

Kenneth continued talking to himself about Christel.

unteela flew around the bend with a red shovel in her hand. "What in the hell are you doing here?"

Omar held his hand close to his heart. A wry grin took the place of edginess. "You're wasting your precious time, Sunteela."

Sunteela grabbed Omar by the arm and took him to an abandoned cottage in the cul-de-sac.

Omar turned his head completely around. His voice was deep and computerized. "Sunteeela!" His forked tongue slewed through brown, cracked teeth. His voice returned to normal. "You came from nowhere," he laughed, "do you have a transport capsule behind one of those log cabins?"

She pinched his muscular shoulder.

"Ouch!" Omar rubbed his shoulder.

"Answer my question," she looked around while talking, "what are you doing here?"

Three of Omar's teeth fell out. He caught them before they hit the ground. "Tee-heet, I heard about what happened to Mr. Joseph Charlemagne. I came to offer my," he unbuttoned his shirt, "support."

Sunteela could barely stand the sight of his muscular generosities. *That's one thing these humans don't have. Their torsos don't look like his torso,* she thought. Thinking about she and Omar's sultry evenings in the cave made her squirt brown liquid at the hairline.

"I hear your thoughts," Omar said as he walked towards Sunteela. "I can see the effect I have on you... those long sultry nights."

Sunteela swung the shovel. "Stay back!"

Omar threw his hands in the air. "It's cool." He buttoned his shirt. "I know how to control myself."

"You shouldn't be here. In fact, I don't want to see you lurking around these grounds ever again."

116

"Tell me, why are you so hostile, Sunteela? Is it because of what happened last night with the real Dana-Lyn? Are you jealous?"

"Fuck you!" She threw the shovel on the ground.

"Oh my, you are jealous. Well, if you were doing what you're supposed to be doing."

Sunteela interrupted him. "I am doing what I am supposed to be doing."

"If you were doing it in a timely manner, there would be no need for me to be here. Does that answer your question?" He sung, "You're slacking again."

"What do you mean, Omar? I just got here last night."

"I've seen you watching him while he sleeps during the day, popping up in his dream bubble, stalking him, peeping at his unmentionables. Admit that you've fallen for Kenneth, and now you're not sure if you wanna complete the mission the way it was planned."

Sunteela turned away. "You'll take me off this assignment."

"So."

"If you know what's good for you, Omar, you loser, you'll stay far-far away from me *and* my family."

"Your family?" Omar laughed. "Which family? You're talking about Dana-Lyn's family. You think you're the real Dana-Lyn. Unbelievable."

Sunteela stared in the distance, face void of any kind of emotion. "You know what I'm talking about. You always do."

"You're right about that. I know everything about you."

She scowled, "I hate our fucking connection." She put her hands in her hands. "Why can't I break it!"

"Sunteela! You've never taken that tone with me before." Omar turned Sunteela around to face him, and then licked her ear. "You'll never get rid of me."

Sunteela roared, "Why you," and pushed him into a pile of logs. "What if someone sees us?"

"You're not worried about that." Omar raised two fingers next to his temple, closed his eyes, and constructed a wooden lawn chair with his mind.

Sunteela plugged her ears. "Stop it." She heard deep demonic laughter coming from under the earth.

Omar joined the laughter. "I saw you at Amy's wedding this morning, at the orange sunrise. That's an example for you. She's doing things in a timely manner. She married the geezer, and now she's on her way to starting a happy little family of devils. Just as we planned."

"How'd you get on this property?"

"Remember? My uncle lives in the clichéd castle down the way. I came through a tunnel."

A vision of a Gothic bride: raggedy white dress, long skull, and cone shaped afro flashed before her. "Stalker! So what if I went to Amy's wedding?"

"And I heard what I heard." He found a brown lollipop in one of his pockets. "Admit it."

"What are you talking about, Omar?"

"Admit that you've falling for that punk ass, deadbeat ass, bastard ass punk Kenneth-fucking-Charlemagne. Tisk-tisk-tisk, not a part of the plan."

Sunteela laughed. "You're jealous. How can you talk about plans? It wasn't part of the plan to sodomize Dana-Lyn!"

Omar attempted to touch Sunteela. "I got needs."

She snatched away. "You salamander."

He looked around in awe. "This is a beautiful place you've weaseled your way into."

"What do you want, Omar?"

Omar moved a park bench with his mind. "Mind if I take this seat? Thank you, thank you very much. Now, as I was saying, I know some things about you that would interest old 'K' to the motherfucking 'C.' Hell, I'll tell him all about the whole underground community."

Sunteela said, "You wouldn't!"

Omar looked at his watch. "Damn, look at the time." He looked around, beating and smoothing every pocket. "Ay look, Sunteela, I have no woolies."

"No! I'm not giving you anymore marijuana and cocaine!"

"I will definitely remember that shit." Omar found an old cigarette in his sock. "You know, you can't hold your shape for long. Joseph can see it right off the bat. However, Kenneth's not short stepping. He's learning how to use his intuition. If he stops hanging around his god-awful friends, he'll see your true form through his third eye."

Omar's words were distorted in Sunteela's mind. "Go back to hell, Omar," she cried, "I've gotta send you back to hell, Omar." She dreamed up a pair of garden shears. She could hear a distant conversation between neighbors: Dr. Orton Maloney and his unpleasant, wife Cynthia. In

118

BLUEBERRY MANOR

Sunteela's mind, she could see Dr. Maloney in his man cave...

"Orton! Dr. Orton Maloney, since you have more help at the clinic, why not go outside and do some yard work. Go on. Get off your big lazy ass," said Cynthia.
Orton protested, "This fucking woman."
Orton sneaked off to his secret man cave. He took a bomber out of the fridge then threw himself on the big and tall leather pillow top. "This is the lullaby I need. The setting sun, the breeze, the door's wide open, and..." He saw his garden shears slide out of the small wooden shed and float through the air. "What the hell's in this shit I'm drinking?" He hunched his shoulders and grabbed another bomber out of the fridge.

Sunteela tore the garden shears out of the air.
"You killing me with those shears won't change the fact that I know what I know." Omar picked his long black nails. "It was a Suntilian ritual, and I heard what I heard." He coiled his finger around a small grapevine.
"And?" She totted the blade. "Get to the point."
"How do you feel? One of your best friends married a handsome millionaire, one you used to date, one that saw your true form because you called yourself befriending him first." Omar laughed. "Remember when we switched places that night?" Omar looked nostalgic. "Oh, that was a night."
Sunteela retched.
"Awww. You still jealous about that night, and sore 'cuz you couldn't close the deal like us."
"Kenneth is more powerful, more handsome, and has more money. He has a good heart. He's smart and beautiful."
"I knew you were in love with him." Omar rolled on the ground. "You know, the lizards aren't happy with your decision to cut them out. And you know how they handle people who spoil perfect plans."
"I don't care anymore."
"But I can help you get closer to Kenneth, that is, if you let me have my chance with him first." Omar's eyes glistened. "Yeah. I can close a deal real fast."
"You're disgusting," Sunteela held her stomach. "Why would I ever let you have Kenneth first? You'll drain him with your charms."
"If that's what it takes to reach our goal."

119

Sunteela could hear Omar's echoed laughter in her head. "Shut up," she screamed. She threw the shears on the ground and picked up a baseball sized stone. She rammed it up Omar's nose repeatedly, causing blood and mucus to squirt all over the pink azalea shrubs.

"Sunteela! What the?"

"I'll be damned if I let any of you take this opportunity away from me again. All I want is a perfect body to live the best life in. The whole lifestyle. It's mine, Omar. Now get the hell out of here and never come back. Wipe this out of your memory. None of it ever existed in this World."

"Sunteela!"

"Fuck you. I know you. I control you, but not anymore. Fuck the organization. This is mine and mine alone." Sunteela pulled a photo of Omar and a lighter out of her pocket. "Your mind is yours, motherfucker!"

"Sunteela!"

"I'm sending you back to the Spirit World with an empty mind," she boasted.

"You can't do that!" Omar's eyes rolled back, he tipped, fell on the ground and began to melt. A book on immortality rolled out of his vest pocket. Sunteela picked it up and threw it in the fire pit along with the photo.

When Sunteela arrived at Parkrose, Kenneth was in the same spot, alone, blending in with the blue and gray wallpaper. "Have I ever felt this much sadness coming from one person?" she muttered.

Through Kenneth's off-balanced groupies, Sunteela saw the shadow of a frightening beast. "Oh my God." She hid behind a shutter room divider. She thought, *they've come for me already. I made sure to send Omar the long way, through the deepest parts of the Universe.* She peeked at Kenneth. "Is that Troll Trollman?" Her breathing became so rapid, that she almost lost consciousness.

When Troll Trollman heard Sunteela's breathing, he conjured up a few Shadow Beasts and sent them to the shutter room divider. A whooshing black heaviness entered through Sunteela's nose, wrapped itself around her voice box, and pulled it down towards her feet. Sunteela could see a fast-moving lump through her skin. Her eyes widened. Rapid heartbeat caused her heart to jump out of its place and skip around her body. After she petitioned a fifth dimensional demon (who contacted Lucifer), the horrors stopped. The whooshing in her ears replaced itself with the sound of a Carrion crow.

Like a robot, Sunteela went into the civilian's kitchen and whipped up a few of Kenneth's favorite snacks: a few honey ham croissant sandwiches with smoked sauce and cheese, a small seafood salad, spiked strawberry lemonade, and for dessert, beignets and black coffee.

When Sunteela presented Kenneth with the food, he said, "Oh, the one who doesn't think I'm worthy of nourishment brings me food, huh? So I have to sit here and nearly die in order to get some food."

"I'll do what I can to help you, sir," said Sunteela.

"Dana-Lyn!" Kenneth was overcome with excitement. "What color is that light around your head?"

"What light?"

Kenneth took the food and nibbled at it like a sour teen. "Thank you, Captain."

"I want to look after you, that is, if you don't object." Sunteela sat in the chair across from him.

"I was tripping earlier, when you brought me the lemonade, Dana-Lyn. At least, I think I was."

"Oh, you know my name?" She twiddled her thumbs and looked around the room. When she locked eyes with a jealous swooner, she ended her stare with a smile and a self-assured head bob.

"I have always been a huge fan, Dana-Lyn, even in the 'Alien Bite and the Heart Chakra' phase."

Sunteela smiled; tried to pretend as if she knew what the hell Kenneth spoke about.

"What was the third track off that album called?" he asked her. "Uh, oh yeah, 'The Incubus Angelic.' See, I know my stuff."

Sunteela smiled. "Yep, you know your stuff, alright."

"You guys were such Gothic Romantics back then."

"Have we changed? So... We're not Goth enough anymore?" Sunteela was genuinely confused. She wondered why Dana-Lyn's music career refused to download with the other memories.

Kenneth said, "I didn't mean it like that."

Sunteela ate small portions of the food Kenneth offered her.

"It seems I know more about you than you know about yourself." Kenneth sported a huge 'I know something you don't know' grin.

Goosebumps made Sunteela twitch. "Just what are you talking about? Secrets already?" She folded her arms. "That's not fair."

"Oops, let me get that for you." Kenneth reached across the table and wiped bits of powdered sugar off Sunteela's cheek. "There we go."

She jerked away. "You strike me as a hip hop guy."

122

"You judging me now?"

"Just an observation," she replied.

"Well, Dana-Lyn, you've always seemed soooo."

"So what?"

"You've always seemed so aloof."

"Aloof!" Sunteela took Kenneth's comment as an insult. "You calling me cold and unemotional?" She stood up, voice barely audible over the loud scraping sound of her chair.

Kenneth grabbed her hand. "Please don't go yet." His eyes were full of never-ending urgency.

"I won't leave, not yet." Sunteela felt stupid for getting angry at Kenneth's benign observation. She returned to her chair. "And I haven't forgotten."

"Forgotten what?"

"You said that you know more about me than I know about myself."

"Me? I said that?" Kenneth continued to gorge himself. "Nooo... I didn't say anything of the kind."

"Yes you did!"

Kenneth thought the way she played with the straw in her glass was adorable. "Um hum...cherry juice and coke. I haven't seen that since my sodie pop days. I've heard the stories about your marvelous drinking abilities. I can't believe you know what a soda pop is, let alone drink one."

"Actually it's sugar water with a lot of caramel coloring."

"What?"

"Oops, I'm kidding." Suntella laughed nervously.

"I didn't think any musicians drank anything outside of alcohol. Guess that's what I get for growing up with a fucking wino as a mother."

Sunteela laughed like a geek, and then looked up at the straight-faced Kenneth. Her look of wide-faced joy turned into one of confusion. "Should I be sorry?" She had a slight malfunction. "Tell me how to feel. Tell-tell-tell, tell-tell tell me how to feee-eeelll."

He mocked her. "*Tell me how to feel-feel*. You're silly."

"What do you mean?"

Kenneth smirked. "I can't tell you how to feel. I promise we'll talk about the heavy stuff some other time, over dinner. Right now, I need your company. It doesn't matter what you say. It doesn't even matter if you talk or not. I just need you near."

"With a smile like that, how could I say no?" Sunteela broke out in song, "*I cannot help but think I need you near. I cannot do this all alone, I feel I'm all alone. I cannot help but think I'm wasting air. You'll never heed my call, I feel I'm in a nightmare.*"

"What song is that?" Kenneth asked.

"One I just came up with. I'll call it *I Need You Near.*"

"It's waaayyy different from some of your other things, but I still think it's cool."

Sunteela said, "I think you're pretty cool."

"Thank you, I think you're pretty cool, too." Kenneth eyed his groupies, "more than I can say for the groupies."

Sunteela scanned the girls' faces. Kelly Vicious, Alana Jemmingson, Callie Reynolds, Memory Nightingale, and Shannon Carmichael, all of which have been jealous of Dana-Lyn since elementary school choir days. She calmed the computerized beeping in her head by picking at her fingernails.

"Those are some long claws, Dana-Lyn, how'd they get so long?"

"Claws?" Sunteela panicked and froze.

"Yeah, how'd they get so long? Hello," Kenneth waved his hands in front of Sunteela's face, "you in there?"

The groupies looked on with hatred as Kenneth and Sunteela recited poetry and sung verses to one another. "Look at that corny mess," said Kelly Vicious. "Who the hell does she think she is, and why does Kenneth beg for her company and not ours?" She gave a group of security guards the finger. "Why are those metal headed security guards keeping us away and not Dana-Lyn? Why's she so special?"

"She's not as pretty as we are. Look at her flat ass," said Alana Jemmingson. "She looks plastic and fake up close. She's ugly as hell in person. You can tell they tweak her photos."

Kelly teased, "But she's a rock star, Alana."

"So what if she is a fucking a rock star? The stupid bitch is a fucking has been."

Kelly uttered, "Bitch." She yelled at the other people in Parkrose's Coffee Break Nook. "Dana-Lyn's the demonic daughter of the Almighty Satan!" Sunteela and Kenneth continued to recite poetry and sing verses to one another.

Kelly yelled louder, "Hail to Satan's daughter!"

Kelly's words triggered something in Sunteela's memory card. She

124

saw a hazy vision of herself dressed in a black and white dress, white apron, and small white hat flash wildly in the distance. Like a robot, she got up, gathered the trash (smashed cheeseburgers and loaded potato wedges) off the floor and took it to the garbage can. She smiled at the groupies before returning to the little round table with Kenneth.

"Why'd you do that?" Kenneth asked.

"Oh, I don't know. Guess I like cleanliness," Suntella answered.

After eating every drop of food, Kenneth spaced out again. Sunteela cleaned the mess on the table, cleaned little bits beignet off his face and attempted to leave him with his thoughts.

The groupies called out to Sunteela...

"Dana-Lyn," Callie Reynolds said.

"Yes?" Sunteela slowly turned around. The silver tray she held was full of paper products.

"You missed a spot."

"What are you talking about, Callie?"

Like a sun baked teenager, Alana said, "Like, look down at the floor, dammit! Like, over there."

When Sunteela looked at the floor, Kelly threw a platform spiked boot from the left, knocking the tray high in the air. The spike scratched Sunteela deep inside the nostril, exposing wires filled with a pinkish bloodlike substance. All of the girls laughed when the substance rushed over her 'O' shaped mouth and slowly dripped on her tight pink blouse.

"Oh wait," said Callie Reynolds, "isn't blood supposed to be red? Why's her blood pink?" The girls paused, and then broke out in ugly cackles.

"Oh no," cried Memory Nightingale, as she pretended to wipe imaginary tears from her black eyes. "You've gotten yourself all dirty. You're a dirrrty, dirty bad girl."

"She's a low level witch is what she is," Alana said. "Fake ass bitch."

. The girls laughed, cursed, chanted, and threw things at Sunteela. They laughed even harder when Shannon Carmichael hit Sunteela's arm with a glass water bottle. It broke hard upon impact, splitting her wrist open, revealing spongy material. The girls threw dollar bills while yelling derogatory things. Sunteela trembled as the scene triggered another weird vision in her memory card.

"That's the shit this whore's used to," Kelly screamed.

Memory Nightingale laughed. "That big flat ass can't ride up and down the pole no'mo."

"Crawl, bitch! I'll give you one hundred if you let me see the place your Jimmy Johns used to be." said Callie Reynolds.

"No," said Memory Nightingale, "give her one damn dollar, dammit," said Memory Nightingale.

Sunteela looked at Kenneth. Through the madness, he continued to space out in the corner, unaware of the world surrounding him. *The fact that he doesn't know how badly the girls are treating me should be a blessing,* she thought, *because if he snaps out of the rut right now, this place would be a butcher shop.* However, Sunteela *was* upset with Kenneth because he did not notice her mistreatment. He did not come riding through her nightmare on a red horse, swinging his stainless steel sword. "If Kenneth breaks," she claimed, "he could kill the groupies with a cradlesong. I've imagined his strength."

"What's your boyfriend gonna do for you now, Dana-Lyn," said Kelly, "who's gonna fucking help you? He can't fucking help himself or his fucking daddy."

Robotic security guards perceived the girls as a threat. They bombarded the café, clubbing the girls like rabid animals. With Officer Quennell's help, Sunteela limped upstairs to the infirmary where they took pictures of the abuse. Downstairs in the café, officers took more pictures and recorded statements from witnesses. Clean up began all while Kenneth sat in a corner blending in with the blue and gray wallpaper completely detached from the world around him.

The motorcade turned down a driveway concealed with privacy screens and vines. Robotic sentries in watchtowers signaled to several men in guardhouses next to the arched entrance gate. Two groups of physicians waited in front of the emergency department doorway. One group took Joseph to the emergency room as soon as the ambulance pulled into the lot, the other group assisted others. Two spokespersons for the Charlemagne family jumped out of the bodyguard's SUV and stood by Christel's side, ready to answer any medical questions summoned.

The doctors were expeditious with foreign looking machines, lots of medicines, and administered tests in order to prevent further damage to Joseph's heart.

When a medical assistant asked a family spokesperson about Joseph's dietary and lifestyle habits, Christel, Bree, and a few others cried themselves to hysteria.

Bree's animalistic scream took everybody by surprise. She went unconscious, bumping her head on an antique bookshelf before falling face down on the floor. Dr. Garcia ordered the house staff to take her to urgent care.

After stabilizing Joseph, Dr. Mario Garcia assisted the house staff in caring for Bree, giving her fluids and salts intravenously.

"I think your favorite niece is pregnant again, Mario," said Christel. "I told her ass about that shit."

"I'll do a pregnancy test along with the other tests. And I don't like your tone, you platinum hussy."

"There's nothing in the world wrong with my goddamn tone, little damn brother."

"By two goddamn minutes. And it almost sounded like you were mocking me, or throwing it in my face that I should have a favorite niece."

"You do have a favorite niece and I don't like that shit, Mario. I have four other children. What about them?"

"Four?"

"No, I have three other children," she laughed awkwardly, "you know what the fuck I mean."

"I love all of my nieces and my nephew," he lowered his voice after a nurse looked at him, "no matter who their biological father is."

Christel said, "I heard that snide remark, motherfucker."

"What snide remark? I didn't say anything snide."

Christel continued to argue. "Speaking of biological fathers, I have a lot I can throw at you, you hypocrite."

"Throw it at me."

Christel pouted. "I don't think you're being fair."

"If you were saying that shit because you really think I'm being unfair, that's another story."

"You're unfair!"

"You're only saying that shit because you feel that Michelle should be my favorite niece, Christel. You know I don't love one child more than the other. I never said anything like that."

"You act like it." Christel pounded the wall, each new pound louder than the last one.

"Stop the madness, Christel! And it's no secret the courts put Bree in my care when she was an infant. All because you were incapable of being a mother and Joseph was off on another one of his 'oil meeting' escapades."

"Are you fucking kidding me, Mario? He's a business magnate for crying the fuck aloud!"

"I know, but you know good and goddamn well you guys were split the hell up; on the verge of divorce. What you told the courts was a lie. He wasn't at oil meetings, speaking engagements, or none of that shit during at the time."

"Well, we didn't divorce, and I got my child back from your thieving ass. Merci beaucoup." Christel tipped her imaginary hat.

"I practically raised Bree from a baby, and the others spent lots of time in my care as well."

"You're making an ass of yourself, little brother." Christel raised her voice. "My children are mine, not yours!"

Mario shushed her. "You're in a hospital." He grabbed her elbow.

Christel jerked away. "Get your hands off me."

"I'm asking, no I'm ordering you to leave urgent care. And don't think about visiting Joseph right now."

Christel questioned Mario. "What makes your ignorant ass think it can give me orders? What are you planning?"

"I'm planning to calm Bree and resurrect Joseph."

"I don't need your shit in my life." She attempted to leave urgent care.

"You're lucky, Christel. I almost told Joseph about Pearlie."

She whirled around, knocking a few utensils on the floor. "I dare you."

"You're a scandalous whore. I can't stand your damn ass. How can you do what you're doing to Joseph?"

Christel snarled in Mario's ear. "You're not telling Joseph a goddamn thing unless you want the whole fucking world on your ass about Andre's birth and his biological mother's death."

"Are you trying to blackmail me? Andre's the innocent person in this. How could you?"

"It's not blackmail. It's a platinum promise, bitch."

Mario put his hands over his ears and screamed." No-No!" He covered his face with his arms. Face glowing with horrors unseen by the other people in the room. "Get the hell out the road!" He crouched to the floor, arms and legs flailing, reliving he and his grandfather's car accident. Several nurses helped him off the floor.

Christel laughed. "You spazzing out, Mario? When are you gonna get it through your head that our drunk fucking grandfather killed the bitch on purpose? You call yourself a doctor and you're sick your damn self." She raised her voice, "What's wrong with my fucking family!"

After Mario's vision, he sent the nurses away. He said to Christel, "I don't know if I'll ever forget what one of your alters did to my ex-wife."

"She still working those sleazy massage parlors?" As Christel walked out of the room, she shouted, "She was a lesbian before Felice showed up, bitchass." She cornered a young nurse, "Tell the other nurses I'm in the sun parlor on the fifth floor."

"Okay," the nurse gave Christel a light up pager and pulled out a pen and notepad, "what's your name, Ma'am?"

Christel slowly cocked her head. She chuckled as fear waved across the young nurse's face. "To answer your question, my name's Christel Charlemagne, bitch. Remember that shit."

Years of abuse had hardened Christel's heart. Whenever the World stressed her out, whenever she was unable to decipher whether she should feel ashamed, or hold her head up high, she morphed outside of herself and spoke to one, or all, of her personalities as if it they were familiar friends.

On the way to the sun parlor, Christel peeked in the indoor Chinese garden next to the step down unit. She was amazed as the vegetation withered in real time. She hopped up and down like a child as psychedelic shapes turned into pure white mist all around her. The temperature intensified, flowing from oppressive hotness to an overbearing freeze. The wind exploded in a storm, driving her into the garden for sanctuary. She found a picnic blanket to wrap around herself; wheezed at the thought of icicles lodging themselves in her heart area.

A loud snake's hiss played through gusty winds. *That sound is familiar,* Christel thought, *soft and partly cloudy. Am I high? Am I in a hazy gray windstorm?*

"Hello, darling," hissed Pistel, one of Christel alter personalities. With the help of the wind, she took the form of Christel's younger, more beautiful self.

"Oh, hello, Pistel," said Christel. "I'll never get used to the dramatic way you choose to enter."

"Did you call me out?" asked Pistel.

"I guess so." Christel was unruffled as Pistel slithered even closer, but still out of reach.

"What is the problem?" she hissed. "I know, but I want to hear it from you, Chrissstel."

"Joseph is sick." Tears dropped down Christel's face.

"What frightens you?"

"I don't like this feeling." She looked at her chest. "Something's there and it feels broken. How can I think of myself at a time like this?"

"What do you think the broken thing is?"

"Love in my heart. I love Joseph."

"Don't be a jackass, Christel," she cackled. "You cannot love."

"How can you say that? I feel like a big fat fool and you say I cannot love? You're not helping me at all." She pouted. "Thanks a lot, ugly old Pistel."

"It's not my job to help you in that way. That's why you called on me and not any of the others."

"They all showed up?" Christel asked.

"I can't control the gate and materialize like this at the same damn time." Pistel danced while humming one of Christel's rock songs. She swayed to the floor then threw her hands in the air, twirling so fast that she caused another windstorm. "Feels so good to be out!"

"You're right." Christel protected her face from flying debris.

Pistel stopped twirling. Her toothy grin melted into a straight line. "I know I'm right. I'm always right."

"What can I do about this strange emotion? There are several emotions all rolled up in a ball."

"You mussst feeeeel them," hissed Pistel. "You've never felt them before, and now you mussst feeel them, Christel."

"Feel what?"

"Anger. Jealousssy."

"I know I have nymphomania."

"How do you know that?"

"The doctors said that I have it."

"Blah, blah, blah. Fuck the fucking doctors. And fuck you too if you think we're a head case with addictions."

"I've cheated on Joseph for years, and I still cheat on him to this day." Christel played with the picnic blanket's ends. "I can't help it. I couldn't help it, not even if I wanted to. And Joseph knows."

Pistel's face crinkled like a paper bag. "Joseph knows nothing!"

Christel winced.

"Tell me, Christel, what do you think he knows?"

"He knows that deep down I don't want to help myself." Christel laughed impishly. "It's such a rush. I like cheating on him." She switched personas as she slid closer to Pistel. "I wish you would help me. I don't know what to do. Help me."

"You're being selfish," Pistel told her.

Christel cocked her head. "How am I being selfish?"

"We all want a piece of the pie. We all want to live." Pistel caressed Christel's face with her long ghostly finger. "Don't kill us like the characters in your Gothic horror novels."

"It's not fair that I use Joseph in order to energize each alter. There's at least fifty that I know of." She cried, "Why must it be me? Why must I have DID!"

"You've been groomed before birth." Pistel provided Christel with flashbacks. "In the right wing, the forbidden door, the third door on the left." Christel looked as though she was hypnotized. Pistel hissed, "Christel, you play the game better than us. Love is a stumbling block."

"I try to be as honest as I can." She struck a puppy dog pose. "There is a secret I have been keeping from Joseph. I feel awful about it. I think it's time to tell him."

"You are honored and special to us. Only you can give us life. And like it or not, Joseph is a big ole dog. He's meaningless."

"I'm sick! That's what I am. And I need help, Pistel." She plugged her ears. "You're not real. La-di-daaa-di-laaa..." She closed her eyes, waving her head back and forth. "No, I'm sick. You're not real!" She opened her eyes, hoping that Pistel would disappear.

Pistel laughed. "I'm still here." She hypnotized Christel with a Herb Alpert track and a golden pocket watch. "We all are special," Pistel hissed. "Lisssten. The myth that we are distant relatives of Aphrodite, the daughter of Zeus and Dione, a god and sea nymph, and a royal mortal who went by the name of Xanthis is very true." Pistel's Spirit entered a statue that adorned the garden. "The gods and goddesses of Greece look favorably on us, though our scent is that of unflustered horror. An icy sea of tears. This physical body degrades us."

Christel put her thumb in her mouth and took a yellow butterfly necklace out of her bag. "Why they use me like so, Ma'am?"

"Shut up!" Pistel popped out of the statue and ran her hands down her tight red dress. "The body of water in which the nymphs frolic degrades us. Neither, we have no desire to frolic with the Nereids, the nymphs of the sea, though they dance, they beckon for us, and we abide by their wishes. The beautiful ones; the legendary, mythological beings who the gods kept at their disposal are pleasant, but the menacing ones, those spawned from ugly old satyrs and beautiful nymphs, those are the ones

BLUEBERRY MANOR

who taunt us. I don't know why, but we're drawn to them, Christel." The place became a dark movie theater. "Listen, Christel. Listen and obey." Pistel's voice trailed off in the distance as if she was leaving.

Christel's glare was glassy, as if Satan Himself was now the Master of her Soul. "We love Pan."

Pistel hissed, "Yessss!" She sounded like a salty sea snake. Her split tongue exuded ghostly perversion.

"We love Pan... We listen and obey. Because of these beings, we've been cursed with the title of nympho. Doctors tell us this disorder is psychological chaos, that fornication cannot be categorized, but, the nymphs who lure us are real. We see them, we frolic with them, and we listen."

"Feed me, Christel!"

Christel's normal speaking voice returned. "Pistel, I called you because I want to know what my real problem happens to be. I want to know."

"That's easy." Pistel hissed and backed away.

"No, wait. Please don't leave me yet. You said the answer to my problem is easy."

"Yesss."

"What is it? What's the answer?"

"You're jealous." She caressed Christel's cheek with a power blue rattlesnake. You need other Energies. You need to give me other Energies."

"Jealous? I'm jealous? Why am I jealous, Pistel?"

"Jealous because Joseph has found love, and you, despite your many johns, have not found love—"

"Yes, I have found love. I love Joseph. How could I not love him?"

"So what if you love him," Pistel replied. "That does not mean that he loves you."

"So, that means I *have* found love." Christel looked down at her chest. "Why is this thing broken inside me if I have not found love?"

"Because Joseph broke it."

"What?"

"Joseph does not love you. Not anymore. Not in the same way you think you love him."

Christel was agitated. "Noooo, I-I don't understand."

Drops of blood sizzled and boiled on Pistel's forked tongue. "And yes... a part of you loves Joseph, but a bigger part of you never will. That part is not capable of giving or receiving love. Not love of any kind. Love is a stumbling block. A nuisance."

"There you go again!" Christel became hysterical. Her cries were sloppy and gross.

"Stop that ugly ass crying!" demanded Pistel.

"Speak English, French or Italian, goddamn you. I can't understand your language."

"What don't you understand?" asked Pistel. "A child could understand the scenario."

"How can you tell me I can't love?"

"You know this already." Pistel hissed, "Christel, you love that part. You live that part. That part rebels against Joseph." "You like it because he reminds you of all the things you were, and all the things you will never be, at least not on Earth."

Christel looked unusually proud. Her spine straightened, and her head raised. "The doctors tell me my nymphomania is psychosomatic, brought on by several molestations and rapes as a minor." She laughed.

"Yesss. Give me more."

"If that's true, then why won't you allow me to get help for it? I want to have a regular life, like a regular person. I feel it inside. I want to be normal. I want to be a good person."

"What the hell is a good person, dammit?" Lightning struck Christel's arm.

She rubbed her arm. "Why can't I be good?"

Pistel said, "Because I live it. Because you like it. Because we all want a piece of the pie. Because this is your calling. Before birth, you were chosen by demons of the third door."

"To be a whore is my calling?"

Pistel's eyes glowed. Her body became transparent. "Nooo!" Pistel's hot breath forced Christel further in a corner.

Christel envisaged a marbleized ball underneath her skin. The ball moved from her stomach, into her esophagus, and out of her mouth. An evil face materialized on the ball before it disappeared. She looked at her trembling hands and screamed, "what the hell is wrong with me?"

"What doctors say may be true, but this does not explain the voices, the visions, and the continuous dreams of being in the sea. Who can explain the lily pads, or something like them? Who can explain the sometimes salubrious, sometimes sullied scent of sea water we smell, the jagged rocks, and the sand, and the murkiness of it? We love it." Pistel's eyes rolled back. "Oh, how we love it."

"Only Joseph believes me when I mention gods, goddesses, nymphs and satyrs, and other personalities. Only Joseph buys the truth, that my condition is more than a head case, and it's as real as the wonders of the Earth, the sun, moon, stars, water, air and fire. Everyone else thinks I'm crazy."

Pistel drifted into a dream of she and Pan's escapades in a lake of fire.

"Pistel! I can see your thoughts." Christel screamed, "what about me?"

"Huh? What?"

"I've managed to run Joseph completely away with my shenanigans. How can I ever make it up to him?"

"Silence!" Pistel backhanded Christel from afar. She elongated her tongue, slowly licked the blood that oozed on the floor. "You're hysterical, Christel. Joseph is weak. He's not going anywhere. He doesn't want to leave you, and even if he did want to leave, he would not leave. Our supernatural hooks are deep." Pistel's slow hiss was hypnotizing. "He isn't going anywhere. It is foolish, that you are so insecure."

"Joseph is my sanctuary."

"It's true, that Joseph has done so much for us. Our secret survives because of him. Because of him, we are able to go on and on, surviving each life like a race of marvelous vampires never to die. Never."

"And never to live." Christel looked as if something snapped inside of her. "Yes, our secret survives."

"Joseph is Christel's sanctuary, but there are other personalities that live inside of you. Me, for instance, and Joseph is not my sanctuary. He will never be my sanctuary. The lily pads are my home. The Lily pads. Our Queen, Lilith. We belong there, and to me, Joseph is merely a dog."

"I'm not a bad person, not compared to what other people tend to do in their lifetimes."

"I know, but you are jealous of Joseph, and everyone else is jealous of your demonic perfection." Pistel's voice became that of a dying snake. "Answer me!"

"Yes?" said Christel.

Pistel opened her mouth. Her forked tongue slithered out of her mouth and into Christel's head, causing a sharp pain.

Christel hit her head repeatedly, until Pistel's detached tongue fell out of her head.

AMINA CAPRICE ANDOLINI

"Chrisssstel, There's something you don't know." Pistel and her tongue left the room in a grayish-black cloud.

"Don't leave, I need your help! Pistel!" Christel bumped her leg when trying to grab Pistel's smoke. She crawled to the window seat, heavy-legged and panicked, wondering about the other alters who will surface.

The quietness in Christel's head was heavy, and shiny, and chrome-like. She could hear her alter selves weighing their past, which was her past, the original personality that came to Earth on December 29, 1958. Christel had her own thoughts on Joseph's recent tragedy, and so she dreamt up a skeleton-headed key and wrought iron padlock. She locked the gate in her head; however, all of the alters had something important to say about an old childhood curse. They slithered between bars like hundreds of raggedy ghosts, flicking their forked tongues in her ego.

"Stop the lashing! It hurts," screamed Christel, while trying to shield herself from the madness. She spoke telepathically to the Creator. "This is dedicated to the stars, so many planets and everlasting things in Your Universes. In Your brilliant jewelry chest, personalities are perfect, while ours (mine in particular) are burnt out duplications of all You are. So many for You to cherry-pick while we, Your Children, are limited to a measly box. It seems unfair." Once the lashing stopped, she laid on the window seat, hands in prayer position underneath her chin. "I don't want to imagine life without my Joe. Creator, You have so many others to pick from. Please don't take my Joe." Her face crackled from dried up tears.

A harsh knock at the doors of the garden took her back to a foul-mouthed guise. It felt familiar, like a one-eyed teddy bear from infancy.

"Mrs. Charlemagne, this is Nurse Miaisha. Are you in there," she asked.

"Yeah, so what," snapped Christel.

"You told a nurse that you'd be in the sun parlor."

Christel put her hands over her eyes and peeked through her fingers. She did not remember how she ended up on the window seat in the garden. "So I'm not in the sun parlor," said Christel, "big fucking deal."

"Is everything okay in there? I heard voices."

"What in the hell did you hear?"

"Voices. That's all. Is someone else in there with you?"

"Did you hear any of the conversation?"

"Ummm...no."

"Addio, nosey bitch," Christel gibed. "Everything is roses in here. Now fuck off. Take your red headed ass back to the other side of camp. I have a light up pager deal. I'll let you know if I need you."

"But I thought—"

"Good to the motherfucking bye, you whore!"

"As you wish, I will leave you to yourself, but if I hear a new word from Bree or Joseph, I will come back." Nurse Miaisha pretended to step away from the door.

Christel felt as if yet another Spirit had taken over her body. She dug around in her purse and pulled out a golden handheld mirror. "They pay me because I'm beautiful. This is the best job anyone could ever have."

There was another soft knock on the doors of the garden. "What the hell is it this time?" said Christel. "Don't be bothering me over no stupid shit, Miaisha."

"Mrs. Charlemagne, your daughter is up now. She is asking for you."

"Okay... Keep your cheap ass dress on. I'm on my goddamn way."

"Yes, Mrs. Charlemagne. And Joseph is stable."

"I'll see him when I see his ass." Christel's alters ordered her to stay on the window seat and look at the early-evening sky. She stared in the distance for what seemed to be several hours, but in reality, only a couple of seconds passed. "Now what?" she said. Instantly, a scene from her past opened like a book.

Fifi-Babette, dressed in a blue pleated dress, tall white socks and black shoes with a buckle, had just returned home from school. The sky was a nice silvery color; pinkish and golden brown hues. While eating her after school snack of fresh bread, fruit salad, cheese, and juice, the sun peeked through the gray drape, creating a tropical island's skulk. As soon as she finished her homework, she climbed up the flowery hill; wild flowers irritated her legs, tall blades of grass stowed away in her white socks.

She hid behind a mountain pine for an hour, watching Florian-Baptiste's long brown curls caress his facial hair. Her older sister held her stomach as she laughed. "Fifi-Babette, I see you hiding behind the

BLUEBERRY MANOR

mountain pine. Make us happy by coming out and joining us."

Fifi-Babette stood on the flowery hill, hoping her sister's gang of friends noticed her. She was taller and had bought a new hat just for them. She felt big standing on the hill with the city of Paris below. Just like her sister's friends, Fifi-Babette wanted to be as beautiful as a portrait, and as picturesque as the sky. She wanted to be just as flawless when she lit the grass and passed it around forming a tiny letter 'o' with shiny beige lips.

Sabine-Odette looked as greedy, shapely, and as big as all of her friends did. The whole gang had a mysterious cat-like aura: curly hair, curves, clothes, and popularity that the others in the village envied.

Fifi-Babette wanted to go on acid trips and pass the strong grass around while spanking her beautiful hair, flaunting her curvy curves in Florian-Baptiste's face. If Florian-Baptiste was a serpent god (he most definitely was), then Sabine-Odette was his goddess. Fifi-Babette's heart developed a blackness, her body glowed of green, her essence spoke of wild red steam. "I want to be Florian's only goddess," she repeated, "and I'll make it happen like so."

Sabine-Odette and her friends spent a good amount of time in the right wing of the house. They came in and out of the third door on the left like gays in the garden. Fifi-Babette dreamt of what they did in there. She went to the threshold of the right wing, and each day, inched closer and closer to the door.

"I see you acting hardheaded, moving closer to the forbidden door. Stay away, Fifi-Babette," said Sabine-Odette. "I'm warning you. You must not enter that room yet."

Fifi-Babette tucked her head in shame and suspicion. "Okay, big sister, I won't enter the room yet."

"Are you lying to me?"

"No, big sister. I will not enter the room."

Sabine-Odette smiled. "Fifteen."

After Sabine-Odette left for the concert, Fifi-Babette spoke to a family friend, Orsino Mosserelow. "My sweet girl, everyone except my brothers and I have left to go to the concert. They're going to be gone for a very long time. Well into the night." He scanned her rail of a physique. "I see you sneaking outside of the forbidden door. Each day you inch closer to it. I've noticed you for months. I have an idea. I have a key to unlock the forbidden door. Do you want to go inside with me?"

"I promised my sister that I would not. She told me I can't because

139

I'm too young and influential. She thinks I'll get confused. She made me promise to wait for her to sit me down. She'll talk to me and she'll answer all questions I have about the door when the time is right."

"When will the two of you talk?"

"Next year, on my fifteenth birthday."

"That's too late. You must know right now, so I'm going to take you. My brothers and I will take you, sit you down, and explain how things work around here." His mouth watered at the thought of shaping an innocent girl into his ideal love-slave.

Fifi-Babette's voice changed. "Do your brothers know about the room? I mean, do they really know about it?"

"Of course. We all know. My brothers, Felice-Paride and Quentin, have been visiting the room every other day for seven years straight. I have been visiting the room for ten years. We are professionals, so we can talk to you better than your sister."

"No, my sister is perfect. She and Florian-Baptiste will talk to me."

"My sweet girl, womanhood is calling you. Your sister is seasoned. She will get jealous of you, of your innocence and she will not tell you everything you need to know. She will cheat. She will not show you everything. Believe me, you'll be sorry if you wait for your sister to sit you down."

Orsino and all his brothers knew Fifi-Babette in the right wing, behind the third door on the left. She learned of all the things she promised her big sister that she would not dwell upon. She visited the room every day, in secret, only with Orsino and his brothers.

Fifi-Babette passed the herbe, and whipped her hair in the faces of Sabine-Odette's gang of friends. Within weeks, her curves began to show. When she flaunted her curves, the gang's special curiosities focused on her. She looked at herself in a special way, and so did all of them. And so did Sabine-Odette's man, Florian-Baptiste.

When Florian-Baptiste knew Fifi-Babette behind the third door on the left, scandalous talk spread throughout the gang. The word saddened Sabine-Odette. She spoke to her friend, Autumn Rivers in secret. "I cannot believe that Florian, the man I planned to marry in the near future knows my little sister in that way. It's so disturbing, I'd rather cling to ignorance, on the off chance that the rumors are untrue."

As the gang stood on a hill and looked down on the city of Paris, they

BLUEBERRY MANOR

spoke with unsettled stomachs, sorrow, and shame. They pulled out the grass, lit it up, passed the herbe around in a circle while coughing, looking greedy, shapely, and big. Since Florian-Baptiste was absent, and they had no child to look up to them in a special way, the group was damaged. Nothing would ever be as it was.

"Sabine-Odette, do you know where your sister is right now," said Autumn Rivers, "do you know where Florian-Baptiste is right now? No, you don't, but we do."

"I've heard all the rumors," said Sabine-Odette.

"But they are not only rumors, they are uncut and uncensored. You must let go of your dreamland," Autumn Rivers passed the herbe, "Florian-Baptiste is no good and your little sister is not so innocent anymore."

Sabine-Odette looked at her engagement ring. "Really, where is my sister and Florian?" Still, she did not want to believe that her little sister had disobeyed her, and entered the forbidden door behind her back.

"She's in the right wing."

"No, Autumn! Not the third door on the left," Sabine-Odette cried thick and sloppy. "I want to remain ignorant regarding the rumors, but it's hard."

"Yes, your little sister is passing the herbe, spanking her long, silky hair, and flaunting her immature curves in the face of Florian-Baptiste." Autumn Rivers advised, "Bless you, and bless your family, for this is the continuation of a curse set in place long ago."

Sabine-Odette stood on the hill, looked down on Paris, and stopped puffing the grass.

She stopped going on acid trips. She did not partake in foolishness any longer. She was ashamed because her sister, the little one that looked up to her so much, had become her. She wanted so much more for her sister.

Fifi-Babette took Sabine-Odette's place on the hill. She looked at herself in a special way, smoked strong grass, and went on disturbing acid trips. She was younger, more beautiful in the group's eyes, greedier, shapelier and more attractive. She spanked her hair and flaunted her curves in Florian-Baptiste's face, and she did not hesitate to do those things in front of her big sister.

Sabine-Odette abandoned the life she'd come to love. She went away to another part of France, all because her little sister, the one who loved

141

AMINA CAPRICE ANDOLINI

her so, had taken her wretched place. *I failed at my job, and now, my little sister will never be all that she could have been.* Sabine-Odette cried, "She has become part of the shameful curse!"

Fifi-Babette welcomed Claire-Colette Broussard into the world on September 5, 1935. She waited until her eighteenth birthday to tell Florian-Baptiste that he was the father. Claire-Colette was four years old. "Do the right thing and marry me, Florian," said Fifi-Babette. "Give me and our baby a rich man's home, and give our baby girl a rich man's name."

"What about your sister?" asked Florian-Baptiste. "I still love her. I would marry her today if she agrees."

"You are wasting your time with her. An accident has made Sabine-Odette barren." Her mind flashed back to the accident at the stables. "Yeah, I know you long to be with my sister, but she has fled to another part of France."

Florian-Baptiste gasped. He shook his head with violent, royal respect.

"What's more is that she can never be me." Fifi-Babette held her head high. "She can never touch a baby of her own, smell its breath, or change its clothes."

"Fifi-Babette, that's not a good thing to say about your own flesh and blood sister. If I was still a betting man, I'd put everything on this: that your evil ass caused the accident that made Sabine-Odette barren."

"So what?" remarked Fifi-Babette.

"Does Sabine-Odette know?"

Fifi-Babette smirked, an ugly smirk one could only describe as demons after the feast. "What do you think?"

Florian-Baptiste slapped her. She fell on the ground and stabbed herself with a nail that jutted out of an upturned horseshoe. "If it had not been for you, your sister and I would have a child right now. Several children." He looked down on her. His face went wild and thin. "Take back what you said, you spider-wasp whore."

While on the ground, Fifi-Babette screamed, "It won't change anything. I am still better for you than she is."

"That baby isn't my baby," Florian-Baptiste snapped.

"How'd you come to that conclusion?" She dusted herself, got up and dressed her wound with an old tourniquet. "Claire-Collette is exceptional at music at such a young age, just like you."

"She is shorter than average, has pale skin, violet eyes, and platinum

142

blonde hair. I, on the other hand, am very tall, dark-skinned, and I have dark eyes and dark hair."

"So?"

"So, she isn't my child. I love Claire-Colette the way an uncle loves his niece. As far as being her father, I am not. She is not of my blood. She does not look like me or any of my dark relatives. She looks like one of the Mosserelow boys."

Fifi-Babette rolled her eyes. "What are you trying to say, Florian?"

"You can clearly see Claire-Colette isn't a black European!"

Fifi-Babette did not speak, and so Florian-Baptiste struck her repeatedly, until her guilty mouth spewed secrets.

"Fine! I do not know who Claire-Colette's father is. Maybe Orsino Mosserelow or Antonio Mosserelow, or any one of the Northern Italians. Perhaps her father is French."

After admitting deception, Florian-Baptiste was so enraged that he threw Fifi-Babette across a small moat. A stable hand who'd been listening to the entire argument grabbed Claire-Colette before Florian-Baptiste could get to her, then ran to Fifi-Babette's aid. When the stable hand saw the anger on Florian-Baptiste's face, he gave the baby to Fifi-Babette before disappearing in the hills.

When trying to grab Claire-Collette, Florian-Baptiste slipped and fell in a mud puddle. Fifi-Babette laughed so hard that she slung her daughter in an alligator's pit. When Florian-Baptiste saw this, he jumped in the pit and saved Claire-Collette, but before he could escape the pit, alligators ripped his body apart.

Fifi-Babette was so distraught that she left Paris, but returned to her childhood home after a few weeks. Spirits of jealousy and lasciviousness met her at the front door, forcing her in the arms of old dealings once again. She was ashamed of the line Orsino and his brothers had on her, but at the same time, she felt as if she could not sever it, nor did she want to.

On Claire-Colette's fourteenth birthday, Fifi-Babette, Orsino, Antonio, and others taught her all they knew about the sickening third door on the left. Four years after her thirteenth birthday, Fifi-Babette and Orsino perished behind the forbidden door. A distraught Claire-Colette ran off with one of her johns, but quickly returned after Antonio Mosserelow's death threats.

AMINA CAPRICE ANDOLINI

When Claire-Colette gave birth to twins, Paulina Denise-Renée Christel Broussard and Felix Giovanni Marco Broussard, Antonio ordered the midwife to hide the girl, sell the boy, and kill the mother. When the midwife stabbed Claire-Colette, the demons that escaped her body entered the baby girl that they now call Christel.

Years later, Christel had grown to be such a beautiful girl, that Antonio kept her, claiming her as his own. At the age of thirteen, he took Christel, and forced her to be his love-slave, releasing Pistel and Felice, two of Christel's most powerful alters. Antonio molded Christel, indifferent to rumors of incest and pedophilia. He kept her locked up, only letting her navigate three rooms of the massive apartment they inhabited.

To deal with Antonio's abuse, Christel created more alters in addition to the demons that inhabited her after her mother was killed. At the age of fifteen, she gave birth to a child. Terrified, believing that the child was her brother, she left him on someone's doorstep. One of the alters wiped that incident, along with so many more incidents out of her head.

One day, the gatekeeper, Pistel, gave a serial killer alter the go ahead to put poison in Antonio's favorite snack. Christel knew about this, and hoped Antonio would die a fitting death. She imagined him struggling to breathe, lashing out at his throat, staring at demonic faces and hearing their laughter as he faded out. After placing the poisonous snack at Antonio's side, she discovered that he was already dead. She saw this as the perfect opportunity to escape, given the fact that she could not remember if she was responsible for his death or not.

Christel and her friend Luigi Mosserelow, who is also the son of Orsino Mosserelow, went back to her grandmother's (Fifi-Babette's) childhood home and set fire to it, then destroyed Antonio Mosserelow's apartment. Afterwards, they traveled to Italy in order to find Christel's birth father. Christel was relieved to know that Orsino nor Antonio Mosserelow was her father, but their cousin, a Spiritual Guru who went by the name of Gianmarco Paolucci Garcia of Rome, Italy was.

Christel lived with her father, but ran away to Paris years later out of boredom. She got involved in her old dealings, that is, until Joseph found her behind a dumpster at a gentleman's club. From that moment on, he vowed to take care of her and to help her deal with and break her family's generational curse.

BLUEBERRY MANOR

Christel's robotic alter was the first to possess her after the vision. "Thisss is my calling," said Cybristel. She bucked her eyes wider than a human being in human skin could accomplish. She climbed out of the window and scooted along the thin ledge until she reached a winged gargoyle, perching herself on its huge neck. Pedestrians on the ground pointed up while gasping and gossiping about her state of mind.

"Is she going to jump?"

"I hope she fucking jumps!"

"Joseph's heart attack has made her suicidal!"

Many people called firefighters and the media who was just around the corner, still trying to sneak into Joseph's hospital room. Flashing lights from cameras seemed to yank Christel out of her robotic daze. She blinked, shook her head, and then grabbed her cellphone while on the gargoyle's neck. The audience below continued to gasp.

What the hell is the matter with Christel Charlemagne!

Christel said, "What in the goddamn hell is this fool Kenneth's new number?" She planted her pointer finger on the corner of her mouth, and took her reading glasses out of the pocket on her short white blazer jacket. "06-77-793... wait a minute, this isn't right." She went on a rampage, cursing heavily and spitting on the heads of the people below.

"Fuck you! Either jump or go inside, you Charlemagne bitch," said an irate spectator. Show us how much you love Joseph and kill yourself!"

Jessica Davis (formerly JessiCorsa Blackberry) felt the ghosts of the Blackberry Klan come after her in the main waiting room of the hospital. Drenched in an invisible sweat, a sour sweat that smelled like old dishrag, she heard the nasty hysterics of her brothers Mel and BeeSquared coming out of the lights, the vents, and the walls.

"You a damn fool, Bee!" Mel stepped to JessiCorsa like a thief in broad daylight. "God, JessiCorsa, yo teef so gat'damn big, you brush 'em with dish soap and a dust rag," he laughed at his own joke, "wash me please, head lookin' ass."

BeeSquared said, "Professional wash and detail, head lookin' ass." He pretended to wash himself.

"Turtle shaped head ass." Mel turned himself into a robot, lips long and pointed. "Wipe on...wipe off lookin' ass. Sit'cho spit shine lookin' ass down somewhere."

Jessica snuck in the Coronary Care Unit. To her surprise, Joseph was sitting up, searching through the nightstand. "Hey, Jessica. Where's the food I asked for when I came to?"

Jessica was overjoyed. "Godfather Joe! Your back is to the door. How did you know it was me?"

"You smell like fresh roses and vanilla," said Joseph, head down, still searching through the nightstand.

Jessica sniffed herself. "That's my rose and vanilla extrait de parfum. It's pure perfume extract. I'm glad to hear your voice. And you know you're not supposed to have fried foods or sweets in here."

Joseph stopped searching through the nightstand, then stared at the ceiling with nostalgic eyes. "Those wonderful Fried Chicken Fridays."

Jessica sat in a chair next to the bed. "You seem to be in great shape for someone who has just," she cut herself off.

146

"I know, but I'm tired."

"I just wanna look at you. Okay... out with it. It seems as if you have something to say."

"Jessica, I have just received a message from the Blind Monks." Jessica looked around for Jeeves. "We want you to go to the confessional on the second floor. We know about your hysteria."

"But how did you know?" Joseph closed his eyes. A shaft of fear shot from her stomach to her heart. "Godfather Joe?" She signed in relief. "You're sleeping."

A nurse circled in the room. Her voice was silent but stern. "What are you doing here?"

Jessica stood up, and swiftly walked past the nurse.

"What a minute, *you*! Come back here." The nurse checked the wires above Joseph's bed. "I've gotta put some guards outside that door," she said, speaking to Joseph as if he was alert. "I don't want to see anyone else in here for the rest of the day. You hear me, Mr. Charlemagne?"

Jessica went to the chaplaincy suite. A group from the chaplaincy department greeted and consoled her as soon as she stepped off the elevator.

She repeated, "I hear the cackles. As clear as present day, and I hear my brothers. I hear them! And Joseph and the Blind Monks must hear it too because they sent me to you." Jessica's eyes rolled around as she heard her brothers razz in her head.

"Jessi? Can't see you, black as tar, black as midnight, there you are!" Mel sung.

"Hey? What the hell you call JessiCorsa in the ocean?" asked BeeSquared.

Mel said, *"I don't know... What the hell do you call JessiCorsa in the ocean, BeeSquared?"*

BeeSquared held his belly. *"She's a goddamn oil slick!"*

Jessica fainted. The monks and nuns from the chaplaincy department picked her up and placed her on a bed. When Jessica came to, she was sitting up and yelling, "I hear cackles and see what I call the devil-bird dance." She curled her fingers, "Their long bent over claws stabbing their ways deep in my psyche." Jessica tried to get up and dance around, but the monks held her down. "I-I left home because of them. I changed my name, my age, and my birthdate, but they forever live in here." She pointed at her heart. Three nuns wiped sweat from her neck, face, and forehead. Jessica shivered. A monk gave her a navy blue afghan.

A chaplain led Jessica to the chapel, a Romanesque room that echoed with the peaceful manifestations of monks, nuns, and springtime incense. He guided her to a little meditation area.

"My child, after examination of your conscience, there is a priest in the confessional." He pointed at the little yellow light.

Jessica was nervous, but thinking about how she had lied to Bernard, thinking about her deep-rooted self-esteem issues, issues with guilt, and the recent panic attacks, she felt the need to confess venial sins.

She asked the chaplain, "The priest is there as long as the light is on?"

"Yes."

Jessica went in the confessional booth and knelt at the screen.

"Peace and welcome," said the priest.

Jessica crossed herself. "In the name of the Father, Son, and Holy Spirit, bless me, Father, for I have sinned. My last confession was one year ago."

"What are your sins?"

"I've been impure, Father. I've allowed myself to be a magnet for demonic manifestation. I hear their voices all around me."

"How have you been impure?"

"I've lied to myself and my husband for years. I've carried guilt, self-esteem, and identity issues which I am afraid have damaged my future growth."

"Go on. Go to the beginning of your impurity."

"It started when I was thirteen years-old. No, before that age, but the last straw was at thirteen." Jessica went into a vision of her family's taunting...

JessiCorsa and her brothers were playing red light/green light when a lowrider Caddy pulled in the path. A tall white lady with matted hair and narrow eyes stepped out.

Mel slapped BeeSquared on the back of the head. "There it is, Bee. We got fresh!"

"Heavy hands lookin' ass slappin' me on the back of the head and shit?" BeeSquared looked at JessiCorsa, rubbing what he thought was a knot. "And what the hell is your Khartoum looking, horse face ass laughing at, Jessi?" BeeSquared mocked JessiCorsa's unusual shoulder movement.

148

BLUEBERRY MANOR

"White lady fuckin' with that white horse and shit," Mel said, "I smell it from here. She's got needle marks up and down her arm."

BeeSquared asked, "How you know?"

Mel pointed at his eyes.

"I wonder what dat junkie hoe want with us." BeeSquared reached for a black and gold basketball but Mel grabbed it.

"She lookin' for some bing pow rolling up on us." Mel punched at the air, "We V.I.P."

"We were only playing a game," said JessiCorsa, "we ain't doing nothing important."

"Fuck you!" said BeeSquared. "Biff Boff lookin' ass." He took the basketball from Mel. "This ain't no fuckin' crack house. We ain't studying that shit. And you ain't V.I.P."

Mel took the basketball back. "Very Important Pig-Dog. Platypus head and neck lookin' ass."

Mel and BeeSquared began to argue about what part of the lady's car to strip.

"Y'all sound like some butt-hurt little girls," said JessiCorsa, "crying 'cause somebody took they seat."

BeeSquared said, "Get'cho shiny black ass away from here. You drawing flies." He neighed like a horse.

"Don't worry 'bout Khartoum, horse head looking ass. All she gotta do is flick'dem flies with her tail," said Mel, "we wasting time arguing when we could be stripping her goddamn car. C'mo!"

JessiCorsa went to a restricted area of the main house to tell her mother of Mel and BeeSquared's attempt at vandalism. When she reached the kitchen window, she heard her mother and Cousin Jaleesha talking about the stranger. JessiCorsa hid behind a big tree.

"Hurry up. Look, Jaleesha." Brenda pulled the blue-patterned curtain back.

"I'm hurrying. What, Brenda?"

She pointed out the window. "Look at that wide-mouthed hoe," Brenda laughed. "That's Cleveland's distant cousin, goddammit. We gone scare the shit outta that bitch. Her racist ass already thinks we do Voodoo in here. I hate her trickin' ass."

Cousin Jaleesha said, "What's going on?"

"Cleveland guerilla pimped that ass last night. Yeah, he branded that hoe and everything. Ain't nothing but she done come round here for

149

money. Dope whore think she above the rules of the game and shit."

"Cleveland's a pimp?" Cousin Jaleesha covered her mouth. "Is that why this area is so restricted? You got some trafficking going on?"

Brenda sighed, "Cleveland's a pastor and manager, dummy." She side-eyed Cousin Jaleesha. "How could you say some sorry shit like that?"

Cousin Jaleesha threw her hands in the air. "Sooo-rrry."

Brenda said, "Look at that shit. Imma show that whore what we about."

Cousin Jaleesha rolled her eyes. "I'm down for whatever. What you got planned?"

"I'll be damned if Cleveland gone catch another case 'cause of her stupid ass. She way outta pocket—"

JessiCorsa said, "oh, the white woman is Cleveland's distant cousin. That means she Mel and BeeSquared's cousin too." JessiCorsa went to the back of the house and saw unfamiliar people dragging huge speakers. "Who are you people and what are you doing here?"

An unfamiliar man spoke, "Go to hell. You're not supposed to be on this side of the bordello, little girl."

"The bord-what-lo?"

"Get outta here, nosey child."

The unfamiliar people turned on the system, and blasted the music so loud that the lyrics were distorted. JessiCorsa tried to walk on shaky ground but fell in fetal position. She managed to crawl to a rusted storage house where she supported herself with rotten beams. She saw a group of people with misshapen faces—black and white swirly patterns on their cheeks and hook noses. They had on long black robes with red splotches on the back. They all had huge claw like teeth.

Some jumped in a pool of mud and splashed around while licking it off one another. Others mutilated animals, and stuck their heads in barrels of offal and honey.

JessiCorsa's eyesight began to fade.

Once Cleveland's cousin caught sight of the madness, she thought she had interrupted a private Voodoo ritual. She screamed, "Oh no, they'll surely put a hex on me!" When someone covered in mud came up to the woman and started jiggle-dancing, she raised up her skirt, had a bowel movement, and then jolted about like she was having a violent episode. The Blackberry Klan laughed as the woman smeared excrement all over her face. "This will ward off the hex." The woman hopped in the frame of her car and sped down the pathway at what appeared to be forty-two miles per hour.

Brenda grabbed JessiCorsa by the hair. She was still shaking, terrified from what she'd just seen. "What the hell are you doing here?"

"Ma, I wanted to tell you something about Mel and Bee. They were going to strip the white lady's car but now it's too late to tell you. She left on the frame."

"I don't give a shitsonian, little bitch. You know you're not supposed to be here. I'm gonna whoop your motherfucking ass for disobeying me." She took JessiCorsa to the main house and locked her in a closet. JessiCorsa beat on the door. Brenda screamed, "Beat on that door one more time and I'll skin you!"

el laughed. "You see that shit. Bitch running on empty head lookin' ass."

"Shiii'it," BeeSquared said.

"That shit was super funny. How she get up outta here in a gat'damn frame, Bee?"

"Dem tires was moving so fast, Dey be lookin like dey shovelin' dirt. I be workin' on a chain gang head lookin' ass." BeeSquared picked up a shovel. "I'ma diggin'neese holes lookin' ass. What it do, Mel?"

Mel said, "That woman so white, she neon orange in this muthafucka, blinding a nigga and shit."

"Lookin' ass." said BeeSquared.

"She wear her sunglasses at night head lookin' ass." Mel got two square ice cubes from the outside freezer combo and held them up to his eyes. "Cold as ice lookin' ass."

"You look like a frog peeping through ice," BeeSquared said.

Mel said, "And you look like that ugly ass dope whore. Pinkeye lookin' ass. Snot mouth lookin' ass. Scratchin' and grinnin' and shit. Mel heard JessiCorsa crying. "What the hell?" He and BeeSquared crawled through a window in the main house and let her out of the closet.

"I heard y'all talking." Tears and slime flowed in JessiCorsa's mouth.

"And we heard you crying," Mel said.

JessiCorsa said, "Y'all both needs ta shut up. I heard Ma tell Cousin Jaleesha de white woman is Cleveland's cousin, so that makes her y'all's cousin too. Her name Sheila-Beth Foxtrot. Ma wanted to scare the Sheila-Beth Foxtrot lady until some diarrhea come outta her. And it did, 'cuz..."

Mel said, "You should be grateful to us. I just saved that black ass. Didn't hafta do shit. I coulda left you in the closet for forever."

BeeSquared agreed. "And I bet she at the main house 'cuz she tried to tell on us. Tattletale looking ass."

BLUEBERRY MANOR

"She always telling on us," said Mel.

"Shut up!" said JessiCorsa.

BeeSquared handed her a pillowcase. "Wipe your face. You're making me sick."

Mel said, "Oh, you done tried it."

"Yeah," said BeeSquared," who the hell is you, telling us to shut up and shit? You so black you look like a cast iron skillet"

"Batter fried fish and chip lookin' ass," Mel said.

"Y'all can't talk about nobody," screamed JessiCorsa, y'all act ugly, you steal, and you're not very nice."

Mel took off one of his tennishoes and threw it in JessiCorsa's face. "Shine these shoes." The fresh smell of rubber dazed her for a minute. Mel threw his other shoe at her stomach.

BeeSquared took off his tennis shoes and threw them at JessiCorsa as well. She stood motionless while BeeSquared abused her with old shoes from a storage bin.

"Bubblin' brown sugar head lookin' ass," said Mel, while eating a caramel sugar pop he found in the storage bin. "Get your shiny black ass away from here."

BeeSquared threw his ant farm at JessiCorsa, but not hard enough to break the plexiglass.

JessiCorsa climbed through the window and headed in the direction of her best friend's fish farm, wishing this was the very last time she'd ever see the place she called home.

When JessiCorsa made it to the Tamoore Family Fish Farm. She asked Mr. Tamoore if she could speak to her best friend Tanequa a.k.a. Tameka. "Yes, she is in the kitchen cooking or eating or something," said Mr. Tamoore. "Just go on in, JessiCorsa. She'll be glad to see you."

When JessiCorsa went in the kitchen, Tameka was eating a fish sandwich and drinking a mango smoothie. "Hello, Tameka."

"Oh, hi, Jessi. Would you like something to eat? I just made it."

"No. I'm in no mood."

"What's wrong?"

"White people this, black people that," said JessiCorsa, "my whole family is a black racist clan. I am so ashamed to be related to them."

"There are lots of racist blacks walking around."

"They always talk about good and bad skin and hair. Well, you know

153

what, Tameka? I don't think there is a such thing as good and bad skin or hair in the first place." JessiCorsa showcased her skin and pulled her hair.

"You're right, JessiCorsa. Anyway, I think they're just jealous of your strength."

"My strength?" She smirked as if what Tameka said was totally ridiculous.

"They don't like the fact that you seem to accept your darker skin tone for one." Tameka took a sip of her mango smoothie and smacked her lips. "They want you to bleach it so you can look more like them."

"Oh no, I'll never do that."

Tameka took a bite of one of her fish sandwiches and told JessiCorsa to get some food from the stove. JessiCorsa declined, Tameka continued. "They want you to seem visibly depressed, because they know as long as they have your mind, they can put anything they want to up there, and you'll believe it." She hit her temple with her right pointer finger. "See, since they've been raised and conditioned to believe that dark people aren't pretty, or aren't supposed to be pretty, they want you to believe it too. They wanna own your mind."

"Yeah, I know."

Tameka's father came in the kitchen. "Tanequa! Give that nice girl something to eat. She looks undernourished."

"Yes, Father." After Tameka's father went back outside, she rolled her eyes and said, "don't worry about that. He thinks everybody looks undernourished."

JessiCorsa laughed.

"What's so funny, Jessi?"

"It's funny when he calls you Tanequa."

"Gosh I hate that name."

"You hate your real name?" JessiCorsa said 'Tanequa Tamoore' several times in her head.

"Tanequa sounds ghetto. I like Tameka better. As soon as I'm able, I'm legally changing my name."

"There's no such thing as ghetto."

"Whatever." Tameka gave JessiCorsa a small strawberry drink and some fresh strawberries in a bowl.

"Ma treats me different because I have a different daddy from Romelle and Bryant," JessiCorsa said.

"Really? I didn't know that." There was an apologetic twinge in

154

Tameka's voice. "I also didn't know Mel and BeeSquared's names were Romelle and Bryant."

"Romelle and Bryant's dad is light skinned. He identifies as either quadroon, biracial or polyethnic. I don't care. All I know is Ma still lets Cleveland Cornell come around even though he puts his hands on her, but she won't let Darkie nowhere near the house."

"Who is Darkie?"

"That's what they call my daddy."

"That's so mean!"

"Well, everybody calls him that. Even his parents."

"Why won't she let your dad near the house? Is she ashamed of him or something?" Tameka was on her second fish sandwich and third mango smoothie.

"Yep, she's ashamed of him because he's dark."

After JessiCorsa finished the drink and strawberries, Tameka gave her a large mango smoothie and filled her empty bowl with freshly cut mangoes and pears.

Tameka laughed. "Too late now."

"I think she really likes him but doesn't want to like him because of his color. Because she's a racist."

"The thing is this, my daddy treats Ma bad, but not as bad as Mr. Cornell does."

"Do you have other siblings?"

"Yeah. Mom had a child before Romelle named Shelly. I don't see her much, not since she got engaged and moved to the Dominican Republic to be with her fiancé's family. And I have two more brothers, Dad's children. I don't see them much either. Their mother is a whole white woman."

"Whole?" Tameka laughed a little. "You mean she's not mixed?"

"You know what I mean." JessiCorsa sighed. "They treat me like I'm not a member of the family at all."

"Who?"

"All of them. There were some good times, but I can count them on my right hand." JessiCorsa held her hand up, fingers spread.

"They're just jealous of the way you look. They don't understand how a person with dark skin can look as good and better than them," Said Tameka.

JessiCorsa beamed. "You're so good for my ego!"

"Just telling it like it is," Tameka said.

"But they continuously tell me I'm ugly. They call me all types of animals, especially a horse. I don't think they have time to worry about me. They're so narcissistic."

"Those kind of people really want to fit in with the in-crowd. In this instance, the in-crowd happens to be red to yellow skin tone. And you're not ugly. And horses aren't ugly."

"I don't think there's a such thing as ugly," said Jessica, "however, a human that looks like an animal is kind of strange."

"I guess," Tameka smacked.

"Their racism makes me tired."

"Me too, girl. You know, I didn't know it was that serious, Jessi. Your grandparents must have been racists."

"Both of my grandparents were biracial. Back then, the people in this town treated the light-skinned blacks like royalty and treated the tar babies like something they stepped in. And some of them still do. A large part of this sleepy little town got stuck somewhere in slave time." JessiCorsa put a forced grin on her face.

"That's messed up." Tameka stared at the rest of her fish sandwich as if it could talk back.

"I don't like thinking like this, but to me, my mamma deserves to get treated bad. She has done a lot of bad things in her life. Most of them involve racial issues and something else I'm not supposed to talk about."

"She needs help."

"Yeah, I know. Still, she needa have several seats for treating me like this. And Daddy foul for letting Ma put a wedge in between us." JessiCorsa slurped the rest of her smoothie. "He's nothing but a deadbeat."

"Your mom grew up with those dogmas. She learned that behavior when she was born, so please don't be too upset with her. Ms. Blackberry doesn't know any better, that's all. I'm willing to bet your dad will contact you later in life." Tameka laughed. "He'll have some juicy stories to tell. You should write a book."

JessiCorsa's voice went up a couple of octaves. "I don't wanna talk to him."

Tameka bucked her eyes.

"Ma has the Spirit of Pure Jealousy. Three of my aunts and two uncles look like whole white people. Ma is a lot darker. She's always been jealous of them."

"And her parents treated the lighter children better?" asked Tameka.

JessiCorsa shook her head, "lots better."

"That's a gosh darn crying shame, Jessi."

JessiCorsa slammed her hand on the table and jumped up. "It's time I break the chain. I don't want my children growing up like this."

JessiCorsa sat down, asked Tameka if she could have some of the food on the stove. Tameka got up and grabbed two fish sandwiches from inside the oven and put some curly fries and hushpuppies in a bowl. JessiCorsa thanked Tameka for the food and continued. "That's why I have to leave Alabama. I'll go stone crazy if I don't. See, nobody knows this but I've secretly been working since I was eight, putting back forty dollars a week with one goal in mind: to emancipate myself at age fourteen. I'm taking on another personality."

"What?"

"Yep. As soon as I graduate from middle school."

"You never told me about that. Where are you working?"

"I help these little old ladies with their shopping and housework. I do just about anything the elderly people ask me to do, from rearranging furniture to cooking, cleaning to taking care of their grandkids and pets. It's great, but when I move, my only regret will be leaving you behind. I wish I could take you with me, Tanequa."

"Hey!"

"My bad... Tameka."

"I can join you while I'm in college."

"Cool! That's what's up. "I have this pen pal in Anaheim, California. She says I can come live with her."

"I don't know about that, Jessi. Why you want to move in with people you've never met before? That's dangerous. They could be serial killers or something."

"But I *have* met her before. You know her too. Her name is Dianna Dionne. Remember? She used to go to elementary school with us."

"Oh, yeah, I remember the Dionne Family. Yeah, they cool peoples. Anyway, when you leave keep in touch with me as much as you can."

At five o'clock that evening, everybody in the house played board games and watched interesting shows on television. Tameka's mother fixed a nice dinner, then all the children danced the night away until they fell asleep from exhaustion.

JessiCorsa called her mother at midnight. In a twisted-little way, she wanted her mother to be upset with her for not calling home sooner.

She let the phone ring and ring, but nobody answered. She looked at the calendar. "Tameka...they said it!"

"Who said what?"

""My family went to the Dominican Republic without me. I heard Shelly tell Ma that she did not want me at the wedding. Romelle and Bryant said they were leaving me, but I didn't believe they'd actually do it."

JessiCorsa's mind flashed back to her uncles' abuse. She cried, and thanked a Higher Power that she would not be in the cabin with those sick pedophiles this weekend. She thought the real reason her brothers picked the argument with her was because they wanted to make her so angry, that she'd run away from home, and then the family could leave her behind in good conscious.

JessiCorsa put her hand on Tameka's shoulder, "Will you explain my situation to your parents. I'm going to need a place to stay for a few weeks, just until my fourteenth birthday."

Tameka said, "What about other family members? Won't they be worried? Will they try'ta sue us or something?"

"No. I'm not that important."

"Don't say that, Jessi."

"I mean, those niggerslicksters don't care about me."

"Then forget 'em, Jessi!"

"I'll try."

Tameka nodded her head. "Don't worry, we got you." After explaining the situation to her parents, Tameka stood speechless as JessiCorsa stared out the window. "I can't believe it. The horrid log cabin on Pickle Ridge Lane. Such a gosh darn crying shame. I'd like to burn the place to the friggin' ground."

essica took a deep breath, held it in for five seconds, then slowly exhaled. "I'm sorry for these and all past sins."

"You should take advantage of the counseling we have available," said the priest, "if not today, come back in three days. I know this is a stressful time for you," the priest told Jessica to check the Bible shelf in the prayer kneeler. Light shining through little holes in the confessional made the solid gold Rosary and brown leather Bible look as though diamonds shone all throughout. "Take the Rosary and the Bible. Pray to Mary whenever you feel anxious and thank Jesus for your future."

"Thank you, Father. Praise the Lord."

"Say four Our Fathers, six Hail Marys, and a personal act of contrition."

The priest anointed the wall of the confessional before the prayer of absolution.

"Amen," Jessica said after the prayer.

"God has forgiven you. You may go in peace."

"Thanks be to God." Jessica left the confessional feeling better about her future, but still unsure about Joseph's. She did not want to go back to the emergency department. The thought of seeing all kinds of people cry, faint, convulse, and fight was triggering; however, seeing others grieve was the perfect time to complete the penance.

While searching through her plaid handbag, a little pink note reminded her of a doctor's appointment later this month, and of the time she spoke to Joseph before his heart attack.

"Hey, Jessi!" Joseph's lower back and arm were stiff from picking tomatoes. "How are you doing? Haven't seen you around here in a while. You sick or something? You look a little blue in the face."

"You saying I'm so black I'm blue?" Jessica laughed.

"Where'd that humor come from?"

He asked, "What has you so worried?"

"It may sound stupid, but," she sat down in one of the wicker chairs nearby, slowly, so she wouldn't fall through, "I feel like I'm losing my mind."

"There's a lot of that going around."

"What do you mean?"

"Nothing." Joseph said.

"Did I say something off putting?"

He grabbed Jessica's hand. "No, I'm not talking about you."

"Of course not."

"But you've gotta get it off your chest, Jessica."

Jessica looked disapprovingly. "Yeah, chest. My breast implants." Jessica checked to make sure the bottom of the chair was still intact.

"What about your implants? Are they leaking?"

"I feel like they are. These things speak to me. They call me to the mirror to check to see if they're still here. Last week I cried, thinking I had breast cancer. It feels like something foreign is trying to get out of me, and," she smashed the palms of her hands on her cheeks, "I don't know. I mean, it feels like something's wrong. I'm depressed all the time, I hear voices, and I just wanna go off and kill myself."

"Nooo!"

She held her wrist out. "One nice cut. I apologize, Godfather Joe, but I feel irrational. What do you think is going on?"

"I would think the real problem is something you've been carrying around for years. The implants are two very convenient scapegoats."

Jessica laughed.

"Are you going to get rid of the psychosomatic demons?"

Jessica looked around. "What demons?"

"The implants, silly."

"That's just it, Godfather Joe. I don't know. I don't know if I can just rip them out now."

"Why not, if they're causing all this trouble?"

"Bernard doesn't know I have implants. He knows about the liposuction, of course, but not the implants."

"I heard you telling Dana-Lyn and Winter-Jem about begging Bernard to pay for liposuction. I shoulda beat his ass right then and there."

"Oh, no, Godfather Joe."

BLUEBERRY MANOR

"You shouldn't have to beg anyone for anything." He said. "Cheap motherfucker. Why does he have to control all the money? I told you about those joint accounts."

Jessica wiped theoretical sweat from her brow, happy that she never told Joseph of the time Bernard forced her to work at a diner in Paris.

"I see it on your face, Jessi. What are you keeping from me?"

"Oh, nothing, it's just that Bernard doesn't like cosmetic surgery."

"Of course not. He doesn't wanna spend the money."

"I deceived him."

"How?"

"By not telling him that I had implants when we met."

"That was none of his damn business."

Jessica looked up to the sky. "I know where you're coming from, but I'm so paranoid. I know I have to get the saline implants out, but how can I after all the lies?" Jessica looked down. "And, um… there's another reason."

"What else do you have to say?"

"Before the implants, they made fun of me in so many ways. You know what they used to say to me?"

"Who used to say what?"

"Other children and family members used to say that I was part of a certain committee. Well, I don't want my itty bitty water balloons because, while some people look perfect with the small ones, I don't think I look right at all. I'm not being superficial or anything. It's just that those thoughts haunt me."

Joseph sat in the chair across from Jessica and poured them both a glass of wine. Through cigar smoke he uttered, "Deal with the thoughts that haunt you, then you'll be able to deal with what you have." He rose up a little.

"People expect nice cleavage. Good cleavage in pretty party dresses." She shook her head. "Without my implants, I'm built like a squash. That's what people will think. They will call me big black ass, squash woman, big squash ass."

They both laughed. "People are strange," said Joseph. "What do *you* want, Jessica? That's important here."

"I want to remove them."

"Then why don't you?"

"I don't know if I could ever be that bold." Jessica lowered her head.

161

Joseph cupped her chin. "It's time to stop running, Jessica. Deal with your demons. You still haven't dealt with that bullying have you?"

"You mean by my brothers?"

"Yes." "Why are you worried about what others expect of you? What do you expect of yourself?"

"It's Bernard."

"I respect you, Jessica, but Bernard's a big dog."

"Godfather Joe!"

"I apologize for that. Still, don't worry about Bernard. Do what makes you happy and stop trying to live up to other people's expectations. The demon has to come from somewhere, right?"

Jessica pointed at herself. "Me?"

"Exactly. Now it's your job to get rid of it."

Jessica looked confused, as if she was trying to grasp the meaning of what Joseph said.

Joseph continued, "If you want more implants, by all means, get them. If not, don't. Do what's best for you. It's gotta be what *you* want. Don't put other people's opinions above your own health and wellbeing. The demon comes from deep inside of you. Deal with it."

"I would like to go natural, but what about my marriage? What would Bernard think? He doesn't know my real size. Our whole marriage is based on a lie."

"Has he ever seen pictures from your past?"

"Not that far back."

"Look, Jessica, don't worry about Bernard, I highly doubt he'll divorce you over a pair of...over a pair of those. And if he does, I'll kick his ass real nice." The boyish grin on Joseph's face amused the both of them.

Jessica grabbed Joseph's hand. "Thank you, Godfather Joe. Like magic, you make an unclear situation crystal clear." She grabbed Joseph's wrist with one hand and wiped tears with the other. "But um, I wish you would tell me about this thing you have against Bernard. Why do you dislike him so?"

"I didn't say that I dislike him."

"Oh yeah? You called him a big dog." They both laughed. "I happen to know you aren't a fan of dogs."

Joseph reminisced about the scar on his arm.

"Godfather Joe?"

Joseph jumped, then tapped the bottom of his glass to make sure there was nothing left behind. "Think back. I think I told you this already."

Jessica put both of her elbows on the table and straddled her face with open palms. "He's sneaky? You said he's hiding something big from me, from us all."

"Yes. He and Christel." Joseph stopped himself short.

"What is it, Godfather Joe? You can tell me."

"It's so hot from the lights." He mumbled. He heard a near accident in his head. He threw his hands crossways.

"Godfather Joe!" Jessica yelled.

"I'm okay," he said, "how's my baby girl, huh? How's my chocolate cookie-cake doing?"

"Um, Cookie wants go to Greece with Pearlie, Kenneth and three of his children this summer."

"Who? DeShawn, Aqua, and Maria?"

"Yes."

"Now that's what I like to hear."

"The trip is very expensive."

"Didn't I tell you about worrying about money?" Jessica nodded. "You know I'll take care of Cookie's end. I've closed my ears to the word no."

"Thank you."

Joseph said, "I'm waiting."

"Is Bernard up for, like, a raise or a promotion or something like that this year?" asked Jessica.

"You ask that same question every year, and every year he gets one."

"He got one last year?"

"Yes. He didn't tell you?"

Jessica jumped out of the chair and announced, "You always know what's best." She stretched her arms out like a loveless child.

Joseph accommodated. "I love you, my goddaughter. My sharp witted angel."

"I love you too."

Joseph wiped a lone tear from his right eye.

Jessica pulled back, pinched Joseph's cheeks, and began to walk away. "See ya later. And thanks."

Joseph spoke as loud as his raspy voice could go. "See ya. And take care."

Jessica walked away heavy hearted. Although she did not see them with her physical eyes, she felt Joseph's tears. Instinct told her that something was going on with his heart chakra; however, she did not know if it was her intuition or her saline implants talking.

The nurse's announcement brought Jessica back to this world. She wiped her wet face with tissue and fiddled around with her rosary.

"Jessica," said Bernard, "I've been looking all over for you. All night long I've been looking." Jessica looked at her watch. "Mario had Joseph transferred to another room."

Jessica gasped.

"It's okay. He's going to the step-down unit."

"Why'd you call him Mario?"

"Who?"

"Christel's brother, Dr. Garcia. It's as if you know him personally or something."

Bernard laughed awkwardly. He kissed Jessica on the forehead. "You're just tired. I'm gonna go see how Joseph's doing. I'll come back. And someone came all the way from the United States to check on you. I'm gonna go and bring her in."

Jessica jumped up. "Wait!" She fell forward on the kneeler in slow motion.

"Jessica? Are you alright?"

Jessica gasped. She rubbed her eyes, "Is this real? Tameka, is that really you."

Tameka laughed. "You're not seeing things. I snuck in when you were on the kneeler, right before Bernard left."

Jessica jumped... "Tameka! What are you doing here?" She gave Tameka a hug. "What about your job?"

"I heard about Joseph. Thought I'd come to France and see about you. Lord knows Bernard isn't."

Jessica heard a small, familiar voice from behind.

Jessica turned around. "Winter-Jem! You made it."

"Of course. And I see Tameka made it out as well," said Winter-Jem. "Dr. Rose-Petal told me you've transferred to the lab in France, Tameka."

"Yes, I'll be working here."

Winter-Jem gave Tameka a hug. "This is a good start. Not like what's going on outside."

Jessica said, "What do you mean, Winter-Jem?"

"A bunch of journalists are blocking the private driveway. There are fights in the parking lot, helicopters circling overhead, grown men lying in the hallway, crying. I haven't been to the emergency department yet."

"According to Bernard, Dr. Garcia is transferring Joseph to a step-down unit," said Jessica.

"Already?" Winter-Jem's squeal echoed throughout the chapel.

"Remember, this is Joseph's hospital, and so I'm sure things are much more elaborate than we're used to."

"You're right, Jessica," said Winter-Jem. "I wish I had a place to unwind before I visit my uncle, though."

"C'mon," said Jessica, "I know the perfect place to unwind." She led Tameka and Winter-Jem to a private meditation room while she stayed in the chapel saying three Our Fathers and three Hail Marys.

hile sitting at a partially concealed table at one of the restaurants on the compound, Kenneth's ringtone—the hook of a folk rock song from the 1970s—looped around six times, garnering the attention of star struck strangers. Kenneth snatched his phone, noticed the number of the incoming call, and respired, "Putain de merde."

A teenage girl, fluffy dark hair, light brown eyes, pointed at Kenneth and said, "Fucking shit!" Her eyes twinkled as if she'd just had a religious experience.

The teenage girl's father slapped her across the face. "I don't care what Kenneth Charlemagne says, I forbid you to repeat his foul language!"

Kenneth answered his phone after a few seconds of contemplation. "Allô?" He put the phone on speaker and positioned it on a cell phone holder.

"And what the hell's wrong with your goddamn number?" Christel asked.

Kenneth dropped his face in his hands. "How'd you get my number?" He cut an eye at Michelle, who was sitting at the bar with Meyer.

"Kiss my ass. I have no time to deal with your drunk-out-the-ass clownery." Christel picked at her iridescent nail claws with a sharp silver file. "While you're running around here with jokes and shit, your sister, Bree, passed the fuck out."

He said, "What happened to Bree? Hysteria? Pneumonia? I told her about the air conditioner and grape juice pops."

"It's not that serious." Christel rolled her eyes, "Mario ordered a group of doctors to take her to U-goddamn-C."

"Not *that* serious, but serious enough for urgent care? What did they do?"

"Hooked her up to the intro-vein shit. She was de-fucking-hydrated

166

BLUEBERRY MANOR

'cuz she's expecting twins in seven goddamn months."

"Twins!" Kenneth laughed. "She's catching up with me."

"That shit ain't funny, Kenneth, and it damn sure ain't a fucking goal. Both of you are some hardheaded shits, you know that? And Bree...I told her ass to get on the goddamn pill. That Haitian gives no damn about her future."

"That Haitian's name is Jon, Christel. How's Dad doing? I suspect that's why you called."

"Stop mumbling! I hate mumbling." Christel said. Several people turned around after hearing Christel screaming through the phone.

Kenneth said nonchalantly, "Whatever."

"Bree was ill for two goddamn days before your father's heart attack."

Kenneth mouthed, "Heart attack."

Christel continued. "The entire time she kept whining to me like a needy toddler. You know I don't play that donkey shit."

People had started to gather around Kenneth's table. Michelle and Meyer alerted Kenneth's security team.

Christel slapped digits on her left hand with her right index finger. "Bree complaining about queasiness, fever, sweating, sleepiness, headache, dizziness, thirst. I can go on."

Kenneth slowly sunk in his seat. "Fuckin' A..."

Christel lit a cigarette; blew smoke while continuing with the conversation. "Some Spanish tourist named Ms. Morales told EMT that Joseph had a heart attack on the hill. He was treated for that, but the heart attack wasn't serious at all."

"What's with you and downplaying everybody's condition? And are you smoking? I thought you stopped that years ago."

Christel continued. "I think I heard Mario mention a stomach ulcer, and liver and kidney damage." Christel heard people talking amongst themselves. "Who are those people talking? Where are you?" She heard dishes clanging. "Do you need me to come to the compound?"

"For what?" Kenneth dropped a few tears. He pushed the women away that tried to console him.

"I told his ass about the greasy goddamn slave food."

Kenneth said, "That's not nice."

"I give no damn. The food wasn't nice to him. He eats like a fucking peasant. Goddamn him. And the painkillers. He pops the shit like candy. All the food, cigars, wine, stress." Soft sobs and an awkward silence took

167

them both by surprise. "Mario said Joseph'll be lucky if he lives another six to seven months."

Kenneth sounded like a fire breathing dragon through the phone.

Christel took the phone away from her ear. "Kenneth!"

He struggled to speak. "Hey... Is the liver and kidney damage that bad?"

"Who knows? Mario wouldn't tell me anything. He blames me for Joseph's condition anyway. It sounds like a cancer that has metastasized. My father died of the same thing."

"Thanks a lot for that picture, you bitch."

"I didn't mean to—"

Kenneth grabbed the phone off the holder and threw it against the wall, emitting a strange noise.

Christel jerked the phone away from her ear. "Bonjour? Allô, Kenneth." She said, "I'm going to the compound to see about my children!"

A sharp piece of phone bounced off the floor and into a police officer's eye. Some people gasped, some people cried, but the police officer stood there, completely composed, as a long strip of odd colored blood traveled down his face and hit the floor.

There were several whispers. Some got their cell phones and snapped pictures with old-fashioned cameras.

The bartender turned the volume up on the television set behind the bar. "Listen," the bartender tried to shush the crowd, "Grim Goresman just interrupted regular broadcasting speaking about what they now call 'Tragedy at Blueberry Manor.' He said several journalists are planning to infiltrate Blueberry Manor Estate and l'hôpital. They will wear very good disguises, very hard to spot." He continued to talk over the crowd. "And there are bomb threats at l'hôpital."

Kenneth sat, unmoved, until he heard strange commotion outside. He looked through the window and saw Christel, ruffled and pink-eyed. She marched up to Ms. Morales and slapped her.

Kenneth ran outside. Michelle and Meyer ran after Kenneth. Several others ran outside, snapping pictures and recording the madness on their phones.

Kenneth said, "Christel, what the hell'd you do that for?"

Christel put Ms. Morales in a choke hold. "Why didn't you give Joseph aspirin, you bitch! It's your fault! Everything's your goddamn fucking fault!"

BLUEBERRY MANOR

Kenneth and Michelle grabbed Christel. Meyer grabbed Ms. Morales. "Michelle, I've got Christel," said Kenneth. "Take your damn ass over there with Meyer. That's where you wanna be anyway. Mean mugging Ms. Morales like you crazy."

Kenneth screamed at Christel. "You smell like $666.00 discount cologne. Where the hell have you been? In Hell?"

"That's none of your goddamn business!"

"You should be ashamed of yourself, fucking around when Dad's incapacitated."

Christel broke away from Kenneth's grip. "How do you know what you know?"

"I know what I fucking know!"

"Fuck you, Kenneth! And don't talk to me that way. You're still my fucking son, little boy."

"Mom, what about the bomb threats?" Michelle said.

"What bomb threats?"

Kenneth threw his hands in the air. "If you were at l'hôpital, you'd know about the fighting and arrests," he raised his voice, "and the fucking bomb threats!"

Christel dried her tears. "Kenneth, has your father told you anything about the family businesses?"

"I know about it already. I've held many COO positions. I've been Dad's understudy for ten years and I've been CEO-in-training for, I don't know, over ten years."

"I've gotta get back to Joseph." She gave Kenneth and Michelle a hug. "And remember, don't say a word to anybody. Joseph will address everybody via satellite."

Kenneth said, "Michelle and I heard from Grim Goresman."

"Grim Goresman knows that Joseph will address everybody via satellite?" asked Christel.

"He has called several times. Entertainment media knows about the meeting, but they know nothing about Dad's condition." Michelle's voice shook. "Mom, do you have any current news?"

"Didn't Kenneth tell you, Michelle?"

"No." Michelle and Christel looked at Kenneth.

"What are you fucking handbags looking at? I haven't had the chance to tell anybody anything!"

"I've gotta go," said Christel, "and Kenneth, I think it's time you step in and stop some of the fighting among the board members." Michelle nodded in agreement.

"They don't like me!"

"It doesn't matter, Kenneth," said Christel, "who gives a fuck about what they like?"

Kenneth said, "Dad has Ross, Cortina, Fat Tito, BJ, Tomas Bravo, and other men and women who can run the businesses."

"But the board wants to see a Charlemagne take over. It doesn't matter if they act like they don't like you."

"But not this Charlemagne," Kenneth pointed at himself. "It's a moot point. After what you said, I don't think I'll be able to do much of anything now."

"What did she say?" Michelle asked Kenneth.

"Christel said Dad has six or seven months left."

In the way to his new room, Joseph told Nurse Miaisha to stop in to see how Bree was coming along.

"Okay, Mr. Charlemagne. Call me as soon as you finish up in here so I can get you to your room and get you hooked up. Dr. Garcia will have my ass if you're not resting comfortably in your room the next time he calls," said Nurse Miaisha.

"From my understanding he's already had that ass." He hummed the 'Benny Hill' music as he pinched her.

"Hey, none of that, now. Just finish up with your daughter so I can put you in your room. So you can rest up like a good little boy." She handed him a light-up pager.

"I heard tell about you, Nurse Miaisha," Joseph laughed, his cheekbones were underneath with his narrow eyes. "If you ain't the most," he closed his eyes, "whoo-wee! I tell ya."

She laughed. "That's enough, Mr. Charlemagne."

"Okay, I'll page you soon." He watched Nurse Miaisha's redheaded endowment walk down the hallway. "And she ain't denied that shit neither." He wheeled himself in Bree's room. "Oh, look at sleeping beauty."

Dr. Mario said, "Joseph! You're not supposed to be in here. I told Nurse Miaisha to watch you at all times. You're in no condition to be wheeling around by yourself!" He reached for his phone.

Joseph swatted. "I feel fine."

Mario gave him an unsympathetic look.

Joseph tried to pull clout. "Who's hospital is this? Who's paying your salary?" He erupted in laughter. "Look, it's okay. He showed Mario his light-up pager. "I asked her to wheel me to the door of Bree's room."

Mario looked around. "Where is she? I'm gonna get on her ass." Mario plopped Bree's folder on the table.

"From what I know, you've already... I, uh'm just gonna see my

171

daughter before checking out the Chinese Garden next to the step-down unit."

"Joseph," Mario slapped his left hand in his right palm, emphasizing each syllable, "you're doing way too much for a man in your condition."

Joseph raised his hand. Mario gave Joseph a stern look. "I'm gonna leave you alone Joseph, but only for a few minutes. Especially if you're planning on visiting the Garden." He looked at Bree. "She's playing possum. I know she's up. She forgets that I raised her for a number of years. I can tell a real sleep from a fake one."

"Thank you, Mario." Joseph turned his attention to Bree. "Hey stranger." Bree opened one eye. "Yeah, you, with that book of names on your stomach. I heard you can take me to my daughter."

Bree squealed, "Dad!"

Joseph looked around then said, "When I see him I'll let you know." Bree laughed extremely loud. "Up...be careful. Use your inside voice." Joseph eased in closer to Bree's ear. "This place is filled with sick people."

"Dad," she put her hand on his arm.

"What is it, Bree?"

"Uncle Mario said the twins are about two months along."

"Whoa, girl," said Joseph. "I'm gonna have to call you 'the old lady in the high top sneakers' pretty soon."

"Dad, you got jokes."

"I'm happy for you, Bree."

"I love you."

"I love you, too."

"But Mom sure isn't happy. She sees it as another one of those 'bash Jon' sessions."

Joseph took a lackluster tone. "That's Christel for you."

"How are you doing? Should you be out of CCU so soon, wheeling around like nothing major just happened?" Bree asked.

"Mario is putting me in a step-down unit."

"So soon?"

"I'm fine, Bree. The heart attack wasn't serious. Nurse Miaisha's taking me to the Chinese Garden before putting me in the new room. I just stopped in for a few minutes to check on you."

"You're great, Dad. Still worried about me."

"You know it. That's one of my jobs."

"Please get some rest. I don't want you to tire yourself out. Save some

BLUEBERRY MANOR

Energy for your new grandsons."

"Mario has run a test to determine the gender already," Joseph asked.

"No, I just feel it." Bree exposed her book of baby boy names.

"Alright, daughter... See you later."

"See you, and if you see Mom could you tell her to come in here? I've been calling her for the longest."

Joseph heard Jose, the security guard, arguing with someone about a cell phone. "Sounds like a Christel right now."

"What does 'a Christel' mean?" Asked Bree.

"Nothing. I'm outta here." Joseph wheeled himself around the corner, stopped to catch his breath, and paged Nurse Miasha.

Mario came around the corner. "Good. I was just coming to get you." They heard Christel's voice getting louder.

"Where's Nurse Miaisha?" Asked Joseph.

Mario cleared his throat. "Don't worry about it. I'll take you to the Garden then call her for you."

Joseph gave Mario a sly look.

Christel raised her voice even louder. "You're pissing me off, Jose! You know what, you can't tell me shit, ya arrogant son of a bitch. I do what the fuck I wanna do. You can't tell me anything ya big black son of a bitch!"

She got in Jose's face. "Fuck with me and I'll take your fucking badge away. I'm on my way to see my ailing daughter and you, you're trying to fuck with me? Huh? I'm Christel Charlemagne, bitch. Go to hell you, ya son of a bitch. Suck on this!" She does a vulgar gesture with her hands.

Jose uttered, "I already have."

"Watch your filthy goddamn mouth, ya asshole. "I know how to close it up real nice."

Jose raised his voice. "Yeah, shut it up, then!"

"Fuck you, Jose!"

The doctor's words were demonic and slow like a back masked record. Each syllable created a psychedelic pattern, turning the darkness in Joseph's head into a queasy reddish-orange.

He thought about all the things he'd miss, and so many goals he hadn't accomplished; however, he was so very thankful for the time he had spent with Nasira Pang.

173

AMINA CAPRICE ANDOLINI

Joseph arrived at the speakeasy at eight o'clock.

Once inside, gorgeous young men decked the halls, muscles fast and frozen under red, white, and blue strobe lights. "I should be ashamed of my old self. What does this young girl see in me?"

Joseph plopped down on a tall, leather, counter stool. With pen and paper, he sketched a barbarian broadsword pierced heart. He thought the picture was symbolic. It spoke of illegal aspirations, of a deadly soul tie, of a soul connection too powerful for words. "It feels like blasphemy, that I should attempt to put this unspeakable joy in a picture." He marveled the ceiling, eyes closed, mouth torn.

"Excuse me."

With his head buried in his drawing, thoughts of the puffy pink stuff adorning his soul, Joseph turned his eyes to the patch of floor underneath the sweet voice. "Yes? I..." At the mere sight of all the cuteness, he heard inexplicable singing. Angelic singing.

"What's wrong?"

It burns, he thought. Joseph's eyes moved up. The voice's legs were pleasantly curvy. Her tight black jeans appeared to be painted on her body. The song in his head got louder, and louder as his eyes traveled up to her wild t-shirt. *This woman is perfect.*

The sweet voice's small oval face was unusually pretty. Her hair was long, black, and covered her left eye. A lukewarm chill shot up his spine. He got excited, straightened his posture, and deepened his voice.

"Hello, Nasira." He started shaking. "You have the most beautiful eye I've ever seen." Joseph started to sweat. He felt as if an anxiety attack was surfacing.

"Eye?" Nasira laughed.

"Yeah, well, I can only see one right now."

"Thank you for the compliment. Years of wearing an abaya in public will do that for you." Nasira leaned in closer. "I've learned to speak through my eyes." She backed off after feeling nervous energy. "Joseph, you're early." Nasira noticed that he looked wet. "Are you okay? You look sickly."

"Yeah, I'm fine." He pulled at his collar.

"You're an hour early I see. I was coming down here to wait for you."

"Then that means you're an hour early, too." Joseph smirked and

174

continued scribbling. "I still beat you."

"Hey, you're an artist, huh? This is a nice picture."

"Thanks. I'm not much of an artist. It's just scribblings."

"I would say not."

"Not what?"

"Not just scribblings. Is it for me?"

"You can have it if you want."

"I want."

"It's just a little doodle, that's it."

"Nonsense. I'll get a frame for it. I consider this a lovely gift from you. Now, I'll have to return the favor."

Joseph said, "What do you mean?"

"C'mon. Let's go."

"Where?"

Nasira pointed up. "We'll have more privacy up there, in the Kingdom." Nasira led Joseph up the stairs to a secret area where red-lit movie houses, a synthetic beach, and massage parlors resided.

"Where are we going, Nasira?"

"This part is camouflaged, set aside mostly for comfort women."

"This *is* a kingdom." Joseph's eyes twinkled.

"You haven't seen half of it, but we'll get to that. For now, we're going to the best part, to my round room."

Joseph's heart went crazy. It felt like it was trying to jump out of his old body and into Nasira's young, fit, beautiful one. He held his chest, gasped for air, fearing he would have a heart attack on the stairwell. *I can see the headlines now*, thought Joseph. *Billionaire Joseph Charlemagne found dead in Camouflaged Quarter...on the damn stairwell.*

Joseph came out of his vision with an open-mouthed grin. His eyeballs searched the room, attempting to find the female voice that rumbled in his head.

He yapped like an injured animal. "No...Nooo, not again!" He pictured a small straw in his head as he wheezed. *No, the pain isn't spreading*. He calmed himself after realizing that he was experiencing a panic attack and not another heart attack. He closed his eyes, studied the psychedelic patterns and moving pictures in the blackness. "Mother of Muses," he said as he raised his shaky arms to the ceiling. "I've been reborn in the pastel." He put his hands on his face. "I have received strong pictures, a master theater, a puffy pink vision. It's time for Christel to know of my magical journey." His voice trailed. "No matter how beautiful the experience between Nasira and I was and always will be, it is what it is—betrayal, a wonderful, beautiful betrayal." He stretched his hands outward. "Horasis... Theia, Greek goddess of sight!"

Christel stood at the doors of the garden. Her voice was chillingly soft. "Joseph?"

"Huh?" Joseph wiped his eyes with the white handkerchief he tucked inside a pocket on his wheelchair. His puffy pink vision disintegrated.

"Are you alright?"

"As well as a man on house arrest can be. I'll be fine." He sung, "I really do-do-do like this garden."

Christel stepped in the garden, looked around as if she could see another dimension. "It's so nice and peaceful. A real paradise." Her voice returned to gruff callousness. "It's too fucking happy in here. It's a goddamn banquet."

Joseph appeared to nod off. His head wobbled from back-side-down to side-back-side.

Christel held Joseph's head in her hands. She then squeezed his trapezius muscle. "Ugly knot. You need a massage?"

"No." He tried to keep his head balanced.

Christel patted Joseph on the back, massaged his shoulders and took a seat on the old wrought iron bench. "What are you stressing about?"

He closed his eyes and tilted his head all the way back, alarming Christel. She lunged forward, ready to soften Joseph's fall. Joseph motioned his arms, "No, sit down, Christel, I'm fine." She slowly sat, holding her hands out as if she was on guard. "Well, I know why my dead parents' ghosts were hanging around."

"Why?"

"They were letting me know of my ill health. Christel nodded in agreement. "On another note, how's Bree? Is she up, ready to go back to the Manor?"

"Yes, Bree is um, finishing up. And you, you should get back to the room. My brother ordered some more of those goddamned tests. How'd you get in here?"

"I asked the red headed nurse. What's her name? Oh, Nurse Miaisha. The nurse with the ass."

"I would hope we all have asses." The jealousy in Christel's voice was thick. "I'm going to have a chitty damn chat with that red headed bitch. Nobody goes over my head. She should have come to me and asked my permission."

Joseph lowered his voice. "Do you ever think about your johns?"

A flash of misery washed across Christel's face. "Joseph, what the hell?"

"I mean, the people you sleep with? Do you care about them when you're through?"

"Sweet orb in the sky, Joseph. What the hell kind of question is that? You've asked me about this fucking shit before and I made it perfectly clear that it is one or all of my alters. They do that shit, not me. Most of the time I don't remember when they come out the gate." She squeezed an imaginary stress ball.

"You're being evasive. All I want to know is do you care?"

"All that goddamn medication has driven you insane. Even more insane than before."

"Even more insane than you?"

"Hardy-fucking-ha, Joseph. Look, I don't know what you want me to say."

"I want you to answer the damn question honestly."

Christel attended to her long satin scarf.

"Don't play games with me, Christel. What's up with you and Clarence the Priest?" After a long silence from Christel, Joseph continued. "And the flexible Trevor. Half the world knows about them."

"No they goddamn don't. They don't because there's nothing going on with Clarence the Priest." She spoke softly, "There was a lot I didn't remember about Clarence before." She flashed back to fifteen years of age, leaving her baby boy on the doorstep of a parish house because she wasn't sure if the baby was born out of incest or not.

"Then why'd you spend twenty-five million on him last month alone, Christel?"

There was a wild twinkle in Christel's eyes. "How do you know about that?" She turned her back to Joseph, and pressed her trembling fingers to her cheek. She gathered herself, "Besides, that's not much when you think about it. We have money on top of money coming in every second."

Joseph's voice slowed. "Are there any others as special to you as Clarence and Trevor?"

She answered Joseph's question in baby-voice. "Trevor and Fabrizio will always be special, but Joseph," she reached out to cup his chin, "they'll never be as special to me as you are to me, 'cuz you're my one and only Joe-Joe." She ended her speech with a ghostly baby giggle.

"Fabrizio? Who the goddamn hell is Fabrizio?"

"Fabrizio?" Christel cut a cheap grin. "He's one of the new gardeners."

Joseph slumped to the side. "Are you talking about the young punk that tried to take advantage of Bree?"

"Joseph! That was proven to be mistaken identity."

"Are you talking about the fucking snake that allegedly kidnapped my grandchildren? Her *three* children!"

"Bree has two children," Christel rolled her eyes, "for now."

"She's raising three!"

Christel's face brightened. "He returned them, unharmed...ah-llegedly. He didn't mean to hurt anyone. He just needed some gas. He had serious gas problems back there."

"If I had caught him, he would have had a lot more than some damn gas problems. Fucking snake."

"What do you mean?"

"I would have blown his ass straight to hell."

Christel popped her tongue. "No, not intestinal. I don't mean those kinds of gas problems. He had a chea'pass car."

"I bet you bought him a new car."

Christel straightened her spine, raised her head to the ceiling in victory. "So?"

"There's a lot of illogical shit, but I understand. I try to understand the shit I don't understand, can't understand, or won't understand. I do understand how the doctors, and a few other professionals can take advantage of you, but the goddamn criminal minded gardener? The goddamn gangsters? Come on, Christel, you're better than that."

"But Joseph, all that should matter is nobody will ever take your place as number one or whatever you wanna call it." She fluffed the small square pillow in Joseph's wheelchair and straightened his short blanket. "Now, that's not what's important. What's important is taking care of you, eliminating stress."

Joseph fixed his voice so that every word struck a curious note. "Christel, years ago I had an affair."

Christel put a deranged smile on her face. "Are you serious? I know you've fucked around on me in the past. We agreed to never, ever talk about it. Ever." She garbled, "That you feel the need to fucking tell me about it now is absurd."

Joseph spoke over Christel's garbling. "Nasira and I have a child together."

"That's the bitch's name, huh?" Christel threw her arms in the air. "Great. You're spilling the beans 'cuz you fucked around and fell in love!"

"Alexis Xiaoling Yu Pang. She was born back in 1998, premature. She's now eight."

"You kept this shit from me for eight damn years? You should've told me back in 1998, fool!"

"You've been busy."

"Looks like we've both been hella busy!"

"Look, my daughter has no health problems, none of that. She's—"

The rest of Joseph's words were thick and dumb. Christel's face became vacant. She interrupted Joseph midsentence. "In the Persian Gulf?" Her voice was harsh and bitter. "I could tell your ass was, um, how do you say...different. The big oil meetings in New York and Florida weren't supposed to be that fucking long. The others who went with you were back at home in a few fucking days." She shrieked. "But you, you'd stay away months at a time. How could you fucking do that?"

"Christel, you damn well can't compare me to them. I have a different position."

"And you went to fucking Dearborn?"

"How the hell do you know?"

"I got phone calls from—" She stopped herself.

Joseph finished Christel's sentence. "From your fucked up ass friends I presume. From Ladina's ass I presume. I have legitimate business in Michigan to this day. They don't know what the fuck I do in Michigan."

"Yeah, you had some business in Michigan, goddammit." Christel said, "You're shameful. You're just, just." She plopped her arms to her side. "You still involved with the hook teef heifer?" She rammed her right fist into her left palm. "Fuck!"

"Calm down." Joseph grabbed her arm.

She jerked away. "Get the fuck off me."

"Stop it with the name calling. There's no need for donkey shit."

"You can't fucking cheat right, Joe. You aren't supposed to be all sloppy with it. You could have caught a disease from that nasty ass slut and given it to Pearlie or me."

"Pearlie was born about four years after the affair."

"You could have taken steps to not include an innocent child in your pissassedness."

"Proper steps? Like you've taken proper steps?"

Christel raised her voice. "You fucking French Guineas are nasty, crazy, slutty, and more crazy. I can't believe you have enough audacity in your aura to—"

"To what? You can't even finish the damn sentence." Joseph scoffed. "To what? To do the same shit you've been doing to me for years? You're the nymphomaniac. If anyone should be afraid of catching something, catching anything, it's me."

"Oh, that's what this is really about, huh? It's about slinging mud?" Christel slung her arms around her body. "Slinging all the goddamn mud in the world, huh? You know all about my medical conditions, Joe. It's been proven by several fuck-king doctors!"

"Several fuck-king doctors you've fucked," Joseph yelled.

"Ah, shut up, Joseph!"

The two talked over each other.

Joseph curled down, almost falling out of his wheelchair. He grabbed onto a small tree in order to keep balanced.

Christel appreciated Joseph's near accident. She imagined kicking the wheelchair and beating Joseph's weak ass.

"I give up," said Joseph, "I've tried for years and years and years. I just had a heart attack and still, there's no talking to you. Nothing will ever change. You'll never understand, you'll never want to see any way except your way. I guess I'll have to die in order for you to see another perspective besides your own."

Christel worked her eyes around the garden. She fought to hold back tears. "What the hell are you talking about?" She mumbled, "Always the victim, motherfucker."

Joseph tried to raise his raspy voice. "You wanna have the last word? You wanna curse the most, you foul mouthed dragon? You don't care about anything except covering your own lumpy ass."

She sung, "*Joseph is jealous-jealous-jealous*! I just had the Brazilian butt lift surgery." She strutted around, showing off her new ass.

"Who gives a damn?"

"You fucking knew all about my fucking problems before you fucking married me you-you fucking motherfucker!"

Joseph dropped his head sharply. He tugged at his hospital gown and then placed his hand over his staggered belly. He threw his head back and screamed as loud as he could (which wasn't very loud)... "Christel!" His face went completely pale, but his eyes were jet black.

"You alright, Joe? You look like a pale asshole. Should I call somebody?" She tried to straighten his head.

Joseph shunned her hand. He showed her the light up pager Nurse Miaisha gave him.

"You stupid French Guinea bastard. Hell, I'm no coward. Hell no. I don't hide my shit. You know everything about me. You know about every last one of my—" She stopped herself.

"You're making a fool of yourself. You know damn well I don't know everything about you. You don't even know everything about you."

"Joe, that was low."

"I don't give a damn."

Christel gave Joseph a cold look.

"At least Nasira didn't ask me for much, just my company. She listened.

She genuinely loves me. That's what I took from this. What about you? What do *you* get from your johns?"

"Nancy doesn't love your dumb ass."

"Her name is Nasira."

"What the fuck ever. She only pretended to be interested in you 'cause you a fucking billionaire, stupid. She saw dollar signs the minute you gave her the time of day. You stupid Guinea bastard."

"You're wrong, Christel."

"You still communicate with that fay'kass, lying ass bitchy, ass-headed bitch?"

Joseph laughed.

"What's so funny?"

"You sound like a child." Joseph giggled, "What's an ass-headed bitch?"

Christel attempted to drink water from a fountain in the garden, but she couldn't get it through her numb lips.

"And don't call Nasira out of her name. She's everything you're not."

hristel poked fun at what she felt was Nasira's childish outlook on love. "I'd be willing to bet my mansion in Vegas that the sappy little girl believes in love at first sight; fairy tales, unicorns, soul mates and Twin Flames." She tickled Joseph's chin. "Does she believe you're her Twin Flame, Joseph? Is she one of those ass aching empaths?" She put her hands on her ass. "She's either a freak or fake. Either way, she's mentally stuck."

"She's gotta be a freak or fake according to your twisted logic," Joseph explained. "You don't think anyone could ever love me unconditionally."

"What about me? I love you."

Joseph could hear the seriousness in Christel's voice. It reminded him of the first time he saw her behind the big green dumpster at a gentleman's club in Paris. "No, you could never love me unconditionally."

"Oh, yeah? And she does?"

"She does."

Christel sat on the ground and stared childishly. "You're not supposed to fall in love, dumb Guinea bastard. I know how to separate true love and things of a physical nature."

Joseph did not feel like arguing with Christel anymore. "I apologize. I should've told you about Nasira, and at least about our daughter much earlier. It's my fault."

Christel crawled to Joseph's wheelchair. "Oh, no you don't, you fat fuck. You're not going to be the martyr."

"It's not like I planned any of this, Christel."

"So what?" Christel jumped to her feet. She hunched her shoulders and twisted her foot like a lost little girl. "It's different for me. You and Nasira are on a whole 'nother dimension, different from me." She turned around with a vainglorious look on her face. "Let me tell you something else. If it weren't for Pearlie, I would have left your ass a million Sundays ago."

Joseph picked up a second wind. He lunged for Christel's arm. His animalistic grunt took him and Christel by surprise.

"Ow! Are you crazy, madman? You're trying to bite me! You're not in any condition to do that."

Joseph slumped back in the wheelchair, struggling to breathe. "I should have left. I should have taken Pearlie, got you the proper help, then left." Joseph spoke slowly. "I'm not a fucking doctor."

Christel angled her head. Her voice went up several octaves. "I would have fought tooth and nail to keep Pearlie. She's my miracle...mine. You don't know the bond we have." Her face was so close to Joseph's that her spittle jumped in his nose. "She's mine!"

Joseph looked in the distance. All of Christel's abortions and miscarriages shot before him like a movie. "I'm sorry. I know this is hard for you. I apologize."

"Stop apologizing, you boob." Christel held her throat while shaking, forcing her eyes to roll toward the back of her head. Her voice deepened. "Oh, Joe, it would have gotten ugly, real fucking ugly. Pearlie would hate you. I'd teach her to hate you. We would have taken you for every penny you have, you bastard. And you, you don't want to meet Felice."

Joseph picked at his fingernails. "So many alters... I tried, but I can't fix you." Joseph held his head as if soothing a migraine headache. "When I was younger, I wanted to be the one to fix you. I wanted to help you, the nice, beautiful girl I found behind the dumpster."

"So?"

"So I had to fight for me and mine by myself. And then I met you." Christel smiled. "I thought I had somebody to fight with me, and everything was roses for a while, until I had to fight for you. I mean, really fight for you. Still, everything was okay, that is until it seemed like I was the only one fighting for you."

Christel attended to plant life.

"And then we had the kids. I had to fight for the kids by myself. And now, I have to fight for my own health by myself."

"Don't be so dramatic, Joe. You know I'll fight for your health. Hell, what do you think I've been trying to do for so many years? Your hardhead wouldn't listen to me about the goddamn food addictions and shit."

"I can't be here anymore if it doesn't satisfy my wellbeing." Joseph wheeled himself to the door, tapping at it in vain until he remembered the light up pager in the wheelchair's pocket. He managed to press the pager before Christel lunged at it.

"You leaving me for her?"

"For Nurse Miaisha? Hell no. Although she does have a nice natural ass and beautiful, natural, fiery red hair."

"I mean Nicole, you lascivious beast."

"Our grandchild?"

"You ribald dog, you."

Joseph threw his head back. "Oh, you mean Nasira?"

"Whatever. You'd rather have that small brained bitch rather than me?" She showcased herself. "Every man in the world wants me. You don't know how lucky you are."

"I'd do anything for Nasira," Joseph remarked.

"How could you do this to me?"

Joseph whirled around in the wheelchair. "You think she's a mindless fuck like your johns are to you? I love Nasira. I love her more than I love myself. And Clarence the Priest, I can't believe you took his ass to Canada. Showing out in front of our children."

"Stop getting so excited. Think about your health." Christel's eyes brightened. She put her hands over her mouth. "You're the one who put ground peanuts in my juice that day, you jealous bastard. You poisoned me so I couldn't go out with Clarence!"

Joseph tilted his body. "What in the hell are you talking about, woman?"

"On the day you and Kenneth and Meyer went to Florida, or some shit you told me."

Joseph held his throbbing chest with one hand and pushed the light-up pager with the other one.

"I fired several cooks that day, Joseph. It hit me just now what the fuck you did. You're the one who poisoned me. You're responsible for several people's unemployment," she shook her head unbelievably fast. "Yeah, yeah you are. All the hate mail I received was because of your evil ass doing. She said, "Youse a ruthless, snake-head bastard!"

"You're always hiring and firing people; throwing 'em off the grounds and whatnot. Congratulations! You earned every piece of hate mail all by yourself."

"Joseph," said Nurse Miaisha, he could barely hear her raspy voice through the pager, "did you hit the call button all those times on purpose?"

"Yes, Nurse Miaisha. I want to leave this," he looked around at Christel, "leave this paradise. Come get me. I need you to take me to the room."

"I'll be there shortly," said Nurse Miaisha.

Within seconds, Nurse Miaisha came in the garden and helped wheel Joseph next door, to his room.

Christel squealed, "I was paining and swollen for a week, dammit!" She attempted to slam the doors, nipping Nurse Miaisha's heel, catching a strand of her hair.

"Ouch, Mrs. Charlemagne! Watch out." She checked to make sure Joseph was not hurt.

"Shut up, you. Fuck both of youse!"

Christel closed the doors and hung her head in shame.

Once in his room, Joseph looked up at the nurse. "Please keep Christel out of here. I'm not ready to see her. I don't think I have the strength."

Nurse Miaisha looked confused. "Okay. We'll put a few guards by the door." She made a few phone calls and checked all of Joseph's equipment before leaving the room. "Now try to get some sleep, Mr. Charlemagne. I'll be back in a few hours, unless you need me before then."

Christel sat on the window seat. She thought about the haunting love Joseph had for Nasira, and wanted to break her pedestal, murder her memory, and reject their lovechild. "Alana, Aaliyah, Alexis, whatever the little girl's name is could never be a real Charlemagne," she said, "I'll see to it that she won't get a penny of our money. That NaShelia, NaSheera, Nasira bitch think she's hit the goddamn jackpot. Ha! I'm kee-hee-heeing on the bitch big time. She's not pissing on me and getting away with it."

Christel morphed into a helpless young girl. She grabbed the picnic blanket she had earlier, put her thumb in her mouth, and lashed out at ugly old Nasira. She sat up straight and rocked back and forth. *The Nasira woman could only be a distraction, just like long business trips and comfort food,* she thought.

Joseph's heart attack played repeatedly in his head. He worried about Christel's dissociative identity disorder (DID), their clusterfuck of an argument, about the Board's disapproval of Kenneth's leadership ability, and about Nasira and their daughter Alexis. He thought of his best friend,

BLUEBERRY MANOR

Fat Tito, and the rest of the Westaman family, one of his granddaughters, his godson, and his niece. There were so many family members and friends to think about. He dreamed of having them all at the compound, a glorious dream that he may or may not be a part of in the physical sense. He said, "If not in this lifetime, then in death throes shall I picture its materialization."

At a higher degree
the psychedelics in Me
will always be in grandeur;
a part of Blueberry Manor,
a part of Blueberry grandeur.
Sun's rays are clear.
Nothing left to fear at this rate.
I've got a lot to say
about my jacked up days
in this crazed hopeless maze.

ABOUT THE AUTHOR

Amina Caprice Andolini (born Shelia Marie Odell) has been writing Gothic poetry and short stories for a number of years while dealing with depression, grief, and symptoms of spiritual awareness. Her goals are to publish other books under the Blueberry Manor saga and release all of her written material in the form of books, merchandise, a musicals, television shows, and movies. She currently resides in Memphis, Tennessee.

To contact the author and learn more about her books and other literary events, visit her

Website https://aminacaprice.wordpress.com

Facebook https://www.facebook.com/Amina.Caprice

Blueberry Manor is Available in Print and Digital